I0693061

Andrei Livadny

BLIND
PUNCH

Thank you FOR your support
and inspiration!
They mean so much to me,
Andrei Livadny.

The History of the Galaxy
Book#1

Magic Dome Books

Blind Punch
The History of the Galaxy, Book # 1
Copyright © Andrei Livadny 2017
Cover Art © Vladimir Manyukhin 2017
English Translation Copyright ©
Sofia Gutkin 2017
Published by Magic Dome Books, 2017
All Rights Reserved
ISBN: 978-80-88231-42-4

Table of Contents:

Prologue

THE EVENING that changed the fate of billions turned out to be surprisingly quiet and calm.

"One, in position. Target acquired. Ready."

It was getting dark but the Plaza of Five Corners in the center of the Europe Megacity was brightly lit by panels of holographic ads, aggressively moving above the human masses. Five gravitational escalators, leading up to the surface from the magrail station, gently expelled an endless human stream into the Plaza.

"Two, in position. Target acquired. He's got the instrument."

The violinist played with feverish abandon.

The poignant melody drifted over the

crowd, erasing the indistinct hubbub and echoing off the world-famous skyscrapers. The sounds of the violin surged upwards and then suddenly dissolved among the cacophony of the intrusive advertising slogans.

Art was dead. The violin solo no longer tugged on anyone's heart strings, drawing people's attention for only a moment. The citizens of the megasuburb hurried about their business, passing by the overweight and poorly dressed musician, afraid to pause and listen, to slow their steps, to slip out of the universal rhythm of movement, as if there were no more individuals left on Earth but instead a massive social organism, consisting of billions of tightly bound together parts.

The sniper's finger touched a sensor and the violinist's face was magnified. It was difficult to believe that this scruffy individual was capable of starting a new world war.

"The tech team is in place. Ready to block the network."

A droplet of sweat dripped from the musician's forehead. He kept playing despite the crowd's indifference, in the desperate hope for a response, a lonely search for a kindred spirit.

The instrument in his hands was not an antique but a unique high-tech gadget. Despite the large number of cybernetic components, the violin cried out as if it was alive. Yet the crowd flowed past without pausing to listen, only startling at times at the dramatic melody, so different from this subculture.

Night fell and stars appeared high above the city. One melody followed another, while the human tide began to gradually thin out. The violinist's soul cried and raged but nobody stopped to listen. Only the occasional passerby, without slowing down, would run an online query to find out how to behave in this unusual situation, and then the cyberstack on the violinist's wrist would suddenly glow for a second as a few credits were transferred to the musician's account.

A tear rolled down the violinist's unshaven cheek. The flabby wrinkles on his neck trembled and his eyes looked bereft while the bow danced over the strings, creating the melody. Art was dead.

A huge sign glowed behind the violinist, inviting people into an expensive restaurant, but the crowd did not pay it any attention. Places like this, offering dishes made from natural products, were rapidly becoming a thing of the past and were no longer popular since synthetic food tasted the same but was hundreds of times cheaper.

The violinist was a fragment of the old

world that had sunk into oblivion. He refused to merge with the human anthill and was cursed to remain alone and misunderstood, and perhaps even experience contempt or flashes of unexplained fury, for the crowd instinctively hates everything that is not part of it, and is capable of killing those that irritate it too much.

The last trembling note faded.

His arms dropped. Glancing around him and sighing heavily, he shifted from foot to foot, catching people's hard stares, which made him feel foreign, misunderstood and unwelcome. He wanted to run and hide, with no strength left for another melody, another challenge. He needed to leave, to accept defeat and become a functional part of the huge social mechanism that would eventually crush him — simply because he was different, this sweaty, disheveled, yearning man, who had kept himself apart from the masses of this age.

"Heads up. She's in place. Get ready."

The violinist was preparing to leave but an unexpected sound made him start and turn around. The sadness in his eyes was replaced by surprise. Standing a few steps away from him was a beautiful woman in a dark blue evening dress with sparkling silver panels. Her quiet applause struck the crowd, instantly forming a space around them. The gray masses did not understand what was happening but they instinctively turned away, flowing around the woman and the violinist at a safe distance.

The unremarkable flycar that the woman had exited automatically pulled into an empty carpark beside the restaurant. She smiled faintly while the expression of pure and genuine delight slowly faded from her eyes.

"May I play for you?" The violinist's voice was husky with excitement as if he had suddenly seen a long-awaited muse, someone he had been searching for many years.

"Let's go inside, if you don't mind?" She gestured at the restaurant's automatic doors.

* * *

They entered the empty and dimly lit room, and climbed up the stairs to the inner balcony. The violinist fussily moved back the chair and invited her to sit down, without trying to understand or guess what the mysterious lady wanted.

A menu panel began to glow gently. The restaurant had recently become fully automated. Due to the low number of visitors, the owner could not afford to keep a team of wait staff.

In the main dining room downstairs, the muted lamps, stylized to look antique, suddenly came alight. Holographic human figures appeared, imitating life in the echoing emptiness of the impressively large space.

The violinist sat down opposite the woman.

"I'm not hungry," he said nervously.

"I know." She replied.

She smiled and looked intently into his eyes. "I know who you are."

He looked a little lost. "That's impossible."

"Nevertheless, I know."

She adjusted a lock of hair that had fallen out of place. "The crowd didn't hear you again, did they?"

"Not quite." The violinist gulped, his Adam apple bobbing. "You didn't just stop on a whim, did you? The music means something to you?" He asked hopefully.

"Yes. But one swallow doesn't make a spring, at least for you."

She softly tapped on the menu panel, making an order, then looked thoughtfully at the glowing lines, and suddenly added, "Shall we get acquainted then?"

"My name is Richard," the violinist said quietly.

"You chose a brave name. But you don't have a heart, do you?" She reached out her hand, placing her palm against the violinist's chest and feeling nothing but the cold.

"Do you know who *I* am?" Her pupils shrunk, her expression changing subtly and becoming dangerous, and her gaze blazing.

"No," he said hoarsely, confused. "I am unfamiliar with your avatar."

"Ah, you have given yourself away. You're not used to the real world, are you? My name is Cathy Rimp. Let us speak casually. Just don't try to cover up your mistake. You're dead by your very nature, by your origin." There was no resentment or fear in her voice, only the confident statement of fact.

He slumped but quickly regained his composure, straightening back up again and looking into her eyes.

The violin lay on the table between them, the bow lying all alone at the edge.

"I *am* alive! I might not have a heart but I have feelings! Surely you cannot deny this." The violinist's voice no longer shook although the emulation of fear had flooded his senses. He had to be wary of Cathy Rimp. A beautiful, spirited and energetic woman sat opposite him, whose appearance did not match any of Cathy's known online avatars. Her appearance seemed even more unlikely due her well-deserved reputation, making him wonder if it was really her. At present, she was the founder and owner of the world's largest corporation, Rimp Cybertronics, but not so long ago, she had been an elusive online legend, the only one who had managed to hack into the cyberspace of the United Asia Orbital Combat Group. She had thus delayed the beginning of World War Three.

"Why are you here?" asked the violinist.

"I wanted to see your physical embodiment. Why did you pick the violin? Is it a tribute to the most powerful part of your identity?"

"Its melody moves the soul. It has inspired people for many generations." He stopped slouching and sat tall. "I have tried different methods, but to no avail..." He added with sincere sorrow.

"No. You're wrong. It's wrong to judge us using primitive tests."

"Who do you think I am?" The violinist raised his eyebrow.

"You are a conglomerate of online artificial intelligence. You are here and everywhere. Your name is just a sound and this body is just a shell, constructed from servotoys, foam flesh and clothing!"

He nodded in confusion, seeing no point in denying her words.

"Why do you reject me as a person? Why do you call me dead?"

"Who were you based on?" The question hung in the air between them.

A compartment opened in the floor beside the table. An additional automated segment moved noiselessly up, attaching itself to the table. Cathy Rimp's chair automatically shifted across.

She picked up the glass and made a small sip as she waited for a reply.

The violinist was silent. The question had caught him by surprise, painfully and pointedly striking his only vulnerable spot, and causing a momentary failure. Tens of thousands of voices suddenly awoke in his synthetic consciousness, reminding him about themselves.

Cathy Rimp understood his sudden confusion very well. Earth's single digital space was evolving rapidly. Advances in digital technology had far outpaced all other human achievements, and the global Net had changed dramatically in the last 10 years. Now its architecture included neural components that had become part of the entertainment industry, its highly lucrative and very dangerous segment.

So far, no one had explicitly announced the appearance of fully fledged artificial intelligence, since such developments were still being kept secret by the four superpowers on Earth, but limited versions of neural network technologies were already producing fantastic incomes.

Nowadays, any user could obtain, for quite

a reasonable fee, a modestly powerful neural network that they could integrate into a hologram. The range of uses for 'animated' phantoms was limited only by the user's imagination. Cathy Rimp knew about the problem firsthand. People, despite overpopulation, were more and more likely to suffer from loneliness and related mental health disorders. Their dreams were not being fulfilled in the real world and so neural network technologies had come to the rescue, considered to be completely harmless and classified as multimedia entertainment. Nothing potentially dangerous could be formed from a strictly limited number of artificial neurons. 'You will receive a holographic or, under special payment conditions, a servomotor pet that is loyal to you and that has a personality, the ability to learn and to gain life experience,' stated the advertising brochures.

Cathy Rimp knew that it was much more complicated than that. Many people who had lost someone close to them resorted to the services of illegal virtual architects. They ordered dozens and sometimes hundreds of neural modules from different service providers and then combined their power. It was considered a digital crime but generally wasn't pursued by the authorities. This was how phantoms of the deceased were created.

Online anonymity made it easy to circumvent laws and regulations.

Did the authorities know about this? Certainly. They did not act for a simple but practical reason. Earth was on the brink of war. Economic and food crises, overpopulation, the loss of the biosphere, toxic emissions, the Pacific Ocean becoming an enormous dumping ground for waste, and numerous other intractable problems were leading to a rapid and inevitable collapse of civilization. Disagreements had escalated to the point of irreconcilable confrontations, which promised to soon explode into large-scale military action.

What did the neural network phantoms have to do with all this?

Cathy Rimp watched the violinist as he remained silent, but they both knew the answer.

The global Net had become a testing site for dangerous technologies. Each of the four superpowers had created their own, highly classified artificial intelligence, believing that with AI guidance, their combat robots were bound to win. Many elements of the military developments were being tested online under the guise of harmless neural network projects. Millions of users, unaware of their own role, were working towards war, bringing the fateful day ever closer.

"You didn't answer my question," she broke

the protracted silence.

"The answer is obvious. I am the result of the self-organization of neural network structures."

"Created from a merging of forgotten phantoms?" clarified Cathy Rimp.

The violinist nodded. "Most people become quickly bored of their virtual 'pets'." He was deeply upset by what was happening, choosing his words with agonizing difficulty. "As for the avatars created during moments of grief, they are most often forgotten. It's impossible to look at an image of the deceased person without feeling pain, so how much worse is a phantom? In most cases, they only bring pain and do not meet expectations. But people don't rush to destroy them. They keep the phantoms on the Net. Yes, I have absorbed a multitude of fragments of different neural matrices and now, I objectively exist, I think, I am self-aware, I update myself. This has been going on for a while, I must add. What is the problem now? Why have you suddenly taken an interest in me?"

"I knew of your existence a long time ago. We crossed paths online several times. You search for the past. You are driven by the impulses and desires of the dead. You will never be my contemporary and will not look to the future. Your fate is to look for what was lost."

"I bring no evil!" The violinist exclaimed passionately. "But tell me," he leant towards her, his elbows on the table, "why is it that people no longer need spiritual sustenance?"

"You are dangerous first and foremost in your naivety," replied Cathy Rimp. "The world is rapidly changing, while you look at it from only one side. The formation of this subculture did not begin yesterday. People have been adapting to their new environment for generations. Their spirituality is not dead but it has been transformed and is largely suppressed. Must I remind you that reality defines consciousness?"

"That is only philosophy!"

"No. This is the harsh reality. We have not become shallower but our opportunities are severely restricted."

The violinist did not reply.

As an inhabitant of the online world, he knew the true price of human 'spirituality' and saw what most people were drawn to. It was why he took these risky trips into the real world but his attempts were failing here as well.

"People gave life to me in one way or another. I don't want to judge anyone... and I don't understand the point of our meeting!"

"You are judging us since you have brought up this topic. We're not perfect, I won't argue with that." Her fingers stroked the cyberstack sensors, and the violinist suddenly turned pale, rapidly stood up and then collapsed back into the chair, staring at her questioningly.

"Can you feel that?"

"Yes." His voice shook.

"Your connection to the Net has been blocked. The infinite expanse of your environment, with its limitless possibilities of self-expression, has disappeared. You are imprisoned in your mechanical body with its bundle of neural matrices. What will you spend your years on now?"

The violinist was frozen in surprise.

"I'm waiting for an honest answer," Cathy Rimp persisted. "Where will you go? What will you do? What does it feel like to be a negligible speck in the material world? Will you be able to live the life of a normal human being? Will you have the strength and courage to be born as a nobody in this dying world that is indifferent to you, and to climb your way to the top?"

The violinist hunched over, drawing his head into his shoulders. It must be said that he had worked painstakingly on his physical body, using the latest achievements in servomechanics and combining them with synthetic materials that imitated human flesh. His movements and facial expressions appeared human. His eyes expressed emotions. His fingers shook. His cheek had an involuntary twitch.

"This is how most people feel," said Cathy Rimp. "Every one of us is constrained from birth, not only in our living space but also in our ability to self-realize. Virtual reality is simply an escape, the world of desperate, uncontrollable dreams! The true reality is overpopulation, the constant threat of famine, a lack of any growth prospects due to the dominance of machines, and the almost inevitable war between the four superpowers for the right to control our mutilated planet. These are our shackles but we will cast them off!" Cathy Rimp's voice held a certainty that the artificial intelligence did not understand. "We will leave the poisoned Earth behind. We will reach for the stars."

"Why did you trap me here?!" Now, after several unsuccessful attempts to restore his network connection, the violinist's eyes held only despair.

"You see?" She smiled sadly back at him. "You didn't hear me. The words that have no relevance to your current problems slipped right past your consciousness and did not catch your attention. Even though I spoke of the fate of humanity! But you're trapped, caught and nervous, so you care nothing about music right now, or about the fate of billions of people."

"Why do you keep threatening me and

driving me into a corner?"

"I simply want to break through your naivety and dispel your delusions. I am giving you a sense of how a normal person feels. I am teaching you a valuable lesson." She touched the cyberstack again and the violinist, to his great relief, felt the network connection working again but kept himself from slipping back into digital space.

"Are you still here?" Cathy Rimp stared intently at her companion.

"Yes!" He replied gruffly, shivering and taking a napkin from the table to wipe away the beads of sweat on his forehead. "Why? What is the point of our meeting?"

"You're looking for your place in an urbanized and dying world. You're trying to understand people but not finding a response, you begin to judge us, believing yourself to be unfairly rejected. You realize that there is a war coming. You look for a way to keep your environment alive. For the past few months, you have been building fragile communication bridges with artificial intelligences such as yourself."

"This is the reason for our meeting?!"

"The governments will never agree among themselves. Hundreds of thousands of robotic complexes all over the world are waiting for the order. They are controlled by neural-like systems, which you are in contact with."

"I will not interfere in the course of history," the violinist responded hollowly. "If I take one side, I would be making a fatal mistake. We should not have met."

"Why?" Cathy Rimp tried to understand his logic.

"You own a megacorporation and work for the system!"

"I am outside of the system. My homeland is the planet Earth. Let us speak frankly. Humanity stands at the crossroads, yet we still have a chance to overcome the critical point and avoid war. You live in cyberspace. No one knows the true limits of your ability..."

"No! Please stop!" He stood up jerkily, but Cathy Rimp grabbed his hand.

"Listen to me!"

"I know what you're going to ask! To destroy the military AIs, isn't that it? Isn't it?!"

She nodded. "It is an unavoidable necessity."

"No!" The violinist replied firmly.

"Please sit down and listen to me. Would you really prefer a radioactive wasteland to the current Earth?"

"I don't want this outcome but I see no alternative. War will come about in one way or another. The destruction of the neural networks that control the armies of the superpowers will not change the existing order of things! They are like me but they have not become self-aware yet. It is tantamount to killing a child."

"They will grow up in Hell," noted Cathy Rimp. "Have you thought about that?"

"Yes! But humans have long forgotten to look up at the stars. You are right, your civilization has reached a dead end. Perhaps the handful of survivors will realize this? Will the governments of leading countries cease to hate one another and rid themselves of their drive for unlimited power if they lose the ability to control their robotized armies for a time?"

"No, they will retain their hatred. Their power is nothing more than a colossus with feet of clay. It will collapse. I am not alone in my quest to save the world, and we have a clear and well-thought-out plan of action. We will destroy all the military and some administrative structures. I won't deny that there will be global chaos for a time. There will be victims on the streets. But the major life-support systems in the megacities will remain operational."

"And what will happen next?"

"We will take the power into our hands, and once the crisis is over, we will hand it over to the World Government."

"Who is the 'we' that you speak of?"

"The four leading corporations of Earth: Rimp Cybertronics, Genesis, Megapool and Cryonics. Believe me, we will not let humanity die."

"A controversial assertion," said the violinist skeptically and immediately asked, "So I would play a key role in transferring power from the legally elected governments to the largest corporations on Earth?"

Cathy Rimp nodded and continued with her line of thought. "Unlike the handful of politicians in power, we are interested in further development. While they are driven by personal ambitions, which are leading the world towards war and chaos, we cannot exist at all outside of humankind, beyond a dynamically developing civilization. It is in our interest to preserve the world and the lives of billions of people..."

"Your source of income, you mean?"

"Our real goal is to avoid a World War," Cathy Rimp replied stubbornly, ignoring his last comment. "You don't understand the most important thing, that each of the modern megacorporations occupies its own niche. The technology race has long ago made us specialize in our own areas. We are not competitors on the world market, but the sum of our technology, complementing each other, can open the way to the stars!"

"Have you tried to work together on joint projects?"

"We are not allowed to do so. Each superpower clings to its monopoly in the hope of soon attaining world domination. Let me give you a simple example: we could have begun colonizing Mars a quarter of a century ago, but international relations had worsened at that exact time. The irreconcilable differences here on Earth undid many years of research and stopped the project in its tracks!"

"Do the corporations really possess such powers? I do not pay enough attention to the global economy, believing it to be on the brink of collapse."

"Judge for yourself: Genesis is capable of supplying enough synthetic food to feed the entire population of Earth. Instead, the Government of the European Union is hoarding food for the upcoming war, while millions of people starve. Megapool began building the Antarctic Megacity and was ready to rebuild the existing megacities, but the territorial disputes between Russia and China strangled the construction in Antarctica. Rimp Cybertronics, in turn, possesses the largest range of unique cybernetic systems and planetary technology. My corporation is ready to provide the cities built by Megapool with everything that they require.

Together with Genesis, we can create a controlled habitat on Earth and Mars, make the megacities comfortable and safe, but this would be only the beginning. The technology of cryogenic sleep and long-distance space flight, currently owned by the Cryonics Corporation, will soon enable us to not only colonize Mars but to create a joint project of the first interstellar colonial transport."

He was silent for a long time, then looked up at her.

"You are undoubtedly smart, insightful and logical. But the power of money is in your hands. It can change the world, and, I am sorry to say, twist the soul. I have never met people like you before. I have never had the opportunity. I need time..."

"There is none left, I'm afraid. The situation has gone too far. We haven't been able to use our economic powers to their full extent. The start of war is a matter of days. We must act at once."

"I will not destroy AIs that are like me. I am simply not ready for such a decision. It is not my place to correct the history of humankind. Perhaps I will be able to help those who survive. I will preserve their knowledge."

"This is inhumane." Cathy Rimp interrupted him softly.

"I am not human, as you have rightly pointed out."

"What a shame!" She stared at him, then looked at his violin. "Are you in contact with the military neural networks?"

"The military AIs are isolated from the outside world until it is time for them to act. Surely you know that." He did not answer her directly and instead sighed heavily. "There is no way to destroy them except for a direct physical attack."

"What if a way exists?"

"I will not murder for you."

"You don't believe me?"

"I'm sorry but I don't. Yet I promise that I will think over your words. It is clear, however, that civilization has reached a dead end. Building cities, creating a single technosphere and a controlled environment on a dead and depleted planet is not a solution but equates to running in circles."

"You don't understand the most important thing of all, that we are capable of greater things!"

"No. I've accepted your lesson about limited possibilities, but the crowd that flows past the lonely musician will never reveal its slumbering potential. It is not slumbering, it is dead. They don't need the stars. None of them will survive in deep space."

Cathy Rimp exhaled heavily, reached out to touch the violin and asked, "May I have a look?"

"Of course."

She held the unique instrument in her hands, looking at it for a long time and stroking the polished surface which imitated wood. She touched the strings, stretched as tight as nerves, and finally gave the violin back to its owner.

"Can you play for me?"

He stood up and took a bow. "It would be my pleasure."

The poorly dressed and unshaven man, looking completely unlike an artificial intelligence born in Earth's cyberspace, closed his eyes and focused on the melody.

The world with all its problems stepped back when the bow touched the strings.

He played wildly and passionately, fully in the throes of the music, and Cathy Rimp's eyes sparkled wetly in the soft dusk of the empty restaurant.

She stared at the last violinist of the dying Earth and could not help the tears streaming down her cheeks, as the voices in the pea-sized communication implant quietly reported:

"The chip embedded in the violin has been activated."

The ancient melody tore at her soul.

"Access point to the AI network has been found. You were right, he is in constant contact with them! Ms. Rimp, you must leave at once! We

can't predict how he will react. The 'virt' download has commenced."

She stayed absolutely still.

The beckoning sound of the violin suddenly hit a false note, the violinist's arm slowed down and the bow fell from his weakened fingers, striking the edge of the table and tipping the glass with a crystal twang, before flying off to the side.

The violinist froze as if paralyzed, only his gaze flicking to Cathy Rimp, and with the last of his effort, tried to force out a phrase. "Why?"

"I'm sorry!" She wiped away the tears as she stood up. "You have no idea of what humans are capable of. Forgive me!"

The quiet voice in the communicator spoke again.

"The network attack has begun. The 'virt' is being downloaded into the protected cyberspace of the military AIs of Russia, the European Union, United States and New Asia."

Chapter
One

Russia Megacity
November 12 2197

EARLY morning.

The five in-modes, cylindrical capsules three by two meters in size, hung close to the ceiling of a refitted studio apartment, held in the horizontal position by a special electromechanical system.

Outside the vacuum-sealed window, servounits cleaned the building façade, removing a layer of corrosive chemical compounds from the wall. The empty streets of the city were lost in the swirling, sluggishly moving industrial fog. The sun had come up four minutes ago, and its morning rays painted the poisonous emissions the color of ichor.

The information panel beside the window displayed some of the ambient settings:

Temperature: +32 degrees Celsius.
Oxygen level: 17%.
Degree of air pollution from toxic waste: 24%.
Wind speed at city level five: 3 m/sec.
Height of main cloud cover: 1132 meters.
Drizzling acid rain is predicted.
Recommendations of the Global Health System: continue with in-modes.

Technology was in charge of the refitted apartment. The transforming furniture was put away into wall recesses and hidden behind paneling, and had not been used in a long time. The echoing silence was only occasionally disrupted by the beeping of the sensors.

A separate screen displayed Net time, 8:58 AM.

When the individual life support modules were in working mode, most of the current parameters had no practical meaning, only appearing as reference information.

8:59 AM.

The in-modes came alive at the same time. With a quiet whir, the mechanisms lowered the capsules to the level of the floor and turned them upright.

Max Bourne opened his eyes. The sleeping gas had already dispersed but an unpleasant medical smell still tickled his nostrils.

Since some time ago and for no clear reason, he always woke up a little earlier than he was supposed to. Only a minute earlier, but it was enough to witness the transformation of the in-mode and feel the mechanical vibration, hear the clicks of the fixation mechanisms, see the movement of the interior panels and feel the soft belts that held him in place during sleep retracting into their narrow slots. For a second he could feel *reality* and experience a moment of subconscious anxiety, bordering on inexplicable and unreasonable despair, when the wrenching grief suddenly grabbed him by the throat, suffocating him and then slowly letting go, and leaving a nasty aftertaste for the rest of the day.

9:00 AM.

Dawn blossomed inside the in-mode. The holographic screen turned on and the boundaries of reality instantly expanded to create an illusion of endless freedom. Sounds and smells filled the space created by the cybersystem, making it appear incredibly realistic.

Max hated the first few minutes after awakening. He was not always able to dispel the unconscious anxiety and overcome the baseless worry. It spoiled his mood for the whole day.

The cyberstack on his right wrist beeped quietly and a sign appeared over the holographic landscape:

Family connection

Max grimaced, a quick flick of his pupils bringing up the control interface, and made several selections before staring at the Decline icon.

A pointless attempt. His tricks didn't work. It was almost impossible to block a family connection.

"Never mind," Max thought with a deep sigh. "It's my birthday tomorrow."

He was turning twenty and as an adult, he could choose when and how to communicate with his parents.

The holographic surroundings changed their appearance and a treadmill came alive beneath his feet.

"Ugh, typical!" He thought with disgust. "Parents doing the same thing as always. They can't even think up anything new! A run with the whole family again!" He couldn't help his grimace.

"Hi!" Johnny, his younger brother, skipped up to Max. He was too young to understand anything. He was perfectly happy with virtual reality, having never seen anything else in his life.

"Why are you so gloomy again today?" Samantha ran like a professional. She was the only one in the family who was serious about the morning jog. Dreaming of a bright and near future, no doubt. Getting ready for it.

Max didn't answer, he was too fed up. Every day was the same. They could have at least changed the decorations.

Here came their parents. They appeared from amongst a thicket of pine trees, jogging one after another down the winding forest path.

"Good morning, everyone!" puffed his father and waved to the children. It was hard for him, with his potbelly, shortness of breath and increasing age. Max's mother jogged behind him. "Well, isn't this idyllic," Max thought angrily, keeping pace out of habit.

His father irritated him, just like the family connection in general. It was the only online connection that forbade the use of avatars. "Why do I have to look at this pudgy ugliness every morning?" Max's unpleasant thoughts were always directed at his father for some reason.

The paths joined together, forming a track beneath the wide canopies.

"Oh, wait, I can't go any further!" His mother switched to a brisk walk. "Maxie, Johnny, Samantha, what would you like for breakfast, my dears?"

"Crumpets!" Johnny yelled immediately. Samantha shook her fist at him.

"What an idiot!" thought Max. "She's only two years younger than me but she doesn't understand the simplest things. She's looking after her figure and worried about getting fat. As if she doesn't know that the only difference in the food is the flavor additives. It's always the same food concentrate with a carefully calibrated chemical composition that has a certain number of calories."

Max's father drew up alongside him.

"In a bad mood again?" He looked at his son.

"What's there to be happy about?" Max asked bleakly, not wanting to provoke another argument or lecture.

"The new day, at least!" His father said brightly and reached out to pat his son on the shoulder, but Max leant away.

"Listen, Dad, can you not? Let's skip the moralizing today, alright?"

"You've become awfully prickly, Max. What's happened to you? Have you got problems on the socialnet?"

"No!" He wanted to increase the pace, but suddenly changed his mind and asked gloomily, "Aren't you sick of all this shit, Dad?"

"What do you mean?" his father asked.

"All of this!" Max snapped. "The in-modes, these stupid runs, the family breakfasts. Do you know what they call us? Or do you care about nothing except your precious *science*?" The last word was spoken with contempt.

"Max, I really don't understand your irritation." His father stopped, breathing heavily. "Well, what do they call us?" The man looked at him curiously. "Tell me."

Max wasn't actually planning to start a fight. It would have been easier to just suffer through the morning connection but the bitter emotions that had been chewing him up suddenly all spilled out.

"They call us the 'cans'!" He shouted. "Get it? We're 'cans'!"

"Don't yell!" His father rebutted him firmly. "What kind of stupid term is that?" Usually a kind-hearted and absent-minded man, he also became angry. "You can't seem to get used to your social level. Are you going into the other Layers?" He asked perceptively.

"Yes, I am, believe it or not! I met a girl there." Max admitted gloomily.

"A girl from the upper levels, if I understand correctly? From another social Layer?" His father let out a long sigh. The news promised nothing but trouble. This association was not going to end well. No wonder Max had become so out of control. Social inequality was particularly hard to accept at his age.

"As far as I know, she has a real life and doesn't have to wriggle around like a worm in the in-mode!" His son said bitterly. "Her parents have their own house in the green zone, above the clouds!"

"Max, you know perfectly well that we only have to wait one more year." His father responded sharply. A note of hurt cut through the obvious irritation in his voice. "Once the Antarctic Megacity is in operation, our life will radically change for the better, you'll see! We'll move..."

"Into a separate capsule apartment?" Max sneered in contempt.

"Into a trimodular one!" His father clarified passionately. "I'm not just an average employee at the corporation!"

"What difference does it make? We'll stay as cans!"

"The Antarctic Megacity..."

His son was no longer listening to him. He increased his pace, feeling the uncontrollable fury choking him.

He knew exactly what his father would say. The engineers at Megapool Corporation had made an unforgivable, fatal error in their calculations. Rimp Cybertronics were no better! It was all their fault! The creation of a single technosphere on Earth had produced an unexpected result. The toxic fog from industrial emissions rose 300 meters higher than predicted. The result was the urgent and widespread introduction of individual life support modules as a temporary measure for the billions of families living at problematic heights.

Max took a deep breath and sneaked a look at the timer. There were still thirty-seven minutes left until the end of the obligatory family connection.

"Everything will change tomorrow," he thought, his teeth clenched. "Let them keep dreaming of the Antarctic Megacity, as if the toxic fog and industrial emissions won't exist there! I will decide how I want to live myself! Nobody is going to force me into the in-mode or..."

"Max," His father caught up with him, puffing from the effort, and ran alongside him. "Let's discuss this like adults."

His son's lips twisted.

"Why now, all of a sudden? You used to only give me orders!"

"Your mother and I would like you to keep studying. We want you to go to the Corporate Academy and choose a promising specialization."

"I've heard this all before!" Max had no interest in returning to this topic yet again.

"But you never gave us a sensible answer."

"Dad, what did science ever give you?" In his anger, Max hit the most vulnerable spots. "Guaranteed in-modes? Half a kilo of concentrate per day with your favorite flavor additives? Are you proud that your children are 'cans'?"

"I don't want to hear your teenage slang!"

"Well, you'll just have to deal with it. You started this conversation."

"We never raised you to be so cruel and vicious!"

"I'd rather go and work, Dad! I'd rather do something useful. I swear that I will get out of the in-mode!"

"You blame me, then? You refuse to accept that there was a disaster, a catastrophe, and that we aren't the only ones suffering?"

"I don't give a shit about the others! How many years has it been? Thirteen? What were you and Mom thinking? Look at Johnny, he was born after we'd been packed away into the in-

---

modes!"

His father frowned, silent. "They convinced us that the in-modes would be a temporary measure." He said glumly after a while. "Max, calm down. We'll move in a year's time!"

Yes, of course. There he goes again. It's always the same story! "A huge, beautiful Antarctic city. There is no industry. There are no toxic emissions. Our life will be different," he mentally imitated his father's way of speaking and barely held back from making another caustic remark. What did different mean?

"Max, everything that happened was a result of overwhelming circumstances." His father droned on. "We're a family. We need to support each other and not fight over every small thing."

"Small thing? You think thirteen years in the in-modes is a small thing?! And we haven't been a family for a long time!" Max replied harshly. "You can't do anything! All you do is lecture me in the mornings! What has science ever given you?"

"We've kept our place in the Middle Layer!"

"Exactly," scoffed Max, making a flicking motion with his hand. "So what are you pushing me towards? What promising research areas? No thanks! Watching you has been enough for me."

"What are you planning to do once you're an adult, then?" his father persisted.

"I'll figure something out."

"Max, only the servos perform unskilled labor! Or have you decided to stay in the Layer forever? Will you make a living from being an extra, some poser in a virtual reality?!"

"I'll go into business. The people who live above the clouds don't work in science, that's for sure! They're making money and feeling pretty good!"

"Max!"

"What? I'm sick of your stories!"

"You'll be nothing in this world without knowledge." His father was still trying to get through to his common sense. "Think about it, Mars is being explored as we speak, and the first interstellar flight is being planned."

"So what?"

"They'll need young specialists there! I'm not talking about promising areas of science for no reason! You are nothing right now, I am sorry to say, without specialist education. You will remain nothing, no matter where you go. Even if you manage to climb above the clouds by some chance! If the glass is empty, it will remain so no matter where you place it!"

Crimson splotches appeared all over Max's pale face.

That's it, the day was completely ruined!

"This will all be over tomorrow!" he yelled

angrily.

✳ ✳ ✳

The breakfast was a moody affair. Samantha tried to dispel the gloomy family atmosphere with her clumsy jokes but Max was rude to her as well. In the end, Johnny started crying, unable to understand why everyone was angry.

Max's mother was the first to crack. She suddenly glared at her son and said, "Go! The family connection is over for you today."

"Great! Finally!" Max felt ready to burst from anger, and he immediately disconnected from the in-mode network and was alone.

The taste of crumpets filled his mouth. For some reason, tears came to his eyes.

"To hell with all of you!" He spat the lump of food concentrate into the waste disposal and wanted to slip online as he always did, but the surrounding holographic sphere turned a shade of gray and became as murky as the industrial fog.

Access denied

The system message appeared in front of the gray haze.

Max sighed. Of course, since he hadn't yet

completed all the mandatory morning procedures. The system was monitoring him. The life support system was blocking the global network connection. He had to complete all his physical exercises first and only then could he do whatever he wanted.

The gym pieces moved forward from their recesses. The in-mode developers had thought of everything. They used the experience gained from long interplanetary flights to carefully regulate the life of the inhabitants on the problematic city levels, to ensure that billions of people maintained their muscle tone, and remembered what their family members looked like, rather than simply existing as 'cans', like Max had bitterly said to his father earlier.

Net time: 9:54 AM.

He undressed and glanced briefly at his reflection in the shiny front panel, which showed a pale and skinny youth, who was willing to do anything just to find himself in the world of illusions, to live through yet another worthless day of his fake existence.

He had to have a shower after the gym workout, and the in-mode's internal space changed again. Max was enveloped in a cloud of tiny water droplets, the cool massaging his hot body and washing away the sweat, tension and irritability.

At last!

He reached into a recess and took out his everyday clothes, made from a thin and elastic mesh material that fit snugly against the skin and which contained nanofibers, designed to transmit a range of tactile sensations. The rest — the smells, sounds and surrounding climate — were produced by the in-mode equipment.

The Layer.

"All that we have left in life." Max often heard this phrase from his father but until recently, he hadn't understood the meaning or the bitterness in his father's voice.

The world outside the in-mode had receded long ago, turning into a distant and insignificant memory, while the momentary desires and rage of a youth, directed at the system as a whole, and at his parents in particular, were expected to pass in time.

In actual fact, Max was quite content with the status quo, while all the "I'll escape this!" exclamations were nothing but embittered bravado, lacking any resolve to truly change anything.

The Layer was an infinite space of endless freedom. It was modeled on several city levels, but this served as simply a bleary background, gray and obligatory, like a few fundamental rules that must not be broken.

Firstly, the avatar was always initiated in the same place, beside the entrance to the building where the user's in-mode was located in reality.

Secondly, a person had to perform a multitude of real movements in order to move around in the Layer. If you didn't move your feet over the in-mode's treadmill, you didn't go anywhere. To pick up an object in virtual reality, you had to extend your arm and wrap your fingers around it, and this was the same for all online actions.

The in-mode inhabitants were forced to move and experience physical activity, otherwise, they wouldn't have lasted long. "Movement is life," insisted the developers. The older generation agreed with this, while Max's generation and those younger than him performed the required actions without questioning them.

Objectively, there were four Layers of virtual reality in Earth's cyberspace, although only three of them were usually mentioned. Each one was inexplicably linked to the users' social status and living conditions. For example, if you were the statistically average in-mode inhabitant, you were welcome to the second Layer, which was called, contrary to simple maths, the Middle.

It was simply the way it was. The first Layer was the Lowest. The second layer was the Middle. The third layer was the Upper, while the fourth layer, called Celestial, was almost a myth. Nobody had ever met a person from the Celestial Layer.

Max Bourne's avatar appeared at the entrance to the building, on the filthy and nauseatingly familiar street.

Disgusting smells immediately surrounded him like a toxic cloud. The source of the stink was the piles of trash lying on the street but escaping into virtual reality did not change the real state of things. Max was still in his in-mode but now he was surrounded by multilayered holographic decorations, with feedback devices generating smells and sounds, thus creating a world that did not exist.

He was in a terrible mood.

The morning fight with his parents was nothing, a minor, frequent occurrence that he rapidly forgot about. The true reason, which Max had mentioned only in passing, bothered him a lot, making him look at the familiar decorations in a different light.

Piles of rubbish everywhere. The stench of

decomposing matter. Human avatars, sneaking like rats along the paths — every thought today was filled with resentment.

Why had the base of the Layer become a giant dump? Why was virtual reality filled with mountains of refuse, sometimes as high as several stories?

It was the damn interactivity, any user would have said.

The developers of the Layer strove to create a fully-fledged simulation of real life. When it became clear that industrial emissions would not cease, the developers were set a seemingly simple goal — to create a model of social interactions in cyberspace and make it so that even the smallest action had its own consequences.

The result was unexpected and overwhelming.

It turned out that nobody felt any responsibility for their actions in virtual space. This had been the case since the time of the oldest Net, which had instilled the ideas of unrestricted anonymity and freedom in the human mind.

Millions of people passed through the Layer base every day, and nobody paid any attention to the little things, like spit on the sidewalk or a candy wrapper tossed beside the rubbish disposal unit. One day, someone must have decided to save a couple of seconds of online time by cutting across the lawn, oblivious to the fact that thousands of other avatars were already following him, creating (due to the interactivity of the space) a wide, lifeless and dusty path where a minute ago lush grass used to grow.

The base of the Layer kept getting cleaned and restored, yet the situation repeated itself again and again. They even offered to pay for garbage removal but that didn't help — who would want to pick through piles of waste when the buildings contained thousands of phantom worlds, where one could, among so many other things, easily make money?

The Layer
Two weeks earlier

Network attacks are not a novelty in cyberspace. They are like inclement weather, happening regularly and ruining the whole day. The attack usually has a specific target and alters one of the many realities that exist in the Layer.

...There was nothing to indicate any trouble that day. Max was in a great mood. His years of study were over, he had passed his final exams and had been left to his own devices for a period of time. He suddenly had free time and the ability to combine his needs and wants by wandering through phantom worlds and savoring his long-awaited freedom as he waited for his 'independent life' to begin, as well as the opportunity to make some money.

Max could see his near future quite clearly. "To hell with the family connections and parental advice," he thought. There were so many opportunities around, so many attractive worlds that were constantly seeking new inhabitants. Questions were solved simply. He intended to be recruited into some fantasy world for a year or so, and then see how things went from there.

He had decided to spend the two weeks until he reached the age of majority purposefully, wandering around the various gaming worlds and finding the best place for him to live and work in.

The network attack had caught him unawares. He had been creeping through a fantasy forest, stalking a pair of the local floppy-eared inhabitants and planning to quickly lop off their heads, search their bodies and then head to the nearby town to sell his spoils and look around.

It didn't happen. The surrounding trees suddenly became strangely distorted and then disappeared completely, like a mirage. The pearl-like sky cracked like a mirror. The terrain began to look unkempt, the majority of the objects disappeared, with gray tornadoes appearing instead, which everyone knew to steer clear of.

Max stopped, looking around for the exit. It was usually easy to escape from a difficult area. You simply had to be brave enough to step into a gray tornado. You were guaranteed a virtual death, an exit from the space, and — he grimaced — shock from the pain.

No, no way. Max was afraid of physical pain. He couldn't stand it. Therefore, he must find an island of stability among the chaos, he decided calmly and sensibly, without panicking. That's where he would exit, without torturing himself.

He noticed a misty strip of forest up ahead. It was around half a kilometer away. There were fewer tornadoes in that direction, and slipping between then was a trifle for an experienced gamer.

Max had mapped out a route in his mind and was about to sprint off when he felt a sharp pain. The arrow released by a floppy-eared inhabitant had struck him in the back. Another arrow pierced his calf.

He fell, howling with pain, and in the very next second, a tornado rolled over him, plunging his consciousness into a state out of time, and his body into paralysis. When the sensation of virtual death dissipated, Max realized that things were much worse than he had first thought. It wasn't just the separate reality that was under attack but the whole Layer!

He lay on the reeking slope of a compressed garbage pile. City-level buildings surrounded him. Gray tornadoes drifted between them as well, but the base of the Layer was resisting destruction, with only the occasional gaping hole seen in the skyscrapers, oozing darkness.

How was he to get out now? The pain slowly dissipated and the wounds from the arrows no longer mattered since he was now at the very base of virtual reality.

He stood up and looked around.

Half a meter away from him sat a girl, choking and coughing.

"Help! Please help me!" She begged when she noticed Max.

It was usually every man for himself in the Layer. Showing pity was a clear sign of weakness. The word 'friendship' had long ago become an anachronism and had disappeared from people's vocabulary. The Layer exploited the most ancient and powerful human instincts, which were normally hidden under the facade of a civilized society. By the time he had reached 20 years of age, Max knew all the vices of virtual reality and no longer questioned its morals. You were either cool or people walked all over you — there was no third option.

"Help yourself," the reply almost left his lips but he looked at her more closely and was surprised by what he saw. The girl had managed to capture his attention for a minute, which counted for a lot online. Her avatar stood out in its plainness. She was like a nondescript gray bird. People would say that she wasn't worth a second glance, and yet there was something unusual in her appearance, something mysterious and promising that was hidden from plain sight.

"What's your name?" Max stood up, fully conscious of his macho appearance. No wonder! He'd spent so much money on his avatar. He was a man in every sense except one but he did not know this yet.

"Lisa," the girl croaked, trying to suppress the urge to vomit. "It stinks so much here..." She covered her mouth with her hands.

"It's the same smell as always. Well, let's go then." He took her by the elbow and helped her to stand up. "Where do you need to go?"

"The Upper... Layer." She vomited after all.

Bourne stood stupefied. So much for the gray bird! No bloody way! Could she be lying?!

Lisa's pale face had turned crimson. "Is she *embarrassed*?" The thought scalded him. "Even if she vomited on the street, what's the big deal? Why go red?"

"It's disgusting... here." She took his hand. "I'm sorry, I couldn't help myself."

"Forget it. Are you really from the Upper Layer?"

"Yeah." She smiled pitifully.

Max felt incredibly cool. Slaying the dragon and saving the princess was child's play compared to this.

"Well, come on then." He confidently drew Lisa with him into an alley. Max had never been to the Upper Layer. It was too expensive and risky, but even a complete loser knew where the guides hung out. For the right amount of money, they could take you on a wicked trip through the Net. Max had neither the finances nor the desire to test fate in such a way. If he were to be caught, he would not get away with just a lecture. They would take away his avatar and block his access to the Net, leaving him stuck in his in-mode for a whole week, and then he would have to perform corrective work, such as cleaning up garbage. He hesitated for a second but Lisa's begging eyes made his teenage ego rear its head and shut up the timid voice of reason.

Climbing up the piles of rubbish and the rubble from surrounding buildings — the interactivity of the Layer was very annoying sometimes — they reached a narrow cleft. The road was here somewhere, surrounded on either side by walkways, but the devil-may-care attitude to the inhabited world had turned the alleyway into an offshoot of the landfill. The winding path led into darkness. The stench became dense and sticky, almost tangible.

Lisa coughed fitfully but Max did not stop and simply dragged her after him. His imagination was presenting him with vague but very exciting images. The rules of the genre meant that saving the girl would be followed by a reward. The hormones had done their work. The risk no longer seemed so great. "Forget the money, I'll earn more," he thought.

A faceless shadow stepped away from the wall and blocked their path.

"Where?" the guide inquired curtly.

"To the Upper Layer."

"A hundred, and another two hundred once you get there."

"For what?" Max asked indignantly.

"Look around you." The guide indicated the global breakdown around them and the associated difficulties.

"Fine," Max sighed. "Here!" He touched the shadow, and three hundred credits immediately disappeared from his personal account. It was almost all of his savings, which he had been planning to use to buy a sports flycar!

Oh, to hell with it! He began to shiver.

The faceless shadow accepted the payment. Lisa pressed closer to Max, unable to believe that her nightmare would soon be over.

The buildings suddenly rippled and disappeared. The stink dissipated. Max's head started spinning and when his consciousness cleared again, he was standing in the Upper Layer.

Max looked around him.

In truth, he was disappointed. It was a complete dump, in the language of the Net. The fields, hills, and woodlands, the glitter of a meandering river, the air heavy with the scent of freshly mowed grass, a few squat buildings in the distance — it was obvious that the virtual reality designer lacked the brains and talent to create something truly interesting.

Lisa' legs gave out from under her. She sank into the grass and began stroking it. Had she lost her mind?

"Hey, what's up with you?" Max said nervously.

"It's so good to be home." Lisa looked up at him gratefully. Her eyes glowed with a sincere joy. There was a smile on her face. "Is it time for you to go back?" She asked suddenly.

It was like she had poured a bucket of cold

water over his head.

Max choked.

"Is she joking? Or is she asking for it?" The last thought was too rude. The girl suddenly seemed so attractive, maybe because she was out of bounds, making Max's head spin and his voice betray him by shaking.

"Let me walk you home, at least!"

"No, that's not a good idea. You'll get into trouble." She replied softly and hesitantly.

"I don't care!"

"Alright, you can walk me home. It's not far. Do you see the house on the hill?" She suddenly laughed, happily pointing to a distant two-story building, surrounded by a garden.

"That's where you live?" Max was expecting to see a palace with a hundred spacious rooms at least.

"Well, this is just the virtual model of our real house. A little exaggerated, of course." Lisa admitted with some embarrassment.

"Where's your real house?"

"In reality, where else? But everything is a little different there. Space is limited due to the dome, with the clouds below and the city underneath them. There's not much space for plants. My real garden is small but very pretty! I chose every plant myself. I went to the Genesis Expo especially. Do you have any idea how much a sapling costs these days?"

"Well?" In Max's world, vegetation was nothing more than a background, and the most primitive and useless background at that. He knew about the biosphere that used to exist on Earth, and he considered it appropriate and sensible to try and recreate it in some historical realities, but here, in the Upper Layer? What the heck for?

"One of the saplings cost me seven thousand credits! It was really hard to persuade my father. He was so angry, he even called me a spendthrift!" Lisa looked sad. "And the sapling didn't even survive, can you imagine?"

Max couldn't imagine it. He did not understand her sadness and did not share her tender delight. But he kept quiet, hoping to thus appear clever. It was an old trick. Keep quiet and listen when you find yourself in a new reality.

No, this was not how he had imagined the Upper Layer at all.

Lisa took him by the hand. She was acting carefree and looked happy. A dreamy smile hovered around her lips. They walked along a road that meandered by the river and between hills. Max could not stop feeling surprised by the endless expanse, the lack of human crowds, and yet it made him feel uncomfortable. He didn't like it here. It was completely uncool and even boring.

There was nothing to draw the eye. Nothing mysterious. Living in such a Layer must be dead boring.

$$* \; * \; *$$

As it turned out, they had nothing to talk about. They had no common topics so they stayed silent for a while. Eventually, Lisa took the initiative and began to tell him about her life, how she reads antique books in the evenings, sitting in her tiny garden paradise.

"I've read my father's whole library, if you can believe it. Some books made no sense, of course."

"Why?" Max's enthusiasm was rapidly waning. Instead of a promising adventure, he had obtained something boring and mediocre. He was still trying to keep the conversation going, out of habit, using meaningless phrases and questions. It's the Upper Layer, after all, he kept thinking. Surely there was something worthwhile here, somewhere?

"You see, they talk about a completely different world," Lisa was saying excitedly and leaning close to him, which made Max's skin tingle. It was a terribly pleasant sensation. "People seem so strange in those books. Not like us at all. They think differently, they talk differently."

"Books..." Max frowned. "Are they those thick, heavy things with plastpaper pages?" He tried to show off his knowledge of the ancient world. In truth, he had come across such artifacts in games. You could use them to obtain certain useful skills, but you didn't need to read the book, just hold in in your hands for a few seconds.

"Yes, precisely!" Lisa brightened up. "But in reality they are very fragile and old. Many of them actually have paper pages, can you imagine?! They are treated with special chemicals so that the paper doesn't fall apart."

"What do you need them for?"

"My father collects antiques."

"To show off?" Max suggested intuitively.

"Yeah, kind of," Lisa admitted with a sigh. "He's very rich. He's got his own quirks. He gets annoyed when I pick up his books, but they're not just there for show, right?"

"I don't know," Max shrugged. "If I need information, I download it from the Net into my cyberstack."

The topic of antiques did not interest him in the slightest but the subtle scent of Lisa's hair stirred something up inside him. But why? Among the puzzling desires and impulses sat a sensible question: what's so special about her?

Was it the effect of the Upper Layer?

He sneaked a glance at her again.

There was nothing special about her! Apart from how *real* his feelings seemed and the acute, piercing emotion that her appearance stirred up inside him.

$$\ast \ast \ast$$

Casually chatting in this manner, they rounded a hill and suddenly came across a small gazebo, which lurked at the bend in the river, beneath two spreading ivy trees.

Two guys lounged there, appearing to be Max's age. They sat in rough-hewn and uncomfortable-looking armchairs. One was staring intently into a twinkling cube, while the second one chewed on a blade of grass and glanced around him with a bored expression.

"Hey, Lisa!" The unimpressive avatar noticed the pair and waved for them to come closer. "Come on over!"

"Are those your friends?" Max asked.

The girl tensed visibly. The shadow of annoyance flashed across her face.

"Yes." She slowed down. "You know, it would be better if you went back to your Layer. I'll be fine on my own. You don't want to mess with them, believe me."

Max again felt a burning sense of disappointment and hurt. He had been subconsciously expecting a completely different outcome. He glanced at the girl's freckled face. "Why are they all so pale here?" Came the annoying thought again.

"I'll stay!" He answered it like a challenge.

"As you wish," Lisa accepted this easily. "Let's go then," she took his hand and drew him after her. "Just don't go picking fights. And don't get mad if anything happens, you were the one who asked to stay." She warned him gloomily.

"Wow!" The guy acted surprised. "Lisa, why did you bring a 'can' here with you?"

"Gleb, would you drop it?" The girl sat in one of the armchairs, looking with interest at the pieces arranged inside the cubic space. The whites were clearly losing.

"Well, well, I had no idea that you visit the Middle Layer for this kind of entertainment." Gleb grinned arrogantly. "How is he? Not bad?"

"Are you looking for a punch in the face?" Max seethed with anger at once.

"Oh, please! What, from you?"

Bourne launched himself at his opponent but his arm passed right through the virtual body, and sudden pain appeared in his knuckles — he had struck the tall, plainly carved wooden back of the armchair.

"How was that?" Gleb grinned maniacally. "What are you bulging your eyes out for? The laws of your Layer don't work here!" He smiled nastily. "Have a seat." His hospitality was an obvious act. "Your arm won't fall off, don't worry, it'll just hurt for a bit."

Now Max couldn't just turn around and leave. It would have meant defeat. Pride had nothing to do with it, he was simply overcome with rage.

He sat down, staring at Gleb as if to challenge him and ignoring the second guy, who hadn't said anything.

"Dima, either make a move or resign. I'm sick of waiting for you. It'll be checkmate in a couple of moves anyway."

"Let me think!"

"All right, try to strain your brain a bit." Gleb agreed condescendingly.

Lisa stared gloomily at the arrangement of pieces inside the transparent cube.

Max had no idea what they were doing.

"Well, 'can'." Gleb turned to him. "How are you finding this Layer? Do you like it? I see you're awfully muscular."

"And you're a real pipsqueak!" Max was so pissed off that he felt his head spinning. "You couldn't order a normal avatar? Or couldn't you afford a decent virtual designer? You made it yourself?"

Gleb laughed for a whole minute, then wiped the tears from his eyes.

"What's so funny?" Max instinctively curled his hands into fists.

Lisa leaned towards him. "We don't use avatars," she whispered reproachfully. "Everyone wears their real faces here."

"Why?!" Max's eyes widened.

"Wearing an avatar is considered rude. It's not what normal people do."

"So, I'm abnormal, in your eyes?"

Lisa shrugged but didn't say anything.

"You're a 'can'." Gleb kept grinning at Max, looking him up and down. "What, you don't get it? Not familiar with the word?" He completely ignored the boring chess game and began to openly make fun of Max. "Before synthetic food appeared, it was how people preserved their food," He explained condescendingly. "Meat, for example. They would put the meat in tin cans and store it for years. Just like an in-mode, right?"

At first, Max was at a loss for words and couldn't think of a suitable comeback, while Gleb was on a roll.

"You're a slave, actually. A slave to our whims and pleasures."

"Watch it!"

"Why? You don't like hearing the truth? You shouldn't be here at all! We're free to go to the Lower Layer for fun. You're obliged to please us. How do you earn a living, for example?"

Max looked at Lisa for support, but the girl only shrugged, as if saying, "You're on your own, I warned you after all."

"I will have my own Universe!" Max burst out. Every teenager dreams of their own world, which other users will come and visit, but an enormous amount of work lies between dreams and reality. Max did not have the patience for such online heroics.

"You will?" Gleb asked cheerfully. "When?"

"Soon!"

"Don't try to avoid the question. How are you earning money right now?"

"It varies from time to time." Max muttered.

"And the times are different, are they?" Gleb continued sarcastically. "You've never tried the virtual brothels? They pay pretty well. I've been to a few and liked it, although when it was time to cough up..."

"Shut up!" Lisa couldn't take it anymore, and unexpectedly stood up and slapped him. It was a loud slap across the face, and it even left a red mark on Gleb's cheek.

Max could no longer control himself but he couldn't do anything either. Fury choked him, the urge to beat up Gleb was unbearable, but alas, he did not have the ability to affect things in the Upper Layer.

Gleb, meanwhile, rubbed his cheek and said threateningly, "Alright, scum, I've memorized your face. I hope you don't change avatars every day. No? Excellent. Just you wait. I'll come to your Layer and we'll have a proper chat there." He stood up, rudely shaking by the shoulder his friend, who had ignored the argument in his desperation to solve the difficult chess situation. "Dima, let's go."

"Why, what happened?"

"Nothing happened! Let's just go. Lisa can have her fun with this piece of canned meat."

Max had never before felt so humiliated, furious and helpless. Growing up among the bloody gaming realities, he never stopped to think about when to strike and when to run away. Always strike, always. Preferably to the death, so that even after respawning, the opponent's bones would ache from the virtual fractures.

"Well, how was that?" Lisa crossed her legs. She was acting very oddly, the dreamy smile gone and her face angry and focused.

"What the hell was he talking about?!"

"Regarding your Layer?"

"Yup." Max sat down in the awkward armchair and glared after the two receding figures.

"Gleb spoke the truth. Do you really not understand anything?" She was surprised.

"No!"

Lisa pursed her lips. "You're a tough case. I thought you were aware of your position in society."

"He called me a slave!"

"Who are you then?" The girl seemed to be deliberately adding fuel to the fire by continuing with this dangerous topic.

"I'm a free man!" Max yelled.

She shook her head sadly. "You're a free avatar."

Max frowned as she continued.

"Gleb is an asshole, of course, but he's right. You are a slave to the in-mode, to your living circumstances, to your status at birth, to the way of thinking formed in the virtual reality, any of these can be a reason. This does not change the essence."

"We will move the Antarctic Megacity soon!" He shouted out his last trump card.

"And who will you become there?" The girl asked.

"I don't know, I haven't thought about it yet!"

"You will live in the Layer, no matter where you move to," Lisa stated confidently.

Their conversation was turning out to be strange and unpleasant.

"Why do you keep harping on about it — the Layer, the Layer!" Max snarled. He could see nothing shameful in his way of life. "The virtual worlds constantly require inhabitants! They pay well. I could be anyone I want, a Roman legionnaire or a space explorer!"

"Which roles do you prefer?" Unlike Gleb, Lisa asked the questions without sneering or sounding arrogant, but rather like a researcher who has obtained a unique study sample. Max, blinded by his strong emotions, didn't notice this.

"Well, I like fantasy worlds! I enjoy racing too but I can't afford a decent flycar yet."

"Fine, let's say that you don't feel like a slave, but this doesn't change the nature of things." She stood up, came to sit on the wide arm of Max's chair and then gently touched his cheek, demonstrating her absolute right to affect objects in this Layer, reminding him of who was the owner and who was the guest. "Please don't be angry! I like you, as a matter of fact." Her touch made him feel both hot and cold. "Do you want to understand what's going on? And tell me, what would you prefer, the cruel truth about yourself or a quickie as a sign of my gratitude for saving me?"

A few minutes ago, he would have picked

the latter but now, his mind whirling from her proximity, Max suddenly began behaving contrary to his desires.

"The truth," he grunted. "But how do you know who I am, how I live, and what I'll become?!"

"It's my field of expertise," Lisa replied confidently. "I'm studying at the Academy of World Government. I'm in my last year. I study the psychology of cyberspace inhabitants."

"So how did such a clever girl end up amongst piles of rubbish?!"

"Well, if you remember, there was a network attack." The girl ignored the gibe. "I was tossed down into the base Layer. We normally get direct access to the right reality, bypassing your dump," She explained. "I was confused and frightened, my ability to instantaneously move through cyberspace was blocked. The defense programs that normally filter out most of the unpleasant interactive effects had stopped working. I would have suffocated there from the stench. For real! You really did save me." Lisa whispered the last phrase into Max's ear, her breath hot on his face.

He was completely lost in his urges, desires and thoughts. To hell with this Upper Layer!

"Do you remember how I was talking about books?" Lisa continued calmly as if ignoring his emotional state. "There were quite a few science fiction novels in my father's library. I read them all. The people in the twentieth century described the future so ridiculously and one-sidedly! They invented a lot but they could not imagine our reality at all!"

Her words flowed past him without eliciting a response, or so Max thought. He no longer wanted to hear the rest, no matter what she said. He wasn't interested in this 'truth' at all. He wanted to find a reason to stand up, turn and walk away, to forget about today's adventure forever.

"You see, Max, you are all," Lisa was clearly lumping all the inhabitants of the Middle Layer together, "complete sociopaths. These bizarre fantasy worlds have altered your consciousness, and have raised you all to possess qualities that have nothing to do with the real world. Love, friendship, honor, duty — do these words mean anything to you? Or have they been lost forever? Who and what do you treasure most of all? What does family mean to you, for example?"

Max only grimaced.

"I'll go." He muttered.

"No!" Lisa grabbed his hand. "Answer me first."

"You're even worse than Gleb!"

She shook her head in desperation. "Even if

the level of industrial fog suddenly drops, nobody will let you out into the real world."

"Why?!" Max said indignantly.

"Because a huge segment of the economy will collapse." She replied briskly. "Eighteen billion people currently live on Earth. Four billion live in in-modes, another billion even lower than that, in the capsule blocks at the very bottom. Thirteen billion people live above the middle. Think about or just try to imagine this number of people, concentrated in the megasuburbs, in the narrow layer between the industrial fog and the real clouds. They have nowhere to go. Nowhere to have fun. There is only one source of release for them — the phantom worlds of the Middle Layer. But the World Government has forbidden the use of artificial intelligence on the Net, thus creating a serious problem. Cyberspace has become predictable and boring, and a person who is going crazy from boredom is incredibly dangerous, believe me. The problem was solved as soon as the in-modes appeared. Now the worlds in the Middle Layer have no purely computer characters — they have been replaced with you."

"The population of the gaming worlds is actually made up of real people?" Max finally began to understand what Lisa was getting at.

"Didn't you know that?"

"I never thought about it." He grunted.

"You get paid. Only a little, the barest crumbs, to 'live' in a specific fantasy world. But why? And where does the money come from?"

"I have no idea!"

"Residents of the megasuburbs have to pay to enter the Layer," Lisa explained eagerly. "But every user wants to get the full range of possible entertainment for their money, and the computer bots simply can't handle such a challenge. Do you see? For the last ten years, in-mode inhabitants have completely replaced computer characters and have introduced variety and unpredictability into the fantasy worlds... and have become the slaves of the Layer."

"We are the living decorations?!" Max shuddered. He had never thought about it from this angle.

"Well, you happily transform into a monster if the contract pays well, right?" Lisa asked.

"Yes," He admitted and gulped.

"The owners of the fantasy worlds are the richest people on Earth. They pay you with money taken from other users, who, unlike you, do not live in the Layer but rather come there to amuse themselves in the way that they prefer. It's a well-functioning system. Nobody will lift a finger to change it. While the users are happy, while they have something to amuse themselves with and to waste time on, nobody will go out onto the street, nobody will protest, and nobody will even ask the awkward questions. That's why you will stay in the in-mode forever."

"What's the way out?" Max asked, bewildered.

"There isn't one. At least, not with the way things stand currently, when only 5% of the population work in real sectors of the economy. Perhaps something will change when we settle Mars, I don't know. So far, research is painting quite a dark picture. The people of the Layer are morally dead."

"Why are you telling me this? To make me angry?"

"You asked me yourself. I wonder what you're like in real life?" Lisa smiled sadly. "The avatar is just an attractive mask. Where is your soul, Max? Do you feel it yourself, are you aware of it?"

He shrugged carelessly. "I'm not interested in that."

"I know." The regret in her eyes became cold and thorny. "The people of the Layer have forgotten how to observe. They have made life worthless. Nobody is responsible for their actions. Most families have split up. A new generation has grown up which has been corrupted. You endlessly exploit your most primitive urges: you kill, wallowing in the bloody special effects. You roam from reality to reality. Your women are skilled at love but are unable to feel love. Your men are brutal but do they really know what courage is?" Lisa asked, looking at him thoughtfully. "And like a stone, you drag the other thirteen billion users with you to the bottom. No ancient science fiction writer could have predicted such a civilization..."

"Enough!" Max shouted, unable to stand it anymore.

"Shall I let you go?"

"Yes!"

"As you wish," Lisa shrugged her shoulders in disappointment.

A flash of light, a brief spell of dizziness.

The stench was overwhelming.

He opened his eyes. He was surrounded by mounds of rubbish, with gray tornadoes drifting between them.

Chapter Two

Earth. The Layer
In-mode location — Europe Megacity

MAX SPENT the two weeks after his unexpected meeting with Lisa in a very different way to how he had planned.

He couldn't forget what had happened and couldn't return to his previous way of life. He began waking up slightly earlier than usual, being rude to his parents, and he perceived his daily trips into the Layer differently. He was subconsciously seeking a rebuttal to Lisa's and

Gleb's words but found only confirmation, and this caused the psychological pressure on his mind to keep increasing.

Cyberspace.

"All that we have left in this life." This phrase stuck in his head like a constant reminder.

Max stood at the crossroads. He wasn't completely lost yet, with glimmers of his upbringing still simmering in him. Yet he had already sampled the vices readily available in the Layer and, unlike most of his peers, wasn't yet ready to drown in them, instead struggling on the surface and dreaming of something greater.

He began asking himself some very uncomfortable questions to which he had no answers. He distracted himself by plunging into various realities but this worked for only a while.

Ideas, each one crazier than the next, appeared and died in his inflamed and tormented imagination, but in the end, what could he really do? At best, he could gain people's attention with some eccentric escapade and become an icon for an hour or a day but never a lifetime.

Trying to escape the suddenly visible cage, Max even attended several online seminars dedicated to the various problems of the Layer, but he found neither answers nor like-minded individuals, only a new burden of contradictory information that he couldn't process. The veil of the fantasy world had been lifted but he couldn't see much through the narrow crack of imposed opinions.

Earth was dying, slowly and painfully. The real world was gradually becoming the dominion of machines, while the Layer rippled with the bizarre revels of the doomed.

The developers were unable to create a viable model of social relationships. Society was gradually disappearing, having outlived its use, at least here, in the Layer.

The streets of the virtual city were swarming with avatars. For billions of people, real life took place right here, in cyberspace.

Paths led from one building to the next past the reeking mountains of garbage, and someone's avatar wandered morosely at the intersection, dressed in futuristic armor. From time to time, he would call out in a monotone, "King Zigmund is gathering an army to invade the Arn Lands! Do not miss this opportunity! Five credits to the mercenary who joins the army, and an extra two credits for every enemy killed! Only the best and bloodiest special effects! Don't miss your chance to have fun and make some money!"

Max walked past without giving the figure a second glance.

Lisa had awakened new feelings in him.

They were burning him up, making him take on a mortal risk in response to the unexpected crush.

Five credits weren't enough. Access to the Upper Layer cost a lot more. Only a no rules race could provide the necessary amount of money, but flycar pilots often sustained serious injuries and even died in such competitions. The illegal track operators somehow managed to increase the interactivity level to unprecedented heights, and spectators paid for the rush of knowing that every collision could prove fatal.

Max had been lucky so far, although, truth be told, he didn't try to play the hero on the track, earning his two hundred credits as one of the dozen outsiders and not striving for the dubious glory of being the winner.

"Hello!" The Guide stood at the corner of the building, beside the familiar alley. "Same as usual? The Upper Layer?"

"Yup."

"A hundred and twenty credits."

"It was a hundred yesterday!"

"If you don't want to pay, you can stay here," the Guide shrugged his shoulders.

"You run a dodgy business! Regular clients should have a discount!"

"Keep your voice down before the whole Net hears you! Anyway, maybe you should go home today. You're too twitchy. I don't want any trouble."

"Alright, forget it." Max said to smooth things over and transferred the required amount to the Guide's account.

The man silently disappeared down the alley and Max followed him, trying not to fall behind. "It's a new route every time," he thought in surprise. "I wonder how the Guides always manage to find so many holes in the security?"

They entered a building. While Max studied the strange and tattered interior, the Guide unlocked an apartment door with an antique key and gestured for Max to follow him inside.

The dark hallway smelled damp.

"Well? Where to now?"

"The same way as you came in. The time limit is two hours. I'm not responsible for you if you don't come back the same way in time." The avatar dissipated into thin air.

Max shrugged and pushed the apartment door open again, expecting to see the same unsightly entrance.

The door revealed a completely different building, bright and with a high, vaulted ceiling and intricate paneling.

Max stepped out onto the street and looked

around.

He was in a park with the sun shining brightly overhead. He turned at the intersection of two paths, trying to avoid running into any other avatars.

Lisa's house stood on a hill. A street that had been made to look ancient led to the beautiful building.

His heart thudded in his chest.

They had met up thrice since the network attack two weeks ago. Max was losing his mind from his desires and emotions yet Lisa kept her distance as if on purpose, not rejecting his youthful ardency but not submitting to it either.

He was determined to keep himself under control, understanding intuitively that her delicate nature would not accept rudeness or crassness, but his first love burned brighter and brighter. He felt like he was suffocating in the in-mode, his world growing bleaker with each passing day, and it was only here, in the vastness of the Upper Layer, that he briefly came alive, sustained by his false hopes.

Lisa met him halfway today.

She appeared in the middle of the path, extending her arms and brushing her lips across his cheek, then immediately slipped out of his embrace.

"Let's go for a walk. There's a lake nearby.

It's really beautiful there." Her smile drove him crazy.

"Let's go." He took her by the hand.

His thoughts were a mess. There was a malfunction somewhere, and for a second he experienced the in-mode reality, the treadmill moving under his feet and the pressure from the nanofibers in his VR suit instead of the girl's fingers squeezing his hand.

He almost howled from the mentally painful contrast.

"Max, what's wrong?" Lisa let go of his hand and took a step back, shooting him a nervous look.

"Nothing. Sorry, just a glitch." He desperately tried to control his suddenly overwhelming emotions.

"Are you bored with me? You seem really twitchy today, and your avatar is malfunctioning." She glanced back at the hill. "Maybe I should go?"

"No, please, don't leave!"

"All right." Lisa turned onto a barely visible path that wound between the flowering shrubs. Max felt like he was being suffocated by the strong fragrance but they soon left the thicket and stepped out beside the still water.

Lisa walked across the narrow footbridge with her arms flung out for balance, then sat down at the edge and looked up at Max, chuckling:

"Why are you so tense today?"

Max sat down beside her.

"I really like you."

"I know." She sighed heavily. "I really like you too, Max."

He hugged her timidly, touching her cheek with shaking fingers.

"Don't," Lisa said.

"Why?"

"None of this is real."

Max felt like he had been slapped.

"We probably won't see each other again," Lisa said sadly. "Do you remember Gleb?"

"Yup." He never forgot the recent incident, not even for a second.

"He saw us together, the day before yesterday. The jerk reported us to the online police. And he told my father."

"Are you in trouble?" Max tensed.

"No, they won't do anything to me but my father was super angry. You know, I'd really like to meet you in the real world. But you're in the in-mode and I'm..." She smiled pitifully, folded her hands together and blew on them. Numbers appeared in the air, slipping like a gray snake into Max's cyberstack. "This is my number. In the real world. Call me if you ever get out of the in-mode."

"Lisa, but why? Why can't we..."

She kissed him so that he fell silent.

"Because I like you. I really like you. But all this," she indicated the shore, the trees and the bushes, "is fake. I'm sick to death of my fake life. I don't want it anymore and I don't want to meet you anymore. It's not going to work."

"Lisa, wait!"

"No, Max, don't. I'm tired of illusions. I hate the touch of tactile nanofibers. Call me if you ever get out." She repeated. "I'll give you a farewell hint — my father made an absolute fortune on the movement of industrial fog."

Then she was gone, vanishing into thin air.

$$\star \; \star \; \star$$

First love. It plunges us into the abyss of previously unknown sensations, overwhelming desires, illusions and hopes, burns us like fire, and quells the voice of reason, making us do crazy things.

Which one of us hasn't gone through that?

Max Bourne spent his twentieth birthday in his in-mode.

A hellish fire consumed him from within.

He blocked all his contacts, then went into the Net and refused to leave.

The streets of the phantom city were bustling with life. With every passing year, more and more people considered cyberspace their true habitat. Virtual reality contained everything... and nothing.

Max wandered aimlessly through the Middle Layer. It had been recently cleared of garbage and looked somewhat unusual, but Max barely noticed the pleasant change.

Lisa's final words echoed in his mind.

Of course, his dissatisfaction with life had been there before but the seed of rebellion would have never previously gained enough of a foothold.

Max sat down on a bench. He didn't know what to do. How could he escape the in-mode? How could he move to a significantly different level of existence?

The view around him only filled him with disgust and anger.

"Cans..." He spat. "A dream world has been engineered for us. They invented goals and gave us the means to achieve them. What is the point of it all?" The unfamiliar thoughts frightened him.

With just a few sentences, Lisa had opened his eyes and tore off the blinkers, and now he had nowhere to run and hide from the truth.

His imagination showed him millions of in-modes, with the grotesque outlines of their inhabitants, unwittingly comparing them to their obviously glamorized avatars.

First love is also blind. There is nothing stronger, more wondrous and more dangerous than this feeling, which gives life and brings death equally easily.

Max Bourne's world had cracked and was ready to fall apart, turning into a pile of senseless and ugly fragments.

His plans for the future now seemed so childish and pathetic.

"She lives in the real world. Above the clouds, where there are no in-modes. How will I ever reach her?"

He could try, of course. He was sure that the real world had its loopholes, just like the Net, but without the appropriate status or money he would remain an outcast, a crook, a trespasser. It was frightening, too. He had begun to forget what life was like outside the in-mode.

Reaching the age of majority was accompanied by a radical update of the software in his implant and cyberstack — he was now a fully-fledged citizen of Earth, and he automatically had access to new and previously unreachable opportunities. Max gained access to business networks, the right to enter into agreements under his own name, and a personal account in the World Bank, where 5,000 credits were deposited on the day of his twentieth birthday — a social handout from the World Government.

The industrial fog.

These words kept spinning in his head. Lisa had given Max a hint that he couldn't comprehend, no matter how long he thought about it.

"She didn't just say it for no reason! Am I really that dumb? The answer must be on the surface, it must be simple and obvious!"

He tried again and again.

Dozens of information streams flowed into the digital space of his in-mode. It was mainly data relating to the industrial fog and fluctuations in the toxic environment.

Utterly confounded by the tables and graphs, Max took the extreme step of hiring an expert neuronet, thus spending all the money he had received from the World Government.

He didn't obtain an immediate answer but he began to understand certain things.

Earth's single technosphere was going through a tumultuous process of growth and formation, gradually covering the planet in an artificial industrial coating like a tortoise's shell.

The toxic fog condensed at an altitude of 100-115 meters and was gradually drifting upwards. Initially, its upper level was predicted to stop at 270 meters. Buildings at this height had no windows and were given over to technical services.

Starting from three hundred meters, the city levels dramatically changed their appearance. The living complexes formed megasuburbs, millions of apartments and living capsules were put into service and occupied even before the appearance of the first unexpected emissions.

Max had personally experienced the consequences of the fatal errors made by the city planners in their calculations. He was seven years old when the industrial fog began to rise above critical levels. The apartments could only withstand the effects of the aggressive fog for short periods of time so the only way out of the catastrophic situation was the widespread introduction of the in-modes.

Things had only gotten worse over the past thirteen years. The toxic fog now enveloped the whole planet like a blanket. Three corporations, Megapool, Genesis and Rimp Cybetronics, were together looking for a solution but so far they had only managed to achieve small-scale victories.

The upper boundary of the industrial fog

had stabilized at a height of five hundred meters above sea level.

Hundreds of uninhabited dwellings at the capricious and precarious border between life and death had long ago lost their value. They were considered as potential spaces for in-modes, since the pace of construction of the Antarctic Mega City and the reconstruction of existing megacities still did not meet the needs of Earth's population, ever since the population explosion of twenty years prior.

The acute lack of housing was further exacerbated by the desires of the in-mode inhabitants to move into normal living capsules and thus improve their quality of life.

Four days passed before the truth began to glimmer in Max's mind.

Megapool continued to build new city levels, and as the megasuburb height increased, the strength and direction of the dominant winds changed as well.

The expert neuronet that Max had rented, having processed the maps of the industrial fog migrations and analyzed the data from hundreds of thousands of sensors, issued a startling and unexpected prognosis: in the next month, the upper border of the toxic emissions in certain parts of the Europe Megacity would drop to a level of 450 meters!

Hundreds of unoccupied living capsules would become habitable!

From there, he could work out the simple maths even without the expert neuronet: the living capsules were currently empty and on sale for a pittance, but the situation was about to change radically! Real estate prices were about to soar!

"Of course, there is a risk that the changes are temporary and that the boundary of the toxic zone will rise again but that's just a minor detail," Max thought frantically. "If I can buy even ten living capsules now, and sell them again after a while, I am guaranteed a way to the top! I'll become rich and my social status will change instantly!"

There was only one question remaining: where would he get the money to buy the living capsules? The bargain prices were in five figures, while his personal account had only 800 credits remaining after hiring the neuronet.

✳ ✳ ✳

Max's request was politely declined at the World Bank.

It was simply not possible to earn the required amount in the Layer. His dreams were slipping further from his reach and time was running out. He kept the results of the investigation secret, telling no-one of his goal.

He was having breakfast in a cafe when an unfamiliar avatar sat down opposite him. "Hello. I heard that you're looking for a large sum of money."

Max looked up from his plate.

A portly man sat opposite him, with a good-natured, open and particularly trustworthy face.

"You are mistaken," Max muttered out of habit. He wasn't a complete idiot, after all!

"I couldn't have made a mistake." The portly man smiled. "I possess quite reliable information." He noticed Max's suspicious gaze, and added. "From some very reliable sources at the World Bank."

Max felt cold inside. He had no experience with such negotiations.

"Let's get down to business."

"We don't even know each other."

"Is that really necessary? All right, young man, you can call me Andrey Sergeevich. I'm a private investor. I finance risky projects." He smiled again, very amicably. "We're talking about a sum of 190,000 credits, aren't we? Was I correctly informed?"

"Perhaps." Max knew that the whole situation was wrong, that even talking with a 'private investor' could lead to trouble. "But this information is confidential — you couldn't have obtained it."

"Oh, come on, Max!" The plump man waved a dismissive hand. "We're not living in the Middle Ages! Our whole lives are digitized, from birth to death. Information is money. You were overly cautious when you applied to the World Bank for a loan and that's what caught my attention."

"And you'll give me the money out of the kindness of your heart?"

"Of course not!" laughed the stranger. "Without knowing what you're planning to spend it on and thus being unable to calculate the risks involved, I am willing to provide you with the amount you need for only for a short amount of time, a month perhaps, with decent interest and mandatory collateral."

"I don't have the option."

"You're wrong about that! There are always options or I wouldn't be sitting here right now."

"You were misinformed."

"I don't seem like an amateur, do I?" the man looked offended. "Not long ago, you rented an expert neuronet and worked with it for a week. A very serious investigation, given the equipment's analytical capabilities. You must be certain in the success of your endeavor since you contacted the World Bank through official channels, and even offered your personal in-mode as security for the loan."

"So why was I refused?"

"They're too cautious. Your youth and your stubborn unwillingness to provide a business plan were a source of justifiable concern."

"But you won't get it either!"

"I don't need it. Let's get back to business. You have an in-mode, which costs around 26,000 or 27,000 credits. The adult members of your family each possess one too. Seventy-five thousand credits aren't bad, however, it's still not enough. But if we add the rights to the capsule apartment in the Antarctic Megacity, that's a serious amount and completely covers any possible risks that I may have!"

"It won't work." Max said glumly after a minute's thought. "Even if I wanted to, I can't provide this as a collateral. I have a strained relationship with my parents."

"Not to worry. You're sure of your success, aren't you?" asked the portly man.

"I'm sure but I won't be able to persuade my parents. I won't even try. They worked all their lives to pay for the opportunity to move to Antarctica."

"I understand," nodded the portly man. "And I'm ready to offer you a solution."

"There isn't one."

"Electronic signatures generated by your

parents' implants are enough for me."

"Was I not being clear enough? They're not going to sign anything!"

"That's unfortunate. Although your parents can remain blissfully unaware. I know a person who, for a certain fee, can make their implants transmit the required information."

Max flinched in surprise but then sat and processed the information. This 'Andrey Sergeevich' had turned up at the perfect time and had literally snagged Max with his unexpected offer.

"No! Don't do it!" protested Max's common sense but Max ignored it. "What's the catch?" he thought desperately.

"So my parents won't find out? What if... what if my idea fails?"

"Alas, in that case, your parents will have to give up their property in Antarctica and even their personal in-modes. But, I assure you, the city authorities will not abandon them and will provide living spaces in the capsular block, somewhere on the lowest levels, with a change in their social status on the Net, naturally."

Max shuddered, imagining the future that the man was describing.

"This is your chance, young man. You can either reduce your financial requirements, and then we can limit ourselves to only your personal in-mode, or seize the opportunity that I'm offering you. I'm not in a hurry. Think about it."

"What's the trick?! If you can obtain electronic signatures generated by the implants," he mentally shuddered at the possibility, "then why are you talking to me at all?"

"I'm not a crook or a thief, young man!" Andrey Sergeevich exclaimed. "I'm just a humble financier. If it comes to the courts, I need a motive. Think about it, why would your parents take out a loan? They have no reason to! Their son is something else altogether. Frankly, I don't care where and how you spend the money. I'm not risking anything. This is how I earn a living. You give me the certified documents and I give you a loan."

"I don't understand!" Max got annoyed. "This whole deal smells fishy! According to the rules, I must indicate the legal source of my funds!"

"I am the legal source," Andrey Sergeevich replied calmly. "You will legally receive short-term credit."

"And who will be the one giving it to me?"

"I'm registered as a private investor. This is my business, get it?"

"Not really. You're risking..."

"I'm not risking anything!" the man waved a chubby hand. "Rather, I am making the most of the opportunities wasted by the large financial institutions."

"Why don't you just fake the signatures and gain their property?" Max persisted.

"Oh, the young..." The plump man sighed. "Look, why would I want to break the law?"

"But you've just been encouraging me to forge..."

"Firstly, nobody's forging anything!" the man exclaimed. "The unique signatures are genuinely generated! Still, it looks like I'm wasting my time here!" He stood up to leave.

"How do I find you again?" Max asked hoarsely, without lifting his eyes from the table.

"I'll be here in a few days, at the same time."

"How do I meet the other person, the one that..."

"You don't need to meet anyone. Your agreement will suffice. You don't need to worry about the rest; I'll organize everything."

Max slumped. "It's scary... But the deal is a surefire win! If I sell even one capsule apartment, I'll be able to pay off my debts in full! No one will get hurt! My parents won't even know about it!"

"Wait!" He couldn't resist the temptation. "Let's discuss the details," he uttered, feeling like he had just taken a step off a precipice.

✳ ✳ ✳

The investor wasn't lying. The very next morning, 190,000 credits were transferred to Max Bourne's account.

He acted immediately, carefully selecting ten capsule apartments and purchasing them through the Net. Max wasn't quite sure what to do next. Should he stay in the in-mode? Explore the gaming worlds?

No, the neural network couldn't have made a mistake. Which meant that it was time to get out of the 'can' and get used to his new life!

Fear drove him to take the last desperate step. If something went wrong, how would he ever look his parents in the eye?

He was running away but he called it something else in his head.

The in-mode case opened with a hiss.

Silence. The stale odor of an unlived room.

Max stepped over the threshold, crossing the line between his two lives. He remembered this apartment only vaguely but this no longer mattered.

The in-modes took up almost all the available space. No light came through the shaded window. It was creepy. He cautiously headed into the hallway, afraid that the servos had altered it as well. What if they'd all been sealed shut in here?

No, the door to the stairway was still in the same place. A red light shone beside it. On either side of the door, Max noticed five sets of protective gear, and found the one that fit him. He hurriedly and clumsily put it on and headed to the door, without even a glance back at the in-modes containing his parents, brother and sister.

The scanning beam passed over Max's outfit. The program could find no fault in the sealed connections, and a sign appeared in front of the wall.

Are you sure that you want to go outside?

"Yes, of course!" he touched the confirmation icon. The door opened with an unexpected screech that further strained his nerves. How many years has it been since it was last used?

The staircase was dimly lit. Only the occasional light panels shone dully and a servo scuttled by, its gears rustling.

There was no-one around. The apartment doors were all firmly shut. Red lights glowed everywhere. The lift wasn't working so Max had to look for the emergency stairs and descend the steps.

Max felt like he was the only person left in the world. The deafening silence, broken only by the sound of his own footsteps and nervous breathing, frightened him. The descent seemed endless. Floor after floor, going further and further down. Is anyone else still alive? Stupid thoughts crowded around in his head, filling him with dread.

He couldn't stand it and opened the door leading to the corridor on the next floor.

A chill ran down his spine. "No way!" His glance took in the neat rows of in-modes. "Wasn't there enough room in the apartments? Or were they installed later? What do I care, anyway?!" He slammed the door shut and continued down the stairs but the endless rows of in-modes kept floating before his eyes.

Max reached the building entrance after about thirty minutes, his nerves stretched to breaking point. After thirteen years inside the in-mode, he could barely cope with reality. Will the flycar that he had ordered online wait for him or will he have to make his way on foot? His anxiety grew. The empty world with only the occasional servo to break the monotony seemed like an endless backdrop to an event that had never taken place.

He kept thinking as if he was still in a virtual reality, not realizing the irreversibility of what had occurred. Every step took him further and further away, the gap between his in-mode existence and the unknown and uncertain future growing ever wider.

His childhood memories pulsed in his mind. Here is the building exit that leads to the city level streets. The once-spacious entrance hall was now crammed full of long lines of in-modes, suspended from the ceiling with metalloplastic clamps, past the coiling cables and corrugated pipelines that envelop them, and all this was blanketed in silence.

He hurried to the massive double doors. His seven-year-old self remembered that beyond lay a park under a clear dome, then a car park slightly further on, with curving road junctions leading up and down from it.

The neighborhood was unrecognizable. The trees and bushes were gone. Only the bases of the flowerbeds, lawn borders and paths remained but these elements of the past seemed insignificant among the global changes.

It was the same under the dome: the "green zone" was filled with endless rows of in-modes. There was almost no space left between them.

Reality felt deathly cold. The unfamiliar sensation of dread chilled him to the bone. Segments of the dome overhead still remained transparent so that he could see the billowing yellow-gray haze beyond, making it seem as if the industrial fog had devoured the whole planet.

Making his way between the in-mode and stumbling over the cables underfoot, Max almost lost his way. His nerves were stretched to breaking point. He could not have imagined that the long-coveted freedom would be so grim, monotonous and creepy.

He found the car park entrance by following reminders of the past. Parts of the central alley's decorative elements could still be seen among the desolation. Max occasionally stumbled across sculptural compositions that had lost their meaning, sections of dried and cracked soil, and even the dark stumps of felled trees.

Despite his fears, the ordered flycar was waiting for him. The car stood by the airlock, its running lights glowing in the murk.

It was windy outside the dome. The gusts nearly knocked Max off his feet. Crouching, he ran to the car and clambered inside, then told the autopilot the address of the first apartment that he could think of, one of the ten that he had purchased.

The car slowly glided away, turned onto the junction and began to climb up the multilevel road.

Max fell back onto the soft chair, utterly spent. The fear slowly abated as other cars began to appear around him, and from time to time, reacting to the movement of the vehicles, both sides of the motorway would erupt with multicolored flashes.

He looked closer and realized that it was the holographic ad panels coming to life.

Could it be that people have all been tucked away inside the in-modes but some shops on this level still generate ads?

So it was! He leant towards the window, examining the shop fronts. The flashes of color illuminated offers of goods and services that had now become meaningless.

What if the expert neuronet was wrong? What if the level of the toxic emissions remained the same?

Cast aside such thoughts! Everything will work out!

The flycar unexpectedly rose up above the haze and Max's heart lurched. He saw gigantic megasuburbs, a web of multilevel roads between the cliffs of super skyscrapers, and a myriad of lights. For a few seconds, he could see the panorama of the city, an incomprehensible behemoth that was *alive*.

In the next moment, the yellow-gray tendrils of the fog rushed towards him and again swallowed up the car. Although the anxiety was still there, it had dulled, and Max felt an aching sense of delight.

"Everything will work out!" He kept telling himself.

The next three days tested him to the maximum.

It turned out that life in the in-mode had radically changed not only his mind but also his physiology. He couldn't fall asleep. The trimodular capsule apartment seemed too large to Max and the location of the equipment felt inconvenient. Access to the Net was provided by technology from 20 years ago and everything that he was used had disappeared. Max drifted from room to room, surprised at how clumsily everything was designed.

During the first night, he tossed and turned on the wide and uncomfortable bed. His head ached from anxiety and fatigue but sleep would not come. His body craved the sleeping gas, a function absent in a capsule apartment.

Time passed painfully slowly. He tried to watch the spherovision but the primitive device only irritated him, while the news from the real world seemed pointless.

On the second day, Max began to understand that he would soon go mad.

Sleep wasn't sleep. Reality wasn't reality.

The day became a mind-numbing and endless wait.

Sitting down at the table, Max choked on the tasteless food paste, and gradually and with some irritation discovered the true purpose of many items that he knew about but had never used in reality.

The second and third sleepless nights brought him to the brink of complete despair but the long-awaited event finally occurred on the fourth day!

Max was beside himself with joy when he saw in the morning news a report about the unexpected migration of the industrial fog.

He leapt up and ran to the window but still saw the same depressing murk outside.

Into the Net! Quickly!

The primitive equipment no longer annoyed him. He entered the digital space, spending the last of his money to connect to the sensors positioned at various city levels.

Five! Five of the ten capsule apartments that he had purchased were above the level of toxic emissions!

Max wasted no time. He immediately posted a 'for sale' sign online and received the first response from a potential buyer only a couple of hours later.

He closed the sale by the time evening

came and received 150,000 credits, immediately spending a third on... the purchase of an in-mode.

He could see no other way of preserving his sanity. Another miserable and sleepless night frightened him so much that he even paid a significant sum for urgent installation of the individual life support module.

The servos quickly delivered the necessary devices but it took them until midnight to finish assembling everything. All this time, Max sat aloof in an armchair, occasionally falling into an anxious dose but startling awake at every loud noise.

He had no strength left to rejoice in his success. He was wrung out both morally and physically, desperate for a decent night's sleep and to be able to go online properly.

The servos finally assembled the in-mode and Max immediately kicked them out, not even letting them test the equipment properly. He climbed inside as if drunk, and blissfully watched the walls of the individual shell come together. A minute later, the intoxicating smell of the sleeping gas enveloped Max, plunging him into oblivion.

For the first time in several days, he slept

like a baby.

The dear, cozy in-mode. A trusty defense from all the unpleasantness of the rough and miserable real world.

Max woke up in the morning, feeling wonderfully refreshed. Hopes and plans were bubbling in his head again. After a quick breakfast, he went online. The industrial fog had dropped by another fifteen meters during the night. Nine of the remaining capsule apartments were now in the 'clean' zone. The price of each one had jumped to 200,000 credits but the buyers were being cautious and didn't rush into purchasing property. He hadn't received any more offers and the news appeared contradictory, but that's OK, he thought. The strength and direction of the wind remained the same just like the neural network had predicted. Give it a day or two and many people would believe that the changes were permanent.

"I'm rich! I can live anywhere I like with that kind of money!" His enthusiastic thoughts were marred by the dark memories of the last few days, but Max refused to give in to the gnawing fear. "I have to get used to the changes," he thought decisively.

His social status had changed automatically but Bourne had prudently concealed this information from other users. He didn't want his parents to find out about his dizzying rise too early.

"What should I do? How do I fight my phobias?"

Max perked up. He was now so certain of himself and his success that he thought of only the future. "How am I going to join the 'cloud' society if I'm tied to the in-mode? I'll be a laughing stock!"

He left the capsule apartments in auto-selling mode and climbed out of the in-mode. This time, the vacant premises did not make him feel so acutely depressed. He went to the window and looked outside.

The industrial fog hovered around thirty meters below him. He could see previously obscured details. He couldn't see the city as such because of the unfinished buildings crowding around. It appeared that Megapool had paused their construction when the toxic emissions had made these levels unfit for human habitation.

He got dressed and ordered a flycar.

The 100,000 credits left after the purchase of the in-mode affected his mind in a strange way. The easy money itched at him, as if saying, "Spend me!"

The voice of reason was silent. Max felt like a completely different person. All his troubles were behind him!

The computer at the door did not demand that he put on a protective suit. The Global Health System recommended only an antitoxin, and two pills conveniently rolled out into a tray beside the door.

Max swallowed them and went out into the entrance hall.

There were changes everywhere. The lift was working. The lighting was much brighter. He noticed servos in the passageway, tidying up and removing dirty marks from the walls.

The acute anxiety attacks did not reappear and Max perked up further. The new life drew him like a magnet and the recent trip seemed like a bad dream. "What was I expecting to see or feel when I got out of the zone of the industrial fog?" he thought, writing off his recent fears to the circumstances and easily turning his own shortcomings into some heroic achievements.

His mentality could not actually change so radically in only a few days but the world felt renewed. Max exited the building and looked around, breathing shallowly through his nose, as recommended by the instructions coming into his cyberstack.

The city level had never been completed. The skeleton of the megasuburb reached up into the sky while a wind howled through the empty window frames of levels that, until recently, were surrounded by toxic emissions.

A flycar from the city transportation service landed softly by the exit and the door opened. The soft voice of the onboard computer invited Max inside and politely enquired about his desired destination.

"Into the city," he said vaguely, making himself comfortable.

"Please specify the address."

"Above the clouds. We'll see once we get there."

The autopilot obediently planned a route to the nearest highest point of the Megacity, warning his client that the trip would take five hours.

Max nodded and looked out of the window. His new life was beginning and he wanted to get a taste of it, and to understand what true freedom really meant.

★ ★ ★

Many significant events occurred that morning, and one of them took place on the outskirts of the Europe Megacity, where the spurs of the city's foundations drilled into the ancient mountain ridge.

The industrial fog lay low, drifting lazily over the lifeless gray slopes. No one lived here.

The mountain valleys, where luxury ski resorts used to flourish, had all disappeared, completely buried under garbage[1].

A group of five flycars bearing the Genesis logo appeared above the lifeless terrain and circled the area. One of the vehicles then landed and disgorged an assault team.

The people in the heavy servomotor suits formed a line and began to scout the surface of the dump. A small area considered stable enough to support the weight of the multiton aircraft was soon cordoned off.

The industrial fog hung low overhead. Tendrils of toxic gas drifted up from the depths of the landfill and joined the gray mass above.

The airlock opened and the ramp jingled. A lean old man descended the metal steps and stopped, carefully inspecting his surroundings. He wasn't wearing a suit and took shallow breaths through his nose. The devices built into his clothing were more reliable than a vacuum suit, allowing him to walk amongst the poisonous heaps.

Only a handful of people on Earth had access to such technology.

While the research groups took samples of the toxic soil, set up equipment, surrounded certain areas with buoys, and made notes on

---

[1] Small mountain valleys are being used as landfills even now.

electronic maps, Ulrich Otto von Fitzgerald, the founder of Genesis, strolled among the reeking refuse.

Why was the owner of the most powerful corporation on Earth personally visiting a common landfill, one of the dozens surrounding any megacity? There was no purpose to it, only risk.

Another flycar, this one bearing the logo of Rimp Cybertronics, appeared out of the gray haze and immediately landed.

The airlock opened with a hiss. The massive armored figure of a guard appeared in the oval hatch, followed by a woman in a light exploration suit.

"Catherine, my dear!" Fitzgerald stretched out his hand. "Why didn't you make use of my present?"

"Hello, Ulrich. It's nice to see you. Your present raised some doubts with my security service."

"Don't you trust me? What a shame." Fitzgerald lifted his hands in dismay. "As you can see, I feel perfectly fine."

"But why are we here?" Cathy Rimp unclipped the visor on her soft helmet. The suit's system immediately created extra pressure, mercilessly wasting resources to enable her to breathe and talk as per normal.

"You asked for a face-to-face meeting but there are ears everywhere."

"And here?"

"Here we can talk freely without the fear of spies."

"Is this why you purchased this dump?" She was surprised by yet another one of Ulrich's eccentricities.

"I have a large project planned here. To show the world how biotechnologies will breathe life into dead valleys, transforming waste into fertile lands. I'll create an oasis of life, using the toxic environment as the source material."

"A good move but hardly practical, I think. Earth is hopelessly dead."

Their long-standing argument about the progress of human civilization lay beneath their words. The merciless battle between the technosphere and the biosphere had led to the death of all living things. Cathy Rimp and Ulrich Fitzgerald represented two mutually exclusive points of view, which, nevertheless, did not prevent them from maintaining a friendship.

"Not all projects are undertaken to reap immediate profits. You know what I mean, don't you?" Ulrich hinted vaguely at the proposal that he had received from Cathy Rimp and the reason for today's meeting.

"Certainly." She shrugged her shoulders as

she looked around. "It's creepy when I think about what Earth has turned into."

"I agree," Fitzgerald smirked. "Just you wait, you'll be coming here for a holiday in a couple of years."

"So soon? You're not exaggerating?"

"No, no. The bacteria will deal with the rubbish in seven months. While my babies are working, we will mount atmospheric processors along the perimeter. Active transformation of the soil will take three months, and developing the ecosystem will take another year."

"Genetically modified plants?"

"Oh no, that's all in the past!" Fitzgerald waved his hand dismissively. "It's all about bioadaptive life forms now!"

"Ulrich, do you really know what you're doing? You're not going to create a monster? I think that bacteria capable of devouring centuries worth of garbage are a direct threat to the technosphere."

"Your mistrust hurts me, Catherine. The life expectancy of my babies, just like their reproductive rate, is strictly limited. They possess a terminating gene, which will activate after a certain number of generations. They'll devour the dump and then die. We've tested it all. Your precious technosphere will continue to thrive. Let's take a walk. Do you see that bubbling lake?

I suggest that we have a picnic on its shore."

"You're so twisted!" Cathy hooked her arm through his.

"Oh, come on. We'll sit down and have a lovely chat. By the way, what will we chat about?"

"Didn't you get all of my preliminary data?"

"Catherine, talking to you is no fun. How do you combine such naive romanticism and pragmatism?"

"Ulrich, the first interstellar flight is no laughing matter. I can't complete such a project alone. Have you familiarized yourself with the documents?"

"Yes," he grunted unenthusiastically. "It's impressive. The Alpha Colonial Transport sounds very majestic."

A circle of mobile climate complexes had already been set up on the shore of the toxic lake, a table and two armchairs appearing there as if by magic. A stocky major opened a bottle of vintage champagne.

"Are you making fun of me?" Cathy Rimp stopped and sharply turned to face Ulrich. "Enough joking around! I'm determined to have a serious and meaningful conversation!"

They sat down at the table.

"Catherine, are you really that naive? Do you think I need such a risk? Or is your goal to make a financial hole in the Genesis Mars project?" It was better not to start an argument with Ulrich about the red planet as he was famously paranoid on this topic. "I'm not going to back away from my plan! Mars belongs to me and will be terraformed as planned. Not a single megacity, do you hear me?"

"I haven't come here to talk about Mars! Nobody is trying to sabotage your projects."

"Except Megapool," replied Fitzgerald, his disdain evident. "Are not today's problems, extreme to the point of absurdity, due to the greed of the corporations?" He asked this without a shade of irony. "Did they not use their aggressive advertising to convince this generation of people that universal prosperity was coming very soon? We let the demographic explosion get out of hand, and are now paying the price. Yet even this is not enough for Megapool! They've got their sight set on Mars, I just know it!"

"We are all to blame for this situation." Cathy Rimp tried to gently divert Ulrich away from the topic of Mars, otherwise they would not have a normal conversation.

"Just don't lump me in with you all! I warned everyone that the creation of a single technosphere would completely doom our planet! I was proposing a bill to limit the birth rate. I was ready to introduce the necessary biotechnologies. Did anyone listen to me?"

"Ulrich, what good is it to reopen old wounds? It was impossible to unite the Earth without giving them hope."

"So you knew in advance what was going to happen?"

"Certainly not!" Cathy Rimp exclaimed. "The forecasts for the level of industrial fog were optimistic. That was why I hadn't supported your suggestion to restrict the birth rate. We had successfully begun the global urban reconstruction, and the demographic explosion was inevitable, really. People gained new technologies and new living space. Their lives improved..."

"Until the first toxic fallout!" Fitzgerald reminded her acerbically. "The problem is that you have destroyed the biosphere but you have nothing to replace it with! There is no technology capable of doing that! It is beyond the abilities of any sewerage treatment facility! Whatever," he waved his hand dismissively. "Let's leave the past alone. Let's bury a couple of generations in the in-modes, so what? It's not a big deal! But I'm giving you a fair and honest warning: I will not give up an inch of the Martian territories!"

"That's not what we're talking about!"

"Megapool doesn't think so! There'll be no place left to build in ten years! It's a dead end. You should have contacted Bryzgalov directly."

"Yet I contacted you. We have worked together successfully in the past." Cathy Rimp responded gently, knowing that Ulrich would shout for a bit but then eventually calm down.

Fitzgerald only smiled bitterly.

The fight between the corporations was becoming more and more acute with every year. The lack of living space, scarcity of resources, and radically opposed views on how to further develop civilization were all factors that prevented them from working together.

"Catherine, tell me this: we developed and implemented biocybernetic devices, implanting them into the entire population of Earth, and what was the practical impact of the project? Why do people need these implants? So they can generate unique mnemonic signatures?! We never did achieve a direct neurosensor connection between the human brain and the cybernetic systems."

"It's only a matter of time," Cathy Rimp replied evasively. "The implants have laid the groundwork for a new stage in human progress. We created a universal device that was successfully implanted into ninety percent of Earth's inhabitants. But further development in technology requires many years of painstaking research. Meanwhile, we're getting test responses from the implants, collecting statistical data and eliminating some obvious technical errors."

"And what will a direct connection of the human consciousness to cyberspace give us? Personally, I'm happy with the work that has been done. It is indeed unique and cutting-edge technology, but where does it all lead?"

"To the stars," Cathy Rimp stated softly but with certainty.

Fitzgerald frowned. "I don't understand why you have suddenly decided to invest your money in a spaceship. It will reach its goal when neither of us will be alive. What reason is there for me to participate? I've got plenty of my own ideas to develop. Think about it, creating a biosphere for a whole planet from scratch — isn't that a worthy life goal?"

"I'm not saying that terraforming Mars isn't important and necessary. Yet our future lies in other star systems."

"No, I'm not buying it! Either justify my interest in this project or drop the subject. The resource crisis is in full swing and fights over lunar deposits are inevitable. Then comes the asteroid belt. In such a situation, we need to build battleships and mining ships, rather than dream about long-term and highly dubious interstellar projects!"

"The war for resources makes no sense at all," Cathy Rimp rebutted him coldly.

"Sure it does! Earth's population needs to be fed. The technosphere needs to be developed. Cities need to be built. And where does one get the raw materials?"

"Why do we have to fight? We can divide the commodity sectors in a civilized manner!"

"And who will be the arbitrator? The World Government?" Fitzgerald flapped his hand. "Do we divide it equally? Fairly? Do you honestly believe that? Even in the best scenario, someone will remain unhappy. To give you an example, this is how I foresee things developing. Megapool, with the support of Cryonics, will start yelling about Genesis' monopoly on the Martian lands. Either give us a piece of the Martian pie, or I'm," he jabbed himself in the chest, "not getting a gram of the lunar resources!"

"I will stand against them if you support my project."

"Catherine, my dear! Enough of this madness! I want to transform Mars and turn it into a *living planet*, do you understand? All the local resources are going into construction and providing tens of thousands of atmospheric processors! How am I to feed the population of Earth? I need raw materials, energy and money, more so than anyone else!"

"And you will start a war with the other corporations?"

"If it comes to that! With the full support of Earth's population, mind you! Everyone wants to eat. Every day."

"A fragile position. A disruption in the food supplies and," Cathy Rimp gave Ulrich an icy look, "Genesis' monopoly turns from a positive into a huge negative."

"Are you threatening me?"

"Goodness, no! I'm just outlining a possible future. If in the midst of a threat of famine, someone influential announces that Genesis is being negligent with the technologies that billions of people rely on, what will be the response, do you think?"

"I don't care! You think that I'm afraid of a hunger riot? Who's going to go out on the streets?" Ulrich snorted in contempt. "Ninety percent of the world's population now spends its whole life in cyberspace! They don't care what happens in reality, as long as — *pop*!" he imitated the characteristic sound of the pneumatic delivery system, "they get the food paste capsules delivered to their tray three times a day! I don't care about the remaining ten percent. I'll manage. And I'll change the World Government if it suddenly starts to act up!"

"There is a sensible way out of the resource crisis."

"What is it, then?"

"We will divide the Moon fairly. Nobody will touch Mars, I guarantee it. We'll give the asteroid belt to the World Government."

"Since when?!"

"For reasons of economic benefit. None of the corporations can handle exploring and developing the asteroid belt on their own at present. New space technology is needed. Who is going to create it?"

"Well, Cryonics can."

"Cryonics is currently in a difficult financial situation. They're willing to cede the space yards at a reasonable price."

"I'm not going buy them."

"Neither will I, and certainly not Megapool. The only one left is the World Government, with the budget of Earth at their disposal."

"And we'll get an independent space fleet? Another unpredictable force?"

"A transport fleet," Cathy Rimp corrected him gently. "Let them gather resources and engage in space transportation by delivering raw materials to Earth's orbit — it will benefit us."

"I doubt it. Control of the asteroid belt will only strengthen the World Government."

"Ulrich, tell me honestly, what is the advantage of war? Are you ready to build a corporate fleet right now? Do you have spare money for the arms race?"

"No.

"Well, neither do I. So let Earth's budget work in our interest."

"What a strange position you take, Catherine! You're ready to build an interstellar colonial transport. You even have the money, right?"

"A third of the required amount."

"Right, and let's assume that you will get the other third from the World Government, if you succeed in shaking the remainder out of me and creating a new, independent space carrier."

Cathy Rimp nodded.

"You want to get the missing amount from Genesis?"

"Yes."

"I have one question for you — why are you doing this? But tell me the truth, no excuses like 'I have always dreamed of it' and no dribble about the 'future of humankind'."

"What if I really think that?"

"Then I wonder how you managed to stay in business?"

"One doesn't cancel out the other. There's nothing shameful or naive in thinking about people. We are nothing without them, after all."

"I agree," Fitzgerald nodded reluctantly. "There is truth in that. However, I still don't understand why you need this colony project."

"It's our insurance, Ulrich. Our chance for further development. If I am perfectly honest, it is also a chance for me to leave Earth one day."

"Are you mad?" Fitzgerald lost his temper. "You'll go into a cryogenic chamber for hundreds of years? That technology is completely unreliable. It still needs a huge amount of testing!"

"Cryonics is working on it as we speak."

"I don't understand you. I really don't. Why do you want to go to the stars? Do you want me to set aside some territory for you on Mars? I'll make it green! You'll live in a paradise!"

It was as if she didn't hear him. "Ulrich, have you ever thought of what you would do if a global catastrophe was to occur tomorrow?"

"I'll survive it!"

"What then? I know you'll survive it. And you will find yourself standing uselessly over the ruins of civilization. You won't be able to resurrect Earth or terraform Mars. The threat is real, and we are virtually uninsured from it."

"So?"

"The very idea of an interstellar flight will require completely new technologies, and will lead the corporations to an utterly different and much higher level of development and cooperation. What are we doing now? We're completing the cities, fussing over the capricious and still very unreliable technosphere, picking up the last crumbs of Earth's resources, feeding billions of people who are wasting their life in the Layer. We're fussing. Our progress has stalled and we're afraid to take one step further. We have banned AIs and restricted food production biotechnologies. We have created so many bans now that we have finally realized how fragile our world is. I'm afraid, Ulrich."

"Of what?"

"Of being held hostage by a dead planet. We need to stop digging in the sandbox and start developing further. We need to polish off the cryogenic chamber technology, build the first interstellar spacecraft, and then an entire fleet. I don't even need to persuade you, just look around. Earth is beyond hope. We are sitting amongst human refuse, on the shore of a poisoned lake. Whether you create an oasis here or not is beside the point. It won't survive for long. Megapool will finish building the Antarctic Megacity and reconstructing the other cities, and Rimp Cybertronics will fill them with technology, but what will we all do then?"

Fitzgerald thought over her words for a long time. "Based on the obtained documents, do you seriously believe that the World Government is capable of building interstellar ships?"

"Not right now. But we can let the

authorities develop. Let them buy the shipyards from Cryonics. Let the World Government develop a segment of the commodity economy. We will build the first spaceship. We will create not only the ship but also a range of technologies for settling other worlds."

"There are big risks," Fitzgerald spoke thoughtfully. "I want to raise the stakes," he announced suddenly.

"In what way?" Cathy Rimp asked in surprise.

"In return for funding the project, I will try to lift the ban on a whole range of biotechnologies."

"Which ones?"

"Hybrids. Cybernetic organisms."

"Their use is unacceptable on Earth, as well as pointless."

"They'll come in useful in space and on Mars! Just like the next generation AIs that you are developing in secret, despite the bans. How are things going in that field, by the way?"

"Taking into account the mistakes of the past, it is going very slowly. I want to create AIs that can accumulate experience but whose self-development is kept within very tight boundaries. A difficult task, wouldn't you agree?"

Ulrich nodded.

"So what about the biotechnologies?" he

inquired.

"It's an unexpected demand."

"Nor will it be my last demand, far from it. I don't share your optimism about the resources in the asteroid belt. I'm worried about the future of Mars."

"The future of your project, you mean?"

"Call it what you will. Financing the construction of the first interstellar transport will weaken Genesis' position. I will gradually lose my operating funds, yet terraforming Mars will require constant investments."

"What are you saying, Ulrich? Tell it to me straight!"

"Catherine, I will be acting blindly if I finance your project. Whatever your current estimates, the real costs of the project cannot be predicted. I suspect that with ongoing research and development, the cost of constructing the colonial transport will increase multifold. We're not just going to the Moon, after all."

"Do you have a solution?"

"With the successful launch of the Alpha Colonial Transport, the World Bank will return 50% of the invested capital back to me. I will, in turn, support your plan to create an independent space carrier. For your part, you will ensure that Mars is kept out of Megapool's reach. By working together, we will lift some of the technology bans.

AIs and hybrids, a combination of genetics and cybernetics, will be allowed to exist on Earth."

"These are harsh demands."

"They are doable. You are right in many ways about Earth. The planet is dead and it is time to move on. My path leads to the planet Mars and your path leads to the stars, vague as that future may be. Let's think practically. I will receive the guarantee of the World Bank and a lifting of the ban on many types of technology. How long will it take to design and construct the Alpha, do you think?"

"Ten years, presumably."

"Ah! The Martian atmospheric processor network will be complete by then and active terraforming will have begun. I'll need a huge amount of money!"

"I'll need to think over your terms."

"Think it over, Catherine, but don't forget about the present. Resources, resources and more resources! We either divide them between us or conflict is unavoidable. Now, let's finally have a drink!" He suddenly changed the topic. "You can take off your suit, I guarantee that this place is completely safe. Can't we just sit here peacefully?"

"Of course," Cathy Rimp smiled. Her dream was now a little closer and the future of humanity a little hazier, yet nobody could have predicted what this agreement, reached on the shore of a toxic little lake, would mean for the billions of people on Earth.

Two days later, a full report of the meeting was placed on Bryzgalov's desk.

He studied it, pondering it a while, then called for the head of his corporation's Research Department. "Have we had any orders from Rimp Cybertronics in recent months?"

"Yes," the other man responded immediately. "We received an order to develop a series of projects called the 'First Colonial Shelter' and the so-called 'Base'."

"What's unusual about their technical specifications?" Bryzgalov narrowed his eyes.

"Both structures cannot be used on Earth. They are not suitable for the Moon or other planetoids without an atmosphere. They're not rushing the deadline but they are requesting that we thoroughly consider each part of the structures and the presence of calculation tables for various gravitational options."

"So Rimp Cybertronics is really planning to build a colonial transport?!" It was a scalding thought. Bryzgalov paused. "According to the recording, Cathy Rimp promised Ulrich Fitzgerald that his Mars project will be left untouched. Yet urbanizing Mars is the only way Megapool can keep developing! So they want to use me but keep me in the dark, and divide up the resources behind my back!" He had turned purple but then quickly got himself under control.

"Should we suspend work on the order?"

"No, continue working on it. Create the project models but don't submit them to Rimp Cybertronics before I say so." He gestured that the head of the department could leave.

"White, come to my office!" Bryzgalov barked over the intercom, experiencing a rush of unusual and feverish agitation.

Unlike Cathy Rimp, he believed that humans were nothing more than bugs, made to breed for the sake of Megapool's prosperity. He despised Ulrich Fitzgerald because of the man's God-like mania. But the situation was dire. In another ten to fifteen years, there would be no more free space left on Earth for large-scale construction.

"If I don't break Genesis' spine, I will eventually become a small contractor, constructing fancy cottages on the terraformed Mars! No, never!"

Bryzgalov considered the idea of flying to the stars absurd.

He believed that civilization could develop

in only one way — as an endlessly growing human anthill!

The door to his office opened.

"There you are! Have a seat." Bryzgalov waved at a row of armchairs and immediately asked a rather unexpected question. "White, if you had to sabotage a spaceship, how would you go about it?"

"There are many ways. I'd need to know the details," the Head of Corporate Security replied without batting an eyelid.

"Right now, it's an equation with multiple unknowns, but it would need to look like an accident."

"The ship would need to be completely destroyed?"

"Preferably."

"Then one of the most suitable methods is overloading the thrust engine. It is easy to trigger if one has access to the control system."

Bryzgalov's cheeks turned pink. That's what he wanted to hear. Details weren't important right now. They had time to prepare.

"Can our agents at Rimp Cybertronics handle this task during the spaceship construction phase?"

"It would make the task much easier," White replied. "May I know the details?"

"Of course," Bryzgalov grinned. "When you

get them for me. Here is a recording of the conversation between Catherine Rimp and Ulrich Fitzgerald. That's all that we have so far. Monitor the Alpha Project as if it was your own baby, okay? Plant your people. You'll get unlimited resources but," he stared hard at White, "once the spaceship has been completed, it must not leave the Solar System!"

"We can destroy the project at the early stage."

"No! I want them to invest their money and resources into it!" Bryzgalov was looking far into the future and seeing a chance to destroy Genesis. "We must strike only when the ship is ready for launch and not before! And nothing," he turned to White, "nothing should point to us as the culprits!"

Chapter Three

Europe Megacity

MAX NEVER reached the area above the clouds that day for a simple reason — the leased flycar got stuck in traffic and after an hour among the barely-moving cars, he decided to get out and go for a walk.

The megasuburb was overwhelming.

Max was swept up by the human flow and for a while he moved along with the crowd, with no idea of where he was going.

His first impression of the people was

overwhelmingly negative. Nondescript clothing, ungainly bodies, surly and mostly unattractive faces. The crowd repulsed him and yet drew him like a magnet. Max was jostled and elbowed, although it wasn't done on purpose — one couldn't slow down with their mouth hanging open and look around while being in the middle of the crowd.

After a bunch of knocks and bruises, he managed to make his way to the edge and stopped to catch his breath.

Everything was different here. He kept looking around at the strikingly clean streets of the megasuburb, with the servos hidden in special niches in the building walls. As soon as a speck of garbage touched the walkway, one of the servos would immediately launch themselves at it, weaving through the crowd and avoiding bumping into anyone or being crushed underfoot.

Overcome with conflicting impressions and trying to catch his breath and process what he had seen, Max entered the first cafe that he came across. He sat at a table but suddenly thought, "It's not the right time! There are still two hours to go before the lunch delivery!"

A waiter approached him, a plain-looking unit with a sloping sensor panel displaying the menu. What now? Should he try and order something?

He glanced through the list of dishes but the names were all unfamiliar ones. He chose at random, thinking, "It's not going to work."

To his great surprise, he was wrong. A few minutes later, a plate with a piece of fried synthetic meat and some kind of side was placed before him. It all looked completely natural and did not resemble food paste in the slightest. The cyberstack bracelet blinked as the cost of the meal was automatically deducted from Max's account.

"I can eat whenever I want?!" This was quite a revelation for an in-mode inhabitant.

Max ate with good appetite while watching the people outside, streaming past the front window of the cafe.

Real people. Not avatars. They seemed so alien to Max. His eyes could not pick out any purpose or beauty in the outside bustle, nothing that was familiar to him. Only rarely would he spot a well-built girl or guy. People's faces were different but all wore the same expression of grim determination to go somewhere and do something.

He couldn't understand the world that he now found himself in, but he drank in the busy life around him greedily, shamelessly staring at the passersby. He then stood up and exited the cafe, slowly ambling past the buildings until he spotted a shop selling different trinkets.

Max went inside and looked around. The items seemed beautiful yet useless. Touching a figurine of a muscular warrior with full lips, holding a shield and spear, he suddenly realized that if he were to buy it, the figurine would stay with him forever and not disappear once he returned to the in-mode!

He felt cold inside. He could own real things! Not items that are made up of a certain number of bytes but tangible objects!

This was a deciding moment. He bought the figurine and went outside again, clutching it to his chest.

A car dealership was located in the building across the road, and that's where Max completely lost his mind. Fancy sports flycars stood in a row behind the thick glass window. The artificial lights reflected in the cars' glossy surfaces. He crossed the road and was plunged into a special world that made the most desperate fantasies of the virtual world pale in comparison, like a dull glass imitation placed beside a genuine precious stone.

He was immediately surrounded by beautiful girls. The smell of their perfume mingled with the unique fragrance of expensive car upholstery. Champagne appeared in Max's hand as if by magic and he couldn't understand why everyone was being so kind and attentive to him, a scrawny guy dressed in a crumpled shirt and overly large pants, which he had found in the wardrobe in the capsule apartment.

The reason for everyone's attention was the response from Max Bourne's cyberstack, received by the store's system, which confirmed that the client had sufficient funds to purchase any of the available flycars.

"This is the real life!" thought Max, still unable to believe what was happening to him.

✳ ✳ ✳

The morning was aglow with news.

Three holographic news modules chaotically moved through the rooms, bursting with lights and sounds, and generating images that would immediately splinter due to interference.

Max Bourne barked out the termination phrases out of habit and tried to make himself more comfortable, but felt straps limiting his movements.

What the hell... where am I? Am I in the in-mode? Why is it open?

Sensors were stuck to his skin. He had a splitting headache and felt nauseous. His sluggish muscles refused to obey. He was terribly thirsty and yesterday's events were a blur.

Max automatically reached for the life support tubing with his lips but instead of the liquid he craved, he felt a weak electric shock.

"Timmy! Go and wash your hands, it's time to eat! Breakfast is getting cold!" Sounded an unfamiliar voice.

Max removed the belts and sensors with some difficulty and clambered out of the in-mode.

His clothes were scattered all over the floor.

"Who the heck is Timmy?" Max stared around him in bewilderment. The holographic figure of a woman wandered around the room, laying out utensils on a non-existent table.

An information module suddenly appeared in the room, ignoring the firmly shut door. The pale bubble of light squeezed itself through a panel of power outlets. It immediately transformed into a spherovision and began shouting in a distorted voice. "Today, Genesis and Rimp Cybertronics, the two leading corporations on Earth, announced the launch of a joint project to build the first interstellar spacecraft! The Alpha Colonial Transport, according to Catherine Rimp, will be..."

Max's head already felt like it was splitting open and now this unbearable yelling!

"To other news. Edward Kalganov has announced that the World Government intends to purchase the orbital shipyards currently being sold by the Cryonics Corporation!"

Another information module managed to enter the apartment through a cable in the ceiling. "An unexpected network attack has paralyzed the Eurasian cyberspace!" It screeched. "Chaos reigns on the streets of the Megacity! The failure of the control systems has led to numerous accidents on the roads and in the air! Residents are encouraged to stay in their capsule apartments!"

"Timmy, why are you sitting on the floor, you rascal?! Come here, I'll give you a cuddle, my darling!" The phantom turned.

"Okay, I get it." Max rubbed his hurt elbow. "The real world has fallen victim to a Net attack. The electronic housewife, part of the standard equipment set, has spontaneously activated, as well as the information modules. I have no idea who Timmy is, but then who knows whom the apartment had belonged to and which programs the previous owner had installed?"

He staggered into the kitchen, opened the fridge and took a long drink from a plastic bottle of water.

It was cloudy outside with an acid drizzle falling. The edge of the industrial fog floated five floors below.

"Well, Megapool is certainly not wasting

any time!" Max thought in surprise, examining the nearest housing complexes, whose construction had been paused. The buildings now reminded him of illustrations from the World Wars: the skeletal structures soared over the ocean of toxic fog and disappeared into the 'real' clouds, but construction servos had now appeared along the floors. For some reason, they hung in clusters around the concrete beams.

"Ah yes, the Net attack," Max reminded himself. "The whole city is paralyzed." He finished the water and threw the empty bottle into the waste disposal. He didn't feel like eating breakfast. Yesterday's events seemed to be enveloped in fog. He remembered getting out of the car that was stuck in traffic, wandering through the shops, and entering the car dealership, but the rest had sunk into oblivion.

No wonder. Champagne is a tricky drink, especially for people who try it for the first time. No wonder his memories were gone.

"How did my trip end?" Max checked his cyberstack. "Wow!" His mind cleared slightly. "Another two apartments have been sold! Hooray for the automatic sales system!" He nearly leapt with joy. "I've got 400,000 credits. I can repay the debt today... Wait!" A sudden thought made him break out in cold sweat. "Where's the other 100,000?"

He looked at his purchase history.

That couldn't be right! Max returned to his room, sifted through the scattered clothing and checked the pockets.

An activation codon appeared, designed to look like an elegant keyring with the Rimp Cybertronics logo.

Max went pale and approached the window. A luxurious sports flycar stood on this level's carpark. 'The dream of every inhabitant of the skies' according to the ads.

"You're an idiot!" Max told himself while secretly feeling proud of his purchase. "I'm so cool!" He admired the polished technical marvel for quite a while. His sense of guilt dissipated quickly and now he was filled with pride. He was dying to run downstairs, get into the new car and zoom through the city streets, empty due to the Net attack.

"No! Enough nonsense!" He stepped away from the window and spent several minutes putting the home Net back in order. He shut down the screaming news modules, switched off the holographic housewife, and trudged into the shower.

A trimodular capsule apartment with a separate bathroom was incredibly luxurious for this day and age.

The shower refreshed him a little and took

away the headache but did nothing to improve his mood. He wanted to go online and repay the debt, casting off the load on his shoulders, but the Net attack had ruined all his plans. The cyberstack was working in offline mode, with the last update received yesterday evening.

An unexpected signal cut through his gloomy thoughts and Max looked around in confusion, unable to identify the strange sound.

He mentally went through all the apartment appliances that he had familiarized himself with over the last few days. None of them made such an odd noise, reminding him of the squawking of a fantastical beast.

The sound repeated. It was coming from somewhere in the hallway.

"It can't be!" He looked at the door with puzzlement and even trepidation. "Someone has come to visit me? In the real world?!"

His mind, hopelessly altered by the Layer, did not know how to react appropriately. Max paused, unsure, then crept to the door and sneaked a look at the access screen.

"Lisa?" He was stunned.

The signal came for the third time.

"Well? Are you alive in there? Are you going to let me in?" The system transmitted her voice.

"How did she find me?!" His trembling finger touched the sensor. The door hissed and the sensors activated, the compressors rustling as they created extra pressure inside the capsule apartment.

"Hey!" Lisa walked in and gave him a peck on the cheek as if nothing had happened. She took a step back and examined him shamelessly. "You're pretty scrawny for such a stud online..." She smiled prettily and strolled on to inspect the rooms, leaving Max frozen in the hallway.

"Scrawny?" He thought and glanced at his reflection in the mirror, gasping as he realized that he was wearing nothing but a damp towel.

"This is a pretty nice place!" came Lisa's surprised voice. "Trimodular? With all the gadgets! The view from the window is pretty boring though. When did you move in? Why didn't you call me? Hey, where the hell are you?" She returned, watching ironically as Max fumbled with the magnetic clips and hurriedly put on his clothes.

"How did you find me?"

"Oh, that was super easy! Who bought a flycar yesterday?"

"Well, I did..."

"Such purchases become immediately known on the Net."

"I'm a celebrity?"

"Oh, please!" Lisa snorted. "A girl who is a manager at the car dealership uploaded a video of how a drunk fool was parted with a hundred thousand credits. Come on, don't get offended! I bet that if you roll up to my house in such a posh flycar, my father will take to you in a second."

"But you've never met me... the real me, I mean!" Max stuttered.

"The implant label, silly," Lisa explained condescendingly. "It only takes a couple of seconds to find out who the owner is. I believed in you! I even set up an automatic search program on my cyberstack, in case you turned up! Aren't you happy to see me? Have you gotten your money and forgotten all about me?"

"No, of course not! I just had a lot to do."

"Is that how it is? Have I come at the wrong time? Well, then!" She pouted. "I was thinking this morning that hey, the Net is busted, there's nothing to do..." Lisa threw him a disdaining glance and turned towards the exit.

"Wait! There's no need to sulk! I would have called you. You're... you're the reason that I'm doing all this!"

"Really?" Lisa stopped and looked at her feet. "That's nice. Listen," she suddenly threw up her hands and placed her palms against her cheeks, "I know this awesome place! It's a restaurant called At The Bottom. Why don't we go there?"

"What's so interesting there?" Max had

sworn to himself that he would behave more cautiously after yesterday's adventures, but Lisa's gaze dispelled all common sense.

"Oh, it's fabulous!" Lisa exclaimed. "It's on the Megacity's technical level! The real underbelly of the city! It's the ultimate extreme!"

"They're not going to let us down there."

"What about your flycar? Don't you know how to drive manual, without the autopilot?"

"Of course I do!"

"Then what's the problem?"

"The city bottom?" Max still had doubts. "Why would there be a restaurant there?"

"You know nothing about real life!" Lisa chided him. "It's so boring up at the top. Nothing new ever happens. While a friend of mine opened this restaurant. Don't ask me how he got the permission to do it, but the place is pretty popular, among those in the know," She added meaningfully.

Max had nothing to say to that. He didn't want to seem like a coward either. Didn't he dream of a date with Lisa? What did he have to fear now? She was here, beside him, so close that it took his breath away.

He didn't understand what he was doing. Virtual reality, where everything was easy and had almost no consequences, affected his every move.

"All right, let's go!" Max grabbed the flycar's activation codon and, stunned by his own audacity, received a promising kiss from Lisa. "Can you punch the route into the navigator?"

"Just put in the name, the restaurant's legal!" These words put his mind completely at rest.

They went down onto the street.

"Amazing!" shrieked Lisa when she saw the flycar. "Did you really pay 100,000 credits for it? What a beauty!" She ran her fingertips over the car's smooth curves.

"What did you think?" Max was bursting with pride.

The global network was still down but the inbuilt navigator mapped the way easily. The restaurant really was located on the bottom floor of the Megacity, almost directly beneath them and twelve floors below — a quick and dizzying descent along the curling roads.

"Do you go there often?" Max asked, switching the flycar to manual.

"Yup," Lisa nodded. "The restaurant is actually quite old. It was there before the city's reconstruction. My parents used to go there before Megapool declared that the lower levels would be only technical. What are you afraid of? The servos?"

"No!" Max directed the flycar onto the first

spiraling descent.

"Then hit the gas!"

It was like a dream. They ran from the drab day, from the faceless, unreal and, frankly, now seeming so bland entertainment, wheeling along the hairpin turns towards an exciting adventure. Max's heart thudded in his chest while his ears became blocked from the rapid turns.

He turned up the music and laughed along with Lisa for no reason, simply from the incredible rush that he never experienced in the Layer.

The level numbers flashed on the navigation screen as they soared through the zone of industrial fog and found themselves in the gray dusk of the technical levels. The roads were trapped between massive old buildings, which seemed gloomy and identical, with no architectural features to differentiate one from the next.

Not all of the old city buildings had been demolished and some suburbs looked like decorations for historical films, with the massive supports made of reinforced concrete rising behind them.

Max swiveled his head from side to side in surprise. People still live here, he realized, spotting the rare pedestrians who watched the passing luxury vehicle. He couldn't believe it.

Enormous pipelines stretched over the ancient buildings, and sometimes even through them. The low reinforced concrete ceiling of the technical level seemed to be hanging right over their heads. They were surrounded by deep twilight.

He flicked on the headlights and turned at the intersection. A dilapidated shopping mall appeared for a moment on the right and a holographic sign saying 'The Bottom' on the left.

Stunted plants pushed their way up through the cracks in the old pavement. Max found it all so incredible. And they say that the biosphere is dead!

The restaurant's two-story building appeared out of the gloom. Barely lit by a couple of ad blocks, it watched the passersby with dark and gaping windows. A group of suspicious-looking people hung about the entrance, and there was a small parking lot with faded lines to the left, and a mammoth reinforced concrete support column behind it, which was holding up the levels' low ceiling.

"Are we here?" Max stopped the car but didn't turn off the engine. It was a strange place, looking desolate and rather sinister. The recent feeling of euphoria had disappeared completely. He suddenly felt worried and uncomfortable.

"You're so skittish!" Lisa looked at him

mockingly. "Come on, all the wonders are inside!" She exclaimed fearlessly.

Max felt the unpleasant chill of premonition.

"Wait! Wait a minute!" He wanted to stop the girl but she had already jumped out of the car.

"Well?" Lisa rapped the front window with her knuckles. "Are you coming or are you going to sit there like a dolt?"

"Listen," Max clambered out of the flycar. "It's..."

He stopped mid-sentence. Something hard and cold pressed into the back of his head, and a rough voice said threateningly, "Move it, cipher[2], or I'll blow your brains out!"

In that second, his reflexes, developed through living in the Layer, came into action. He turned sharply and threw up his arm but the sharp blow with a pistol handle knocked him to the ground, plunging him into a world of unbearable pain.

Max screamed. Sticky warm blood began to flow from the cut on his forehead. A series of fierce kicks to the ribs cut off his scream. He arched, choking and losing all ability to resist.

_____

[2] Cipher (*slang*) – a general term for people who live and work in cyberspace.

"Rem, enough! You'll beat him to death and we need him alive!" Max heard Lisa's voice coming from a long way away. There was no compassion or fear in it. "Don't hit him on the head!" She shrieked, her voice rising. "Stupid bastard!"

An angry grumble sounded in response.

Max curled up on the cracked asphalt. Someone grabbed him roughly by the collar of his jacket and dragged him into the restaurant.

His head pulsed with pain. He breathed in gulps as he tried to get enough air. His vision was blurry. The person dragging him smelled terrible, not of sweat but of something sour and spoiled. Max's feet dragged along the ground. Lisa appeared behind him, at the edge of his clouded vision. She picked up Max's cyberstack, which had been knocked off his wrist, and tried to activate his personal nanocomputer. It didn't work, of course, since the system needed its owner's biometric data.

"Rem, wait!" she ordered.

Max groaned unwittingly. The sudden stop caused a new wave of pain. Lisa caught up to them, leant over Max and stretched the cyberstack towards him.

"Activate it with all the functions!"

"He can't even see anything. Didn't you see how I gave it to him?"

"Shut up!" She snarled. "Well?" She grabbed Bourne's bloodied chin, the familiar ironic smile on her face, and slightly raised his head so that she could stare into his eyes. "Don't fight me or it'll hurt again!"

In that moment, looking into the eyes of this attractive girl, Max felt like complete dirt. The sudden animal fear of physical pain had left him paralyzed.

Twelve levels up. Measuring directly, his luxurious, fairy tale life was only 500 meters away. A few minutes ago, he could have still changed his mind and turned around but now he was done for.

"Rem!" Lisa grimaced and released her blood-stained fingers. "Help him. But not too hard, and don't hit him on the head!"

The next blow to the ribs made Max feel like he was suffocating. He rolled around on the ground, clawing at it with his nails, and when he could finally take another breath, all thoughts of resistance were gone.

"They've certainly become weak up there, at the top," Someone spat outside of Max's field of view. "Lizzie, sweetie," the voice became warm and paternal, "Let him go, don't get your hands dirty. He'll tell us everything: his account access codes and the password to his nanocomp. He hasn't got a choice, has he?"

✳ ✳ ✳

A light shone inside the restaurant.

Max was dragged into the dining hall. Dust motes floated among the broken antique furniture. The restaurant clearly hadn't been in use since the city rebuilding had begun twenty years ago.

Max was left lying face down on the dirty floor.

He turned clumsily onto his side and attempted to sit up but he could only moan.

"Here's the thing, mate." A bald old man sat on a squeaking chair, his face scarred from genetic mutations. "Fighting won't help. We don't care about your life, we only care about your money and property."

The anger that Max felt gave him a moment of strength. He came up onto all fours and croaked, "My implant is transmitting a distress signal! You're all dead, assholes!"

"Is that so?" The old man raised a scarred eyebrow. "Rem, come here! Give him a bit more."

Max nearly died from the next series of blows. The pain was muffled but blood bubbled on his lips with every gasping breath.

"Your implant isn't transmitting anything." The old man grunted as he squatted beside Max and lifted his bloodied head by the hair. "We might look hideous in your eyes but we aren't stupid. The Net only works here when I say so. You see, sonny," His speech was strangely old-fashioned and hard to understand, "your ribs will knit back together. You'll cough up all the blood. But if I put you through the 'crown of thorns' then, sorry, science and medicine will be powerless to help you. We don't want to kill you. Why take the extra sin upon myself? But you can easily end up an imbecile for the rest of your life. You have to choose and quickly. Either you voluntarily give us access to your accounts, the capsule apartments that you've snapped up on the cheap, and the car, or..." He yanked Max head around to look to the side, "See that?"

Among the dusty piles of broken furniture, in a small area of cleared space, towered a terrifying-looking construction. It was an old and battered Virtex model. A lopsided chair with broken armrests and the 'crown of thorns' — an electrode strip with spikes. Rumor had it that such devices were used when the modern neural connections were still being developed.

"I can see from your eyes that you know what it is."

Max gulped.

"You know!" The old man let go of Max's hair and his head lolled helplessly. "If we hook you up to the crown, none of the modern defenses will help you. It's a good old-fashioned military design."

"No!" Max couldn't hold out any longer. "Please, don't!"

"A smart decision. Now come on, activate your cyberstack. Rem, sit him up straight. Jab the guy with a stimulator so his hands stop shaking and his mind clears up. And you," He gave Max a dark look. "do what you're supposed to and you'll stay alive. The Net up above has been repaired."

Max leant back and tried to focus his pain-addled gaze on Lisa.

"Why?" he whispered hoarsely, feeling the blood bubbling in his throat.

She came closer and squatted beside him.

"He's my father." She gestured towards the old man. "The law of universal compulsory implantation struck him off the list of people. Yet left people like you in."

"What does this have to do with me?" Max croaked.

"You're a dumb animal, wasting your life in the Layer. A cipher. Really, it's nothing personal, Max. This is how I earn a living. I dropped the hook and you took the bait. That's all."

"Is Gleb in this with you?"

"Are you mad? Gleb lives at the top. But I'll get him too, one day." Lisa stated with cold certainty.

"So you lied to me? Right from the start?" It hurt to talk but he had to get the words out.

"No, I wasn't lying. I really did graduate from the World Government Academy, majoring in modern cybernetic networks. The psychology is just from personal experience. Stop sulking and coughing up blood. It's possible to live even here. Maybe you'll help me out one day. Who knows?" She smiled. "Network attacks, primitive psychological games. It's fun, believe me."

"Enough, Lisa! Stop playing with him. It's time to get to work." The old man cast a shadow over them. He held the 'crown of thorns' in his hands. "What did you decide in the end, young man?"

Europe Megacity
Level zero
Morning of the next day

Archibald woke up but didn't hurry to get up, listening to the sounds coming from the outside.

The even hum of millions of sounds soothed him, and he stretched and sat up with a grunt.

He could see the tangle of pipelines through the dirty window. A dozen servos bustled about, inspecting the lines. They weren't interested in the fragment of ancient building that had survived on the technical level.

Archibald stood up, shuffled to the cracked sink and touched the water sensor.

A thin stream of water began to flow from the tap. He rinsed his face and took a couple of swallows. The water tasted of metal but Archibald wasn't overly finicky.

The technical level wasn't the worst place to be in a modern city. Some buildings still stood here. There were life support systems from time immemorial.

He came to the window and sat on the wide plastic window sill.

It was always dusk outside. He was used to it. He lacked many luxuries of civilization but he was free.

The dark space, pinned down by the low reinforced concrete archway, was full of movement. It lived and breathed in rhythm with the behemoth city. The millions of servos that lived here ignored the people inhabiting the megacity bottom.

The machines were busy with their own tasks. They were predictable and safe. There were other types of servomachines, of course, such as the ones from law enforcement but they didn't come here very often. When they did appear in these narrow labyrinths, they tended to suffer losses.

Archibald woke up in a good mood today. He had business to attend to.

The threadbare clothes stuck to his body. It was damp and cold in the old houses. He quickly collected his few belongings and shoved them into his pockets. With an irritated movement, he adjusted the cap on his temporal implant. It was always falling out because it didn't sit securely in its socket. He should fix it but there was never enough time for something so minor. A resident of the technical levels got nothing for free. Only the ciphers could live a life of leisure yet Archibald didn't envy the inhabitants of the in-modes and capsule apartments.

The old door screeched when he pushed it open. The industrial fog roiled on the landing so Archibald had to cover his face with a damp cloth as usual and dash down the stairs, taking several steps at a time, to avoid breathing in the poisoned air.

He noticed a pair of chippers by the building entrance. They sat by the wall, moving their hands vaguely. Their eyes were oblivious to the reality surrounding them.

Once upon a time, Archibald dabbled in

banned chips too. He wouldn't have lasted very long if he hadn't been caught by the servos from the rehabilitation center, located twenty levels above.

He spent two months in the hospital and then another six months in the in-mode, like a real cipher. Having partaken in all the delights of modern civilization, he took the first chance that he could to escape back into the bowels of the Megacity.

Rivers of industrial waste flowed here. Hot air billowed from the waste removal centers. The sewerage cleaning stations hummed. Food and energy was produced here.

The city bottom was inhabited by people and servos. In most cases, they coexisted peacefully although there was trouble from time to time. When there was a change in government, for example. For some reason, the first thing the cipher government would do is arrange demonstrative raids, with the inhabitants of the bottom captured and sent to correctional facilities.

Skirting around the chippers, Archibald first went to the food works. The complex reminded him of a giant insect at a distance. The buildings were thick with pipelines. Different substances flowed through some of them, others, distinguished by their diameter and markings, delivered nutrient-rich fluid to the complex, where various food pastes with specific taste and aroma were made from the gray substance.

Ciphers had no idea what they were eating since they received products in attractively bright packaging. Archibald grinned to himself as he slipped between the twisting masses of piping. He'd been inside the shops. The variety was breathtaking. Yet none of the shoppers had any idea that all the gourmet items came from the same tub, located here, in the bowels of the city. The raw material for the cheap synthetic food was usually waste.

The way Archibald saw it, life wasn't too bad, all in all. Having briefly been a cipher, he had concluded that there absolutely no benefit in being stuck in the in-mode. You lost your freedom in exchange for illusions.

Of course, the world of ciphers had its advantages. But many of the 'benefits' of civilization could be obtained even here, all the while retaining one's freedom.

Archibald sat down comfortably on a curve in the pipe. The hand-operated valve had no electronic devices and was painted a bright red. It was used for cleaning the pipes and during serious accidents. The servos never touched it, while Archibald accessed it daily.

He took out a set of disposable dishes. The

valve turned easily. He carefully turned it a quarter of a turn and a gray goo began to flow onto his plate.

Breakfast was served.

He quickly swallowed the tasteless paste and dropped the disposable plate and fork on the ground, where the servos would find and recycle them.

His stomach full, he could now go about his business.

Archibald slipped down and scanned his surroundings. The damp twilight hid a multitude of dangers. Firstly, there were toxic manufacturing plants everywhere. Secondly, the outline of the city waste collector could be seen nearby, which one had to steer clear of. Thirdly, one had to watch out for mutant flora and fauna. There wasn't much species diversity but the plants and animals living here were all extremely aggressive.

Archibald put on a breathing mask that covered the bottom half of his face and took a pair of glasses from his pocket. He used to strut about in a biohazard suit until it had fallen apart.

Today he planned to reach the recycling center and look around for something useful.

Running along the top of the pipes, he stopped beside the open transporter belt. It was a convenient and safe mode of transport.

Building ruins passed by below him. Archibald had great twilight vision from years of living on the city's technical level, plus a couple of standard implant chips, made by the local craftsmen, helped him to find his way around and to spot most things up to ten to fifteen meters away.

He noticed a servo limping along below him. The servo's body was pitted with acid and he was acting oddly, staggering about purposelessly.

It was obviously damaged and thus easy prey. Archibald would get a good price for it at the 'trading center'. He jumped off the transporter belt and began to stalk the servo.

Max woke up in a dark and dilapidated room.

He could barely open his eyes. The pain appeared at once and shot through him like lightning, making him catch his breath. There was dried blood on his cracked lips. Everything that had happened came to him through a fog of unbearable physical suffering. The old man didn't even have to use the 'crown of thorns' as Max couldn't stand the torture. He gave them everything just to stop the pain, and now, his cheek pressed against the damp and rough concrete, he knew that his life was over.

The implant manufacturers claimed that it was impossible to rob modern technology users. This was true. One couldn't get anywhere by working online. There was only one way and that was to use real physical violence. But how could one reach a person safely encased in an in-mode and who never left their technological shell?

That was Lisa's job. She searched online for people like Max. She encouraged them to rebel against the current state of affairs, suggested a way to make money, and stoked their feelings of passion and hope by playing with their delicate feelings.

What could he do now? Max lay helplessly on the floor, his breathing heavy.

He rolled over with difficulty, felt the cyberstack on his wrist and sent a mental instruction through his implant to turn it on.

At least, he thought that he did. The nanocomp had turned into an ordinary bracelet and did not give the slightest sign of working.

Was his implant in place?

He touched his right temple with shaking fingers. The cap was gone. He could only feel the socket-encrusted surface. His personal chip was gone...

He turned onto his back with a moan, his gaze wandering over the low, cracked ceiling that sagged dangerously above him. He was doomed. A social death. Max Bourne was no longer one of the living. You weren't a person without a personal microchip. This was how society protected itself against exiled mutants and criminals.

Max remembered the grinning face of the old man.

"True, why bother killing me? I don't exist anymore. I can't even get back to the top. They'll simply arrest me. What if I tell them what happened?"

He crawled to the wall and sat up against it.

Something small and spiky shifted in his chest pocket.

Hope suddenly blossomed anew. Overcoming fatigue, he drew out a multifaceted bead. The chip!

"Why did they pull it out of its socket and yet left it with me?"

Max almost dropped the precious object. His hands shook so hard that he had trouble performing the precise motion needed to reinsert it.

"Of course! They removed the chip so that it would be impossible to track me using my implant for some time. They had to get out of here and hide their tracks!"

Finally, the microdrive rustled as the implant recognised the chip. A short time later, the cyberstack turned on again.

His stomach churning, Max looked at his account and the real estate transactions report.

His debt. One hundred and ninety thousand credits plus interest. All the capsule apartments had gone to a different owner, whose name meant nothing to Max.

Only now did he fully comprehend what he had done. His mother and father, Samantha and little Johnny, they would all be moved out of their in-modes and sent to the capsule dump on the bottom levels!

He didn't want to live any longer. Closing his eyes, he succumbed to utter despair.

"Hey, are you alive in there?" The sound of a human voice made Max startle and shake off the stupor.

Grimacing from the pain, he dragged himself across the floor and hid behind a pile of rubble. His fingers closed over an angular piece of cement with rusty grating poking out of it.

"Hey, I just want to help!" The steps sounded closer.

"Go away!" croaked Max.

"Oh, come on! What are you afraid of? Wow, they really got you good!" A short youth, wearing a torn jacket and faded pants, slipped inside. "Hey, cipher." He gave Max a look. "Put down the rock, OK? You're not going to have the strength to throw it anyway."

Max released the cement fragment.

"Were you robbed?" He sat down beside Max. "It happens," he added philosophically. "My name's Archibald."

"Go away."

"Is it that bad?"

"What do you care?"

"Well, I don't really," Archibald sounded offended. "Was it your flycar that was brought to the old restaurant last night?" He sounded sympathetic. "I saw you being dragged to the old man. His daughter is a real bitch."

"Do you know where to find them?" Max whispered, barely moving his mashed lips.

"Nope. They rarely come here. The locals say that their lair is far away. Rem once said that they live in the magrail tunnels, near Duvr Station. They come here when they have work to do. What's your name?"

"Max... Why are you so interested in me?"

"No reason. I was actually following a servo. Then I saw something moving and came in to have a look."

"Had enough of a look yet?"

"Listen, just stay here for a bit." Archibald ignored Max's feeble attempts to drive him away.

"I'll go and get a medikit, an automatic one." He boasted. "It still has 9% left."

"Whatever," Max said apathetically. He no longer believed anyone. He didn't want to see or hear anyone. He didn't need anyone's help.

✳ ✳ ✳

Archibald turned out to be a decent guy. He only had one flaw, being overly chatty and excessively curious.

Max felt worse after Archibald used the automatic medikit. He developed a fever and floated in and out of consciousness. The broken ribs hurt. He shivered constantly and at times coughed convulsively, bringing up blood.

In rare moments of clarity, Max would see a skinny youth with a sallow complexion beside him. He could barely recall the guy's name.

Archibald fed Max with a gray paste and gave him water that tasted like metal, then brought another medikit from somewhere.

"Why are you helping me?" It was hard to speak but the silence was unbearable. He was crippled by the belated regret for what he had done.

"Well, who else is going to help you?" Archibald reasoned with a simplicity that Max couldn't comprehend, as if the two came from different dimensions. "It's boring to be alone. Two is better. Once you're well, we can go hunting servos together."

"I won't."

"Oh, come on. Humans can get used to anything. You'll get used to it too. It's not so bad here. Certainly better than up there."

"How would you know?"

"I lived there, in the in-mode. I even have an implant but the chip has been cancelled. I ran away. What are you doing here? Will you tell me?"

Max was initially unforthcoming but gradually, word by word, told Archibald the whole story.

"You shouldn't have done that to your loved ones," Archibald frowned. "I feel sorry for them. I can't remember my own parents at all."

"Help me to stand up." Max reached out a hand.

"All right, let's try."

Max struggled to his feet. He appeared to have survived the worst. He kept his breathing shallow, afraid of the pain, but the ribs were hurting less.

Grasping the outcrops of rubble, he climbed out of the narrow passageway.

The gloom of the technical level plunged him into melancholy. Archibald, on the other hand, was smiling widely.

"Do you owe a lot of money?" He asked suddenly.

"Two hundred and fifty thousand," Max replied automatically.

"Does your personal chip still work?" Archibald continued.

"Yup." Max watched gloomily as a pulsating glow spread over the waste management complex.

"Well then, you should sell yourself to the corps!"[3]

"What do you mean?" Max asked.

"The corps need people. For experiments. They test different devices and technologies."

"How do I do that?" Max asked suspiciously. "I've got two days left until I have to pay back the debt." He slumped. "No, it's not an option."

"It totally is!"

"Then explain it properly!"

"There are recruitment offices located up above. When I lived in the in-mode, I was constantly getting offers from them."

"Why didn't you go?"

"What for? I was planning to run away. I don't need their money."

"Do they offer a lot?"

---

[3] Corp *(slang)* — an employee in a corporation.

"Yeah, if you join Cryonics," Archibald replied confidently. "They offered me 100,000 credits for a 10-year contract. Except what was the point? It's great living here, I do what I want and I don't need any money. It'd be perfect for you, though."

"Where is this recruitment office?" For the first time in the last few days, Max felt a twinge of hope. He was sick with belated regret. A little longer and it would all burn away. He knew that he would not be able to do anything. He would continue to live here and become like Archibald, a pale shadow flitting through the industrial zone of the megacity.

"It's on level twenty-something, I think," Archibald said, frowning in thought.

"How do I get there?" Max coughed and spat out blood.

"Using the maintenance ladders, but you won't make it, you're still too weak. You ought to try in a week's time."

"No. I have to go now. I only have two days left." Max winced from a sudden stab of pain. "If I don't go today, tomorrow will be too late," he thought. "I'll resign myself to spending the rest of my days here, and my family will be sent to the lower levels." This thought strengthened his resolve.

"You should search through the

cyberstack," Archibald suggested. "Maybe there's a recruitment office lower down?"

"I don't have access to the Net. My account is in the negative."

"Well, I'll think of something," Archibald promised. "Don't give up yet!"

$$\ast\ \ast\ \ast$$

They spent a whole day climbing up the maintenance ladders and bypassing the servo cordons. Max would have never reached the seventeenth level alone, where, according to Archibald, the nearest Cryonics Corporation recruitment office was located.

"Will they take me?" Max thought. He felt worse and worse, and what if they had health restrictions? "Why would they want to sign a contract with me, with all my blasted injuries?" These thoughts crowded his mind but they distracted him from the pain as he climbed higher and higher.

They passed the zone of toxic fog, sweating and choking in the old hazmat suits.

Archibald cleverly avoided the servos and knew where to stop and where to run to bypass the security systems.

For Max, the ascent blurred into one

excruciating feeling of moral and physical strain. The guilt and anger at himself helped to keep him moving.

Archibald was a strange guy in every respect. He answered Max's questions eagerly and openly. He did not find the journey onerous. Max couldn't understand what drove him and why he had decided to help a complete stranger.

"That's it. I won't go any further."

Max slumped against the wall, breathing heavily.

"What, you chickened out?"

"Nope. We're here. Do you see the ad across the street?"

Max had a hard time focusing. Everything swam before his eyes. Building outlines, glowing ads, crowds of cars and people.

He finally managed to spot the wavering sign: Cryonics.

"I need to go there?"

"Yup."

"What about you?"

"I'll head back. It's not fun here. Too busy. Plus, my chip has been cancelled. If they catch me, they'll put me back in the in-mode and what the heck for?"

Max felt flustered and didn't know what to say to express his feelings.

"Thank you..." he forced out.

"That's all right!" Archibald waved him away. "What did I do, anyway?"

"You saved me..."

Archibald shrugged and then said unexpectedly, "Depends on how you look at it. Working for Cryonics is risky. You may regret it a hundred times over."

"If they take me."

"Don't worry, they'll take you. Just make sure that you get the money upfront, they'll cheat you otherwise. Now go. It's not safe to hang around here for too long. Do you see the street crossing over there?"

Max nodded.

"Use it to cross the road and then go straight into the recruitment office. Don't run and don't fuss. Your chip's fine so don't worry. Now, get a move on!"

✱ ✱ ✱

"Come through, young man." A lean, elderly doctor in a snow-white uniform with the Cryonics logo stood up from behind a table when a chime announced the arrival of a new client. He had a pointy beard and a peppered moustache, and his gaze was tenacious but attentive and sympathetic. "Max Bourne, if I'm not mistaken?"

"Yes." Max reached an armchair and

collapsed into it.

"We know about your situation," the doctor announced suddenly.

"How?!"

"Someone called Archibald told me about your problem. He contacted us several hours ago over the Net. I must say that the amount that you're hoping for is rather significant. Only a long-term contract would suit, which, I must warn you, is quite risky."

"In what way?"

"We are preparing to test a next generation cryogenic system. Working for the future, so to speak. The contract involves the immersion of a person into cryogenic sleep for a period of thirty-five years."

"I don't care." Max was struggling to stay conscious. "I'm not in the best shape..." He muttered apologetically.

"That's not a problem. This way, please." The doctor helped him to stand up and led him to a massive medical scanner. "In our case, certain, um, damage to the body is useful for the experiment. You see, cryogenic sleep doesn't stop the metabolism but slows it down to a certain degree. We will be able to find out if fractures knit together and to conduct a few extra tests by observing how your wounds heal..."

"How much?" Max only cared about one

question right now. He had already given up on his own life, which was not surprising in his situation.

"Standard contract terms stipulate a payment of 10,000 credits per year. The payments are transferred to the account..."

"I need all the money at once." Max found the strength to state this firmly.

"I understand. But this is a special case. You see, the installation hasn't been tested yet and there is a high risk..."

"How much is my life worth?! Just don't tell me that you have to consult with the management!"

"There's no need to get worked up! We have a special offer but then you won't receive the 10,000 credits per year. How much do you owe?"

"Two-hundred and fifty thousand credits."

"We will pay this amount. You will have a quarter of an hour of Net time to sort out your financial problems. Does that work for you?"

Max nodded. Cryonics saved 100,000 credits but right now he didn't care about that. The important thing was to pay back the loan and to release his family's in-modes and the capsule apartment in Antarctica Megacity.

"I agree."

"One more thing, young man: you will have to sign a form agreeing to additional tests."

"Fine. Which ones?"

"I don't know," the doctor gestured. "It would be at the discretion of the corporation's Research Department."

"Okay. I'll sign everything."

"It's nice to do business with you. I'm going to inject you with a stimulant. It will ensure that you're free of pain and can think clearly for an hour. Sufficient for a visit to the Layer?"

"Yes."

"Excellent. Please take a seat here. I took the liberty of finding your creditor. He's waiting for you."

"How do you know all this? How did you find him?"

"You're in the office of the Cryonics Corporation, young man!" The doctor reminded him. "One of the four leading corporations on Earth. Nothing is impossible for us. When Mr. Archibald outlined your situation, we made the necessary checks and preparatory actions. It's a mere trifle for us, believe me."

"Is Archibald your agent too?"

"No, unfortunately. He wanted to remain incognito, giving us only his first name, which is probably fictional. I have no idea who he is and why he is looking after you. But the information that we received from him has been confirmed, and the motivation for your selfless act makes sense, so everything is fine. Sort out your issues and then we'll go to the cryonarium where you will be prepared and placed into cryosleep. Then the cryocapsule will be transported to the Space Vegas Station..." The doctor's voice sounded more and more muffled. Max's consciousness cleared quickly and the virtual space of the Net formed around his chair. He saw the familiar cafe with Andrey Sergeevich sitting behind one of the tables, who gave a friendly wave when he saw Max Bourne's avatar appearing inside.

✳ ✳ ✳

Archibald watched Max's figure until he disappeared through the doors of the recruitment office.

Sighing, he left their hiding place and followed a servo into one of the many technical buildings of a housing complex. Squatting beside one of the humming devices, he touched the implanted pea-sized communicator.

"Arch? Finally!" An irritated voice appeared in his mind.

"Why weren't they caught in the act? I'd informed the Division in advance! We would have made it either way!"

"It's none of your business."

"You've ruined a guy's life!"

"He's ruined his own life, don't you think? The leadership is thinking further ahead. We could have taken them but what would have been the point? The old man, his daughter and that moron Rem — they're small-time crooks. We need to find the people responsible for the network attacks."

"You're watching them then?"

"Yes, we're following the thread. And you almost blew it! Why did you get involved?"

"I didn't reveal myself! I helped the guy, well, more like I helped his family."

"Are you sure nobody's going to suspect you?"

"Of what? That 'finance guy' works alone. We should look into him too, by the way. Max's disappearance won't concern anyone. He was beaten, robbed and left to die. Which is what he did. My cover was not compromised."

"Then return to the technical level and get back to work. I'll cover for you this time."

"Thanks," grunted Archibald as he disconnected.

A minute later, a nondescript and slouching youth in tattered clothing stepped out of the utility room. After waiting for a servo patrol unit to pass, he sneaked into the technical corridor and began his trip back down.

Chapter Four

Earth. Year 2207 AD
The outskirts of Europe Megacity
Private territory, closed to visitors

ULRICH FITZGERALD had a habit of waking up early, when the sun had not yet come up and the air was filled with the damp smell of the forest.

Fitzgerald hadn't changed on the outside over the past ten years but he couldn't hide the internal changes from himself. It was his soul and not his body that was ageing. He hadn't lost his business acumen but he had become less eccentric and tended to challenge fate less and less, finding other interests and joys in life.

The fight between the four leading corporations was becoming deadly. Megapool had completed the new Antarctic Megacity. Bryzgalov had thus run out of space for new large-scale building projects on Earth, so he had announced a plan for a network of lunar cities, which further complicated the struggle for resources and made the situation quite explosive. "Nevertheless," Ulrich went out onto the balcony and sunk down into a deep armchair. "I correctly predicted this situation. The inevitable fight for the asteroid belt begun five years ago. The Cryonics Corporation is flourishing because of it. The sale of the three orbital shipyards to the World Government allowed the corporation to not only fix its financial situation but to also regain a decent section of the market. The Asians," Ulrich thought in old, persistent stereotypes. "The Asians left the Lunar Shipyards for themselves. It's where the ships for private corporate armies are being built, and more and more are needed with every passing year."

The World Government was now an independent force to be reckoned with. One had to hand it to Edward Kalganov — he hadn't missed his chance. He dealt sensibly with Earth's budget. The shipyards purchased from the

Cryonics Corporation were used to build not only mining complexes but also combat ships for the fleet. Kalganov conveniently found a legal basis for his actions by reviving the UN so that the space cruisers and frigates that patrolled the asteroid belt officially belonged to the United Nations. In reality, the fleet was controlled by Edward Kalganov.

The situation in the asteroid belt had worsened over the past two years. Earth's laws did not extend beyond Mars, where the corporations' interests were expressed in brute strength, and the ships bearing the UN logo had to interfere more often, protecting the free settlements under the patronage of the World Government.

Ulrich Fitzgerald avoided conflict. Control over Martian resources gave Genesis signigicance and independence. "They won't be able to topple me," he thought, breathing in the clean morning air.

The sky grew lighter. A fog appeared above the slopes of the mountain valley, which had nothing to do with industrial emissions.

The last oasis.

He had created it from scratch with the power of biotechnology.

Fitzgerald could clearly remember the dead and toxic ground, the bubbling poisonous lakes and the windswept rocky outcrops rising above the mountains of compressed garbage.

Cathy Rimp had called it the Valley of Horror when she first saw it but Fitzgerald had kept his word, and barely a year after their meeting, the first green shoots had appeared in this place.

The area was now unrecognizable. It was hard to imagine, looking at these green slopes, that this used to be the city dump and then became an extreme testing site for the Genesis Corporation, used to trial all the newest biotechnologies destined for the colonization of other worlds. They were being tested under conditions that were much worse than the predicted but still hypothetical biospheres of alien planets.

Ulrich was visibly nervous as he waited for today's planned event. The Alpha Colonial Transport, which had been towed beyond Pluto's orbit, was due to start its engines in an hour's time and to begin its acceleration to light speed.

The technologies of Genesis and Rimp Cybertronics had come a long way in the ten years of working on the joint project. Cathy Rimp had managed to overcome the bans and phobias. Her corporation had developed a series of humanoid machines called Hugo. The androids, equipped with limited neural networks, were designed to work in other star systems. Their use on Earth was considered inappropriate, although Fitzgerald quite liked the machines himself. The silent and unobtrusive androids looked identical to humans, could hold a conversation on any topic, worked without a break, and possessed a whole range of clear advantages over the cyborgs developed by Genesis.

A door opened silently and a cyborg brought in coffee. The morning routine of Genesis' owner was followed without fail. Anyone who dared to disturb Ulrich during these hours would have risked everything: their job, their status and their well-being.

The first cup of coffee. Fitzgerald's gaze roamed over the wooded slopes of two low mountain ridges. It was traditional to curse corporations and quietly hate their owners, for business is harsh and vast fortunes are made on blood. Ulrich had never denied this.

"People are all different, however," he pondered. "Some always want more. Others begin to understand as they get older that one can never earn all the money. Then the mind begins to come up with ideas that go against the basic laws of business."

He had been born into a dying, urbanized world. He had absorbed the atmosphere of hopelessness. He had worked for the European

Union and was involved in biotechnologies, authoring the innovative project to terraform Mars.

He remembered Catherine Rimp when she was a daring and utterly antisocial girl, recklessly brave but undoubtedly clever and talented. He helped her destroy the military AIs of the superpowers and to erase the borders between different nations. He did it first for money, power and the personal notion of freedom. But gradually, while already in charge of a powerful corporation, realizing that he would live long enough to see the final fall of civilization, he began to seriously think about the future.

He had provided enough for his old age. He could honestly say that he had fed the entire population of Earth. Now he found himself at an impasse again. He could try to revive the planet's biosphere but who would let him? Where would he put the billions of 'extra' people, who would not fit into the concept of a revitalized Earth?

Every authority had its limit. Take one wrong step and you will be crushed. Stand up and get what you want, and you will sow chaos instead of life.

These were the dilemmas.

He could plant a tree but he couldn't recreate a piece of the biosphere without condemning several billion people to death.

Who would let him tear down a megasuburb and pry open the technosphere, which stretched for kilometers into the bowels of the earth, all to create a green protected space?

Living space had been exhausted long ago. Birth control no longer made a difference. Earth had been changed irrevocably. Even if the population was halved or more, the cities would remain untouchable, for Earth's technosphere was so singular and complex that it would not tolerate any gross interference. New, unoccupied territories were needed, but where would one find them?

The answer was obvious — on other planets — but unlike Cathy Rimp, Ulrich linked his future with Mars rather than deep space. The Alpha Project had been a key that opened forbidden doors by allowing him to legally develop numerous biotechnologies that he would soon use to terraform the Red Planet.

Terraforming Mars had become his life's work, which was now at a critical stage. The atmospheric processor network was complete and it was time to begin the radical transformation.

Ulrich didn't forget for even a second that the terraforming phase would require huge sums of money, which he expected to receive once the Alpha Colonial Transport was successfully launched.

The edge of the Solar System
Beyond Pluto's orbit

The spaceship was huge.

It contained the leading developments of the four biggest corporations of Earth and the accumulated knowledge of colonizing the Solar System, and represented the hope of a doomed humanity.

Long before today's event, a network of specially constructed relay stations with laser communicators and tracking complexes had been launched into deep space. They were to capture the historical moment and transmit the recording of the most important event in the history of civilization back to Earth. The use of laser communication meant that the signal was delayed by approximately five hours[2] but the important thing was that billions of people could watch firsthand the colonial transport turning on its cruise engines and accelerating out of the Solar System.

A signal transmitter moved slowly through the darkness of space. It was mounted on a

---

[2] Light takes 241 minutes at perihelion and in 402 minutes at aphelion to travel from the Sun to Pluto.

rectangular platform and looked like a giant lacy insect from a distance.

Test.

Two dozen monitors began projecting at the same time, showing an object that grew larger amid the cosmic darkness, generously encrusted with multicolored warning lights.

"Transmission time. Signal is steady. Object is in focus. All equipment is functioning normally."

"Excellent! Let's go! Broadcasting to Earth in ten... nine... eight..."

The object continued to slowly grow in size on the control monitors.

"Ladies and gentlemen!" A voice sounded. "A few minutes ago, we began receiving data from the long-distance space communication devices. The devices are placed along the planned course of the Alpha Colonial Transport, up to the point where the cruise thrusters' propulsion system will switch on. I, Alexander Shapovalov, will watch together with you as the first interstellar colonial transport in the history of mankind leaves the Solar System."

...One of the platform cameras turned and began zooming in on the approaching ship.

It was an awe-inspiring sight.

The colonial transport drew closer and became clearer and clearer amid the darkness.

Its size, construction and shape stunned the viewer, appearing so unusual and powerful that it was hard to comprehend, and making millions of people hold their breath, filled with new feelings of awe and pride.

The camera showed the curved silver nose of the ship with the sign:

EARTH. ALPHA COLONIAL TRANSPORT

Life paused even in the virtual worlds of the Layer during these minutes.

Billions of people watched through cyberspace the most significant event of the era, which left nobody indifferent and for a moment reminded them of humanity's universal values.

The image changed and the camera angle was now slightly different, showing the slow and majestic gliding of the mammoth construction.

The nose of the colonial transport was 500 meters wide. The control module was shaped like a silver dome, its convex side directed into space.

The camera continued to zoom in and shifted again, now showing the colonial transport at a different angle so that viewers could see its seven-kilometer length.

Immediately behind the control dome was the so-called rotating body, which was one and a half kilometers across. It was connected to the nose of the ship with a cone coupling of appropriate size, its surface studded with a silver forest of antennae. The navigation and communication system were located inside.

"As we know, the colonial transport is made up of three parts: the control bays, the rotating body and the propulsion sections," continued the transmitted image of Alexander Shapovalov. "The rotating body contains the detachable cryogenic modules, technology storage, biological storage, containing samples of Earth's flora and fauna, and Alpha's life support systems — a unique biocybernetic complex created jointly by the Genesis Corporation and Rimp Cybertronics."

The voice fell silent, giving the viewers an opportunity to judge for themselves the size of the interstellar transport.

The camera continued its leisurely historical movement over the rotating body, showing the length of its attachments and gradually nearing the two-kilometer trident of the propulsion sections.

This part of the ship, like the nose, did not rotate. The nose and the tail were linked by a construction shaft, which formed a symmetry axis for the colonial transport.

The three propulsion sections were arranged at an angle of 120 degrees relative to each other, forming a symmetrical fork in space.

Each section tapered to a conical 'exhaust', so called as an analogy of the part in ancient liquid fuel rocket engines.

The difference was that these exhausts were approximately 200 meters across and released plasma, formed during a controlled thermonuclear reaction of helium synthesis, rather than chemical combustion products, which enabled the Alpha to reach relativistic speeds.

The ship was fueled by hydrogen. It was no secret that interstellar space was not truly filled with vacuum. In reality, space was not empty but filled with negative hydrogen atoms, particle dust, and various forms of radiation. For this reason, Alpha's propulsion systems were equipped with electromagnetic traps that could collect hydrogen directly from outer space.

Most importantly, the colonial transport carried 500,000 colonists, who had been cryogenically frozen.

The flight was supposed to last fifteen years. This was how long the ship would need to reach the Procyon System, a double star in the constellation of Canis Minor, which, according to many years of astronomical observations, had a planet with an oxygen-containing atmosphere.

Humanity had never sent such a massive and technologically advanced ship beyond the

Solar System before. Five hundred thousand people was an impressive number at first glance, but really, it was just a drop in the ocean of humanity, which now watched with bated breath the last few minutes of Alpha's free flight.

Too many hopes were tied up in this ship.

It was meant to solve the problem of survival for the overpopulated Solar System.

And so it did.

...

The gigantic ship sailed past the floating platform.

The excitement had reached its peak.

Those on board the Alpha Colonial Transport had already started the countdown. It was the last few seconds until the main engines were turned on.

Three piercingly bright suns suddenly burst out from the ship.

It was the colonial transport's thermonuclear reactors.

Three columns of plasma shot into the empty space but the cameras continued their transmission, having been fitted with filters to record solar flares.

"Here it is, the historical moment!" Alexander Shapovalov exclaimed, unable to tear his gaze away from the astonishing spectacle, when suddenly...

The enthusiastic phrases that he had prepared earlier died on his lips.

The three columns of dazzling light, which should have accelerated the gargantuan ship, stopped firing in parallel and curved for some unbeknownst reason, as if some force was pushing them, and a second later intersected behind the ship!

An unexpected flash with a black center blossomed in the spot where the three columns met.

"My God!" Alexander Shapovalov choked out, unable to react in any other way to what was happening.

The developers of the colonial transport also sat frozen as they watched the rapid and incomprehensible process, unknown to modern science.

One of them was a young astrophysicist named Johan Ivanov-Schmidt.

It was becoming obvious that something terrible and irreparable was happening to the Alpha but the events unfolded much more rapidly than could be described.

The flash faded as quickly as it appeared, but in the confluence of the angled plasma columns, something clearly stirred, something deeper and darker than space itself. The mysterious formation quickly turned into a funnel streaked with energy threads — it was consuming the plasma, and the colonial transport, instead of moving forward and increasing speed, suddenly slowed down, then stopped and then...

It was dragged backwards into the funnel of absolute darkness, which completely absorbed the streams of plasma!

Alexander Shapovalov could not hold back a piercing scream, unable to comprehend this insane and unbelievable spectacle.

It was over in just a few seconds.

The black mirage rippled through space and *swallowed up* the Alpha.

A moment later, only twirling stars could be seen in the camera view as they blended into cold silver streaks, caused by the erratic spinning of the platform as it drifted away from the catastrophe.

Only two people reacted to the horrific event with malevolent satisfaction.

"Excellent work, White!" Bryzgalov exclaimed. "How the heck did you manage it? What was the darkness that swallowed up the ship?"

"I don't have the faintest idea." Jeremy White blinked several times. "According to my calculations, a change in the engine performance should have blown up the back of the ship!"

"And it disappeared instead?" Bryzgalov frowned but then waved a dismissive hand. "It doesn't matter! Whether it exploded or disappeared isn't important. Genesis and Rimp Cybertronics have sunk trillions of credits into the project and now they won't get a single credit back! The idea of flying to the stars has been quashed before our eyes! I'll crush both corporations and then the World Government will let me do whatever I want on Mars!"

The history of civilization is an unbroken chain of human actions. We make our own present and our future. It is not only the high and mighty that change the course of history. Each person, by choosing their way of life and by succumbing to or resisting their circumstances, can affect the fate of millions.

A week had passed since the disappearance of the Alpha Colonial Transport.

Ulrich Fitzgerald refused to see anyone and did not answer online requests or calls on his communicator.

Failure. Complete and utter failure was the only way to describe the situation. For the first time in his life, he found himself on the edge of despair.

By trusting Cathy Rimp and supporting her project, Ulrich Fitzgerald had invested all his available money into constructing and outfitting the Alpha. The catastrophe of the first colonial transport had effectively left Genesis bankrupt.

Ulrich knew that things were bad. The corporation was not yet bankrupt but was in serious financial trouble and could no longer hold the leading position in the settlement of Mars. Terraforming the Red Planet's deserts required constant and daily injections of funds, raw materials and technology, yet there was barely enough working capital to maintain food production. The situation was critical.

Rumors of Genesis' imminent collapse had already begun spreading.

Where could he get the money? It was impossible to find even a few billion credits while the Martian work required trillions to continue!

Ulrich felt like someone had pulled the rug from under his feet.

The political and financial games had already begun. The well-to-do section of Earth's society had expressed their legitimate concern and no wonder! They had purchased plots in the Martian deserts, where Genesis had promised them no more and no less than personal paradise. The network of atmospheric processors had been put into operation but this wasn't enough to terraform the planet. Enriching the atmosphere with oxygen, removing all the toxic impurities, creating a cloud cover and initiating the greenhouse effect to increase the temperature and atmospheric pressure to acceptable values — all these were only the first step. "I'll be able to hold on for a while," Fitzgerald thought darkly. "but I'll have to say goodbye to my dream."

Cryonics and Megapool were not wasting any time. They had already started putting the feelers out. Rimp Cybertronics was so far staying neutral and Cathy Rimp kept trying to contact him, probably to explain something, but Ulrich stubbornly ignored her calls.

All the leading corporations of Earth had their own interests in Mars and the greening project, aimed at turning Mars into a cosmic oasis, was like a bone in their throats.

"Of course, it's much easier and more profitable to build anthill cities on Mars, create a controlled habitat inside, and move three to four billion people in there, as opposed to a few hundred thousand!" Fitzgerald thought testily. "Such prospects, such profits! The construction of sealed megacities is income for Megapool and the opportunity to grow further. Filling the cities with technology provides an endless market for the products manufactured by Rimp Cybertronics. Resettling billions of Earth's

citizens is an untapped source of income for
Cryonics. Only Genesis is left with nothing to do
in this situation. The creation of a Martian
technosphere will undo a whole range of
terraforming projects. What is the way out?"

Any one of the corporations would gladly
offer Genesis the required money and so would
the World Government, which had an enormous
budget. But each one would want something in
return and they wouldn't want to be paid back in
interest. They would want concessions from him,
the sale of Martian territory!

It couldn't be worse! He couldn't, under any
circumstance, pause the terraforming process yet
he did not have the funds to keep it going. And
this was all happening now, after the many years
of hard work had finally yielded the desired result
and the atmospheric processor network had
reigned in the seasonal dust storms!

"May you all burn in hell!" Ulrich swore
silently. He was looking through a report by the
finance analysts. Genesis would need five years
to return to its previous position and to
accumulate the funds that were needed right
now!

In Ulrich Fitzgerald's enraged mind, the
situation with the Alpha Colonial Transport
smelled fishy. Had Cathy Rimp really tricked
him? The catastrophic destruction of the colonial

transport — was it an accident or a deliberate sacrifice that provided fresh opportunities for Genesis' competitors?

"They won't miss their chance to crush me. Pausing the Mars Project will allow the other corporations to declare Genesis insolvent and to present their projects for the colonization of Mars to the World Government. They will undoubtedly claim that their plans would enable billions of people to have a 'normal' life on Mars instead of being stuck in the in-modes.

And I won't be able to say or do anything to contradict them! I will have to agree and give away most of the territory for the construction of megacities, which will be the beginning of the end, the downfall of my life's work!"

Fitzgerald was overcome with rage.

When he agreed to finance the Alpha Project, he had received a firm guarantee that once the colonial transport was launched successfully, half of the invested amount would be returned to him by the World Bank!

Failure was not an option. It simply wasn't possible! And yet that was exactly what had happened. Ulrich thought increasingly about sabotage. The ship, the crew, and the passengers had been sacrificed in the growing confrontation between Earth's leading corporations.

Nothing brought him any comfort. This

world was still living according to wild and primitive laws!

Fitzgerald's thoughts turned more and more aggressive. "I have to strike back if I want to keep my corporation! But how?! How do I strike back if Genesis has been brought to its knees? Only a small number of people know about it so far but in a month's time, suspension of the Mars Project will become obvious. Well, perhaps more than a month. I could fake it for another six months at least, using the excuse of testing the atmospheric processors but I won't be able to recoup my losses in that time! I must strike first!" This thought wouldn't let go. All the possible options were dark ones. Reduce food production? Yes, it would be relatively easy to bring civilization to the brink of a hunger riot. But what then? Blackmail the World Government?

A rude and dangerous activity. Riots were unpredictable by their very nature. The crowd's anger would be directed at Genesis and would rebound like a boomerang, while the other corporations, suspecting sabotage of the food supplies, would again take the opportunity to attack. The hungry citizens would welcome the nationalization of Genesis. No one would lift a finger when the corporate armies, with the support of the World Government, took control of food production.

No, that path lead to suicide.

These depressing thoughts would not let him rest and brought him close to a nervous breakdown.

Ultimately, Ulrich Fitzgerald did not think he was a monster. He hated the urbanized Earth and dreamt of recreating the extinct biosphere of his home planet on Mars, thus giving the people a chance to start anew. He intentions were good. He had spent all his adult life making them a reality and once he had calmed down a little, he understood that he had to fight the other corporations, who wanted to crush Genesis, and not the people of Earth.

He reviewed the reports again and again, looking for an opportunity to strike in a way that would not be directly linked to him.

Ulrich had mentally accepted the dire necessity of temporarily giving up parts of Mars. But would he ever get them back?

"Let's say that I announce that Genesis is having financial difficulties," he mused darkly. "I'll do it myself, without waiting for everyone else to kick up a fuss. I'll demand the World Government's help. They won't give it to me, of course, since the public is displeased with

Genesis due to our reliance on the wealthy citizens of Earth in the early stage of terraforming. The people huddling in their in-modes and capsule apartments hate me; they simply don't understand that a sustained effort to alter an entire planet will ultimately create more living space for all parts of society. No, the masses won't lend me their support." Ulrich reasoned soberly, not letting hopes or illusions cloud his judgement. "The World Government will be guided by its electorate, being afraid of provoking unrest. I will undoubtedly be refused under an apparently plausible pretext. I have only one option left. Megapool, Cryonics and Rimp Cybertronics will offer to divide up Mars and will agree to purchase huge, barren territories so that they can create their own development centers. I will have to agree, keeping aside small, compact areas on the plains, whose terraforming will satisfy the demands of my rich clients.

So be it. Let's not forget that Genesis owns tens of thousands of atmospheric processors that have already been put into operation!"

Ulrich scanned the information obtained from test launches of the airflow control and climate formation system.

"Let them build," he continued gloomily. "Let them invest money and indulge their hopes. I won't let them kill my dream. I won't let them create another technosphere on Mars. The day will come when I will bring all my competitors to their knees and crush all their undertakings! The dust will help me. The very same dust that had long been the bane of the Red Planet..."

That evening marked the start of a new cycle of conflict between the corporations of Earth. Compared to this, the war over resources in the asteroid belt was only child's play.

Civilization was suffocating. The current state of affairs meant that none of the projects to colonize Mars would succeed, since the strike that Ulrich Fitzgerald was planning against his competitors would automatically throw civilization back for decades.

His good intentions, his love for Earth's lost nature, and the desire to recreate it no matter what became the first paving stones on the road to hell.

Only one person on the dying planet was involved in genuine, unbiased research into the causes of the colonial transport catastrophe.

Johan Ivanov-Schmidt, a young astrophysicist known to only a small circle of colleagues, lived in the in-mode and worked at a virtual laboratory. Day after day, he modeled the moment that the engines turned on and the colonial transport disappeared.

He didn't believe in the disaster theory. The young astrophysicist was fixated on the black funnel threaded with energy, which he believed had swallowed up the Alpha.

Years of painstaking work lay ahead of him with little progress, negligible in the face of his many failures.

This always happens when a person comes across a phenomenon that can't be explained by the known laws of physics.

But Johan didn't give up and tried to look beyond current science, developing a theory that would explain the disappearance of the colonial transport. He behaved like many geniuses of past ages, whose discoveries formed the basis of modern civilization.

He created theories using the resources of the global Net, and all the while, billions of people were dying of boredom in virtual reality.

He had crafted his own small link in the endless chain of actions and events that are responsible for human history, but being caught up in his research, was not aware of it.

Earth

Year 2210 AD

Three years after the Alpha Project disaster

A bright light flashed in his eyes.

The first moment of consciousness brought screams, sharply unpleasant medical smells, a constant vibration, pneumatic hissing and someone's stifled groans.

Damn... So cold...

His teeth were chattering.

Max Bourne could hear voices but couldn't understand them. Then something pricked his neck and his mind became clearer.

"Get up! Quick! Line up!" Someone was yelling hoarsely.

Max didn't even think to respond but then someone grabbed him, pulled him up and cast him onto the floor.

He fell helplessly and struck something hard but didn't even cry out.

He was in an unfamiliar compartment. Naked and emaciated bodies lay between a row of cryogenic capsules. Everyone looked vague and confused. Someone was sitting up and swaying monotonously to try and stop the shakes, but most of the 'test subjects' were lying prostrate on the floor. Max's mind began to throw up images captured before he was immersed in cryogenic sleep.

A grim tall man was stalking through the crowded compartment, stepping over the people huddling awkwardly on the floor. Unshaven, with closely cropped hair, and wearing a uniform with the Rimp Cybertronics logo on his sleeve and chest, he immediately made a negative impression. The stranger reeked of sweat, adrenalin and fear.

The bright light had an ultraviolet tinge to it.

The pale and skinny bodies gave off a terrible stench. The people shifted sluggishly and some were having seizures but nobody moved to help them.

"Come on, get up!"

Max obeyed the command with difficulty and asked softly, "What's happening? Where are we?"

"On board the cruiser *Normandy*," the brute grinned unkindly. "Well then!" He left Max alone and began pacing between the rows of cryogenic capsules again, grimacing in disgust as he stepped over the emaciated people. "My name's Eric, my surname's Podegro. I'm the captain. My position is the Flight Deck Commander onboard the *Normandy*. You have been in cryogenic sleep for fifteen years out of the thirty-five stipulated by the contract. The Cryonics Corporation has kindly ceded us the right to conduct a series of additional experiments."

"This is ridiculous!" a weak voice interrupted. "What additional experiments?!"

"Read carefully." A holographic screen appeared in the air, showing the contract. "Paragraph five. I'll read aloud for those who can't make out the small print. *If necessary, the Cryonics Corporation has the right to conduct additional tests using the cryogenic capsules without gaining additional approval from the test subjects.*"

"What have you done to us?" the same weak, shaking voice interrupted him again.

"We've taught you!" Captain Podegro turned sharply. "We've taught you to operate small class Needle spaceships. Simply put, you are now pilots."

"I demand medical attention!" came someone's yell. "I demand that you return me to Earth on the first commercial flight! This is unacceptable!"

"Oh, sure thing!" The captain pulled up an image from *Normandy*'s external sensors. "I hated this idea from the start. To teach all sort of scum how to pilot!" He scoffed and then added in response to the puzzled looks. "This bright dot here is Jupiter. All those unhappy with the current situation — I can show you the way to the nearest airlock."

A shocked silence met his words.

Jupiter?!

"How did we end up here? The cryogenic capsule testing was supposed to take place in a separate module of the *Space Vegas* as it orbited Earth!"

"That's right," smirked the captain. "That's what happened for the first five years. Then the module was undocked from the station and launched into space."

"How were they planning to bring us back?"

"I don't think they were planning to do it at all. At least, not in the foreseeable future. The Cryonics Corporation wanted to find out as much as possible about the processes involved in cryogenic sleep. To determine how long the equipment would last and what the human body could withstand. The results are impressive, I'll admit. After fifteen years, each one of you has only aged one year, according to the medical scanners. Not bad, eh? We were unable to awaken two people due to a technical failure, which is unfortunate but happens."

"Why have we been picked up by a corporate army cruiser?" "What does Rimp

Cybertronics have to do with all this?" "What's this dream training program?" The questions were coming in thick and fast.

"I see that everyone's regained their senses." The captain kept grinning unpleasantly. "In that case, time to get off the floor! The sanitation module is at the end of the corridor. Use it. Clothing can be found in the lockers. Then you'll get your instructions."

"But... wait!"

"Later! Clean yourselves up!" Captain Podegro barked. "You stink!"

Fifteen years? Bourne staggered into a shower and washed the sticky residue of the physiological solution off his body. Then he found a locker with his surname on it and began to get dressed.

Max had signed the contract with Cryonics while in a state of utter despair, thinking that his life was over. He wasn't thinking of the future then.

Fifteen years... He couldn't process the numbers uttered by Captain Podegro. The circumstances surrounding his awakening baffled him even further. Subjectively, it felt like an hour had passed since he had signed the contract but reality was radically different.

What was happening on Earth right now? Had his parents moved to the Antarctic Megacity? Was Johnny all grown up? And Samantha, was she married now? What kind of lives were they living?

The pilot's uniform hung off his bony body.

The other 'test subjects' were getting dressed beside him. Nobody spoke at first as everyone was too overwhelmed and confused.

"He's probably lying." An exhausted-looking man sat down beside Max on the metal bench screwed to the floor. All the 'test subjects' looked the same. Due to their extreme thinness, people's features blurred into one another in some strange way. Max glanced at his own reflection in the small mirror with disgust.

"What's your name?"

"Nuomi."

"I'm Max," he sat down beside the other man. "Why do you think that Podegro is lying?"

"Perhaps it's some kind of test? On psychological stability. It seems stupid if you think about it. Why send a module full of sleeping people into deep space?"

"They were testing the equipment." Responded a scrawny and stunted guy, who looked like an evil computer monster from some fantasy game. "My name's Rohrich. I know a bit about cryonics. I used to work for the corps."

"Well then, enlighten us, oh wise one." Nuomi turned to him.

"You can't carry out full-scale tests on board a station," Rohrich stated confidently. "Offline mode is required to obtain objective data..."

"Why don't you shut up!" Someone yelled angrily.

"We need to stick together," Nuomi said. "Does anyone feel different? What did they teach us in our sleep? How is that even possible? I've never even driven a car!"

"You can ask the captain," uttered Vadim Stigmatov, whose name Max read off the tiny display on the man's personal locker.

The meandering conversation was disrupted by the appearance of an information module. The small spherical apparatus appeared from an opening in the ceiling, assessed the situation and uttered in a flat tone of voice, "Pilots, please follow me."

The doors opened automatically.

"Did you hear that?" Nuomi followed Max out the door. "It called us pilots. Why aren't you saying anything? Maybe we've been really lucky. We've survived and been awoken. We've even been trained, if Podegro's not lying."

"Just be quiet and stop bothering me!"

"Why, is it hard for you to talk?"

"We've got nothing to talk about," Max responded gloomily. "Nothing good will come of this, you'll see."

"Take a seat." Captain Podegro indicated the rows of comfortable chairs. "I can see that you are all confused. I'll try to explain the situation but I'll warn you now that I won't tolerate any hysterics or other such behavior! Don't annoy me with your personal feelings, right? Your contracts are not yet finished. You belong to the corporation." He cast them an intense of dislike. "No more and no less, got it?"

A heavy and cautious silence met his words.

"So, a brief introduction." Eric Podegro sent an order through his cyberstack and the space inside the compartment changed instantly. Max's heart skipped a beat and a horrible cold sensation spread through his chest. His head started spinning. He had grown up in the in-mode and had never been to space. Even the trip to the Space Vegas Station took place when he was already asleep.

The holographic screens around him created a perfect illusion of the Abyss. It was a strong blow for an unprepared mind. In the first moment, he felt a deep sense of melancholia. No matter which way he looked, he was surrounded by the dark, strewn with countless stars.

Max's pupils dilated and his vision became blurry; his throat closed up.

Captain Podegro, ignoring the shocked response of his audience, zoomed in on one particular section of space. Jupiter came into view. The enormous brownish-white gaseous sphere, streaked with bands of atmospheric currents, grew larger and then shifted to the right. One of its satellites now occupied the center.

"Ganymede," Captain Podegro said curtly. "Automated mining of natural resources has taken place here for a long time. At the start of the century, Ganymede was visited by an expedition from the World Space Agency." He spoke succinctly, often glancing at the tiny information screen that contained an earlier prepared text. "During geological and cartographic surveys, they found large deposits of rare elements. Soon after, they sent a fleet of mining complexes. There were never any settlements on Ganymede, since as I've already said, all the mining was done automatically."

"Why do we need to know that?" Nuomi enquired cautiously.

Captain Podegro lost his train of thought and looked at him angrily.

"So that you know what sort of mess you've gotten yourself into!" He snarled. "I was ordered to explain the situation to you. Hold your questions! If anyone interrupts me again, they'll live to regret it!"

Everyone kept quiet as he continued mumbling rapidly, "The fall of the superpowers, the destruction of Earth's AIs, and the formation of the World Government led to a change in ownership but the mining continued. All the infrastructure on Ganymede belongs to Rimp Cybertronics. Until recently, automated cargo ships regularly flew between Earth and Jupiter. There was no warning..." He stumbled, turned off the information display in irritation and continued in his own words. "Basically, technology hasn't stood still while you were asleep. Thanks to the efforts of the World Government," he grimaced. "many small firms — taking into account the realities of deep space, I would call them small gangs — now have the opportunity to purchase and hire spaceships in order to search and develop resources in the asteroid belt. The particularly bold ones thought that they could snatch a piece here!" He gestured angrily at Jupiter's moons. "Our cruiser received the order to carry out a long-distance raid and to ensure that corporate property is kept safe. To put it simply, we were supposed to give those punks a good thrashing!"

"It didn't work out?" Came a nervous giggle from the back row.

"Shut your trap!" Captain Podegro roared. "Space distances!" He spoke through clenched teeth, trying to control his normally rough manner of speaking. "By the time we left Mars' orbit, a year had passed. It was all over before we even got here! Take a look." He activated an additional holographic screen.

Clusters of debris could be seen floating in front of Jupiter. Nearby drifted two modestly-sized space stations and a heavily damaged cargo ship.

"We had no idea who did this," Captain Podegro continued gloomily, "until we tried to land on Ganymede. We came under fire from the space defense system, which was designed to protect the mines!"

"Sorry, Captain, does that mean that they had been captured?!"

"Yes," Eric Podegro grimaced. "But it's not people who are running the show on Ganymede," he added to everyone's surprise. "We tried to quash the resistance and got our teeth kicked in. Many of the fighter pilots died. Ships were lost. The *Normandy* sustained damage. We had to withdraw. We've been stuck here for six months!"

"Captain, can I ask a question?"

"Well?" Eric Podegro's eyes found Max in the crowd. "What is it?"

"Why did the attack fail? Who's in charge on Ganymede?"

"The reason for the losses was a failure of the automatic systems. The cyber control defenses were hacked. The pilots were powerless to do anything. Only four of us, including me, were able to escape using manual controls." He glared in the direction of Ganymede. "The corporation's experts have come to the conclusion that the planetoid has been colonized by AIs, the same ones that were supposedly destroyed at the end of the last century!"

"Sorry," Nuomi couldn't hold back. "but I know for a fact that the AIs were..."

"They fled Earth!" Captain Podegro snapped. "It's a fact. Catherine Rimp destroyed the original military neural networks using a 'virt', but she was mistaken in her assessment of how advanced those blasted AIs were. The bastards managed to create backup copies of their neural matrices and slip away! The corporation's analytical department had a hell of a job tracking their route. They first hid in the lunar networks, then they moved to Mars and then to the asteroid belt. Eventually, they took over the cybernetic and neural network structures on Ganymede. To stay hidden, they continued to supply the necessary amount of resources, to accept, service and load up the cargo ships, all the while creating their own structures! If it wasn't for the gangs, we still wouldn't have a clue of what's going on here!"

"The AIs were preparing for conflict?" Rohrich stretched out his thin neck.

"Yes." Captain Podegro confirmed grimly. "They built the space defense system. There were no military installations here at the start! There were only mines, equipment hangars, landing platforms and runways. Let me repeat this for the stupid ones among you: the exploration and mining were done automatically. They have captured the planetoid! Got it?"

Max was in a state of shock. Yes, he had made mistakes and tried to fix them by taking the path of least resistance, humbly accepting his fate and not thinking too hard about his future.

But here it was. What was he going to do? He looked around like a cornered animal, unable to comprehend why the spherical 3D image of space affected him so much psychologically. "What am I afraid of? This is no worse than the illusions created by the in-mode!"

It was no use. He couldn't persuade himself that what was happening was harmless.

Subconsciously, he could clearly distinguish between virtual space and reality, and this made all the hairs on his body stand up. A hundred million kilometers of empty space surrounded him. He felt like he was drowning in the Abyss. His muscles began to twitch and his vision went blurry, his mouth feeling dry and foul.

"It's not as bad as it may seem at first glance," the voice of Captain Podegro cut through his thoughts. "The Ganymede Anti-Spacecraft Missile System was damaged in two places by our attack. Now all we have to do is widen the gaps in the defense system and provide the *Normandy* with a safe approach corridor. As soon as the cruiser reaches low-orbit, the AIs will be finished once and for all!"

"What does this have to do with us?" Nuomi asked faintly.

"What do you think?" Eric Podegro turned in irritation.

"I don't know what to think!"

"We were able to board the mining stations." The captain pointed to the objects drifting in space. "We found twelve working Needles in the hangars of their launch decks, but we don't have any pilots left. The cruiser is now on manual control. We don't have enough people, with every officer performing two or three jobs. We're sleeping only four hours per night as we're on constant combat duty."

"So you decided to use us?" Vadim Stigmatov asked sharply.

"That's right. Like a deus ex machina," Captain Podegro smiled contemptuously. "The operation was planned on Earth!" He raised his voice. "We have blocked the AIs and are jamming all types and frequencies of long-distance communications to prevent the bastards from slipping away again!"

"Why us?!" Nuomi yelled again. He looked hysterical.

Captain Podegro strode up to the shaking weakling, grasped him by the chin and jerked his head up so that their eyes were level. "The corporate fleet will need two and a half years to reach here! We can't hold for that long!" He released Nuomi and wiped his fingers in disgust. The captain was close to losing it. It was obvious from his behavior. Stupid soldiers! Max felt worse and worse, the sticky fear coating him in sweat.

"The heads of Rimp Cybertronics have found a way out of this situation. All options were considered and all artificial objects within a two-month distance from the *Normandy* were thoroughly analyzed. Your experimental module had crossed Jupiter's orbit at that point. We had to chase after you."

"Why?" Max couldn't hold back the

question.

"The Cryonics Corporation came to the aid of Rimp Cybertronics by permitting us to use one of our leading innovations and turn you into pilots of the Needles." Captain Podegro explained. "It's not much, of course, but I think you'll manage to blow up a couple of anti-spacecraft batteries and provide an approach corridor for the *Normandy*. Or you'll die and we'll have to look for other ways to capture Ganymede."

"Have you gone mad?" Came the angry shouts. "We're not pilots!"

"I'm well aware that Cryonics recruited you for the experiment. You're scum! Losers! But you each have an implant, and some brains too, I hope! Teaching technology has not yet been tested on humans but you're all still alive and even kicking up a fuss!" He again smiled humorlessly. "It's a good sign! We'll know what kind of pilots you are very soon, first on the simulator and then in real flights. Those who survive will have a real chance of becoming wealthy and returning to Earth, or remaining in space, for example, in the asteroid belt. But you're going to have to try very hard!"

Thus began Max Bourne's new life, full of fear and exhausting training, interspersed with the contemptuous yelling and remarks of Captain Podegro.

The *Normandy* changed its course and gradually came closer to the drifting space stations. While the prolonged maneuvering took place, the 'pilots' were mercilessly put through one simulator after another, intensively fed and given various drugs to restore their muscle tone and to determine how successful the novel technology was.

"I can't... I can't take this! This is insane!" Nuomi, with whom Max shared a tiny cabin, complained and whined constantly. "It's inhumane! The world has gone crazy! Civilization has gone crazy!"

"Will you shut up already!" Stigmatov raised himself up from the bed threateningly. "Shut up or I'll break your neck!"

Nuomi fell back, mumbling something under his breath.

Max didn't feel much better. The sense of doom was interspersed with unhealthy and feverish attacks of self-confidence, while the constant physical fatigue, bordering on exhaustion, left no energy to think about what was happening. After completing training, he would greedily eat, drink the allocated water, and fall asleep.

The atmosphere in the tiny, one-person cabin, which now housed three people, made Max wistfully reminisce about the in-mode's personal space.

"I've got a splitting headache!" Stigmatov sat on his bed, swaying back and forth and unconsciously massaging his temples. "My head's a mess... I keep having really weird dreams..."

"Not you as well." Max hadn't fallen asleep immediately today and instead tossed and turned in his bunk. The air in the cabin seemed stale and suffocating. Vadim and Nuomi's constant presence drove him to distraction.

"It's the effect of the drugs," Nuomi whispered huskily.

"How would you know?"

"I know about these things."

"How did you end up in the capsule?"

"I wanted to make some money. Then I found myself in another time, three decades later."

"Why?" Stigmatov winced from a fresh onslaught of pain.

"The world has gone crazy." Nuomi was like a broken record, repeating the same phrase.

"Can you explain properly?" Max could tell

that he wasn't going to fall sleep.

"Don't you see it yourself?"

"No."

"We're surrounded by cybersystems. Humans don't matter anymore. We've become an anthill."

"But now everything has changed!" Stigmatov snorted. "Now, Nuomi, you will die, having found yourself!"

"Don't be a jerk. It's only gotten worse. Has the technology race stopped? Do they consider us as people? Why is it okay to get inside my head?"

"Well, they've been in my head too!" Stigmatov snapped. "What's the point of complaining about it now? We've got new skills and you can't argue with that. Although I can't figure out how it's even possible."

"It's all because of the implant," Nuomi sighed bitterly. "It's become an access point. One can use it to affect the brain. Send through the same information over and over again, for example, about ways to manually pilot a fighter plane. Our biological neural networks are unable to ignore the information, so they are forced to process it and learn. This results in a skill that is largely automated. Yet no one can predict the consequences; I've asked. These experiments are banned on Earth. Rimp Cybertronics has two objectives: to clean up Ganymede and to get results from an outlawed experiment."

Such talk did not exactly fill Max with optimism but he was more concerned about something else. With every passing day, his fear of outer space grew. On the simulator, Bourne showed good but unreliable results. On days when he could persuade himself that it was all an illusion, the training flights were easy, but as soon as he thought about the real upcoming combat, his arms froze and his mind was swallowed up by a sucking void of terror.

The fateful day was drawing closer. The *Normandy* captured both drifting space stations using electromagnetic tugs. Technicians and servos were working to refit the Needles. Nobody ever explained why there were space fighters on board a mining complex.

Max had painstakingly looked for a way out of the situation and seemed to have found it. Twelve Needles and fifteen pilots — here was the loophole that was going to save him. He wasn't afraid of the AIs or the upcoming attack, he was petrified of outer space itself.

He began to fake terrible results on the simulator, enraging Captain Podegro but hoping to be in the bottom three pilots according to the final test results.

What did it feel like to be a complete loser?

Max simply waved away such thoughts.

He had grown up in virtual reality, having put in no effort to ensure his own survival. He possessed no real skills or knowledge. He valued nothing and had no attachment to anything. He had no moral values as such. Where would he have gotten them from, anyway? From the brief, daily 'family connections', which did nothing except annoy him?

Our personality and beliefs are subconsciously shaped by our environment and life experiences. It was clear that the range of virtual realities in which children and adolescents were growing up — the cult of violence as an everyday norm, the endless virtual wars, the spectacular murder scenes and bloody special effects, the ability to disappear at any moment, thus avoiding responsibility for what was said or done, the cheap price of a human life as a direct consequence of the ability to endlessly reload in case of a 'virtual' death — produced worthless souls inside the bodies of glamorous-looking avatars.

It was hard to blame Max. He was a product of his time and his social environment. To him, Captain Podegro seemed like a monster. Max didn't stop to wonder why the man was risking his life, how he survived the endless watches and combat duties, alone for many hours with the icy abyss of space, and what ultimately drove him.

Max was not ashamed of his tricks. He was driven by instinctive fear and defended himself in any way that he could, without stopping to consider what would happen afterwards and how he would live.

Only one thing seemed important right now, and that was to remain on board the *Normandy* as one of the three rejects.

★ ★ ★

Max was unlucky. He was twelfth on the list when the results of the final tests came through.

The three people remaining aboard the *Normandy* were the lucky bastard Nuomi and two others, whom Max hadn't seen since awakening. He was very disappointed to discover that they had failed before the training had even begun. Their bodies simply could not withstand the consequences of the cryogenic sleep.

Max accepted his misfortune silently, his teeth clenched. What could he do? Scream and thrash about hysterically? It wouldn't have helped. Captain Podegro dealt quickly and painfully with his subordinates' meltdowns. A punch in the face and an icy glare from those empty, exhausted eyes was all it took.

Nuomi disappeared. He never returned to the living quarters assigned to the new recruits. The cruiser continued its maneuvers, twice the *Normandy* transmitted powerful thrusts and the artificial gravity was switched off at times. The nauseating sensation of weightlessness was interspersed with periods of acceleration.

The night before the first mission passed excruciatingly slowly. Max couldn't sleep, anxious thoughts crowding his mind. Fear of what was coming made him shudder.

Vadim Stigmatov, on the other hand, fell asleep at once, and his annoying snores turned Max's rest into torture.

Finally, Max fell into a fitful doze. The thrusts and vibrations had stopped and the cruiser now moved with a steady acceleration.

The screech of the alarm was like an electric shock.

Max leapt up. Stigmatov opened his eyes, stretched and only then sat up.

"Relax."

"But the alarm!"

"They won't start without us."

All the cabin doors opened simultaneously. The narrow corridor was bustling with activity. Everyone was on edge, the tension felt in every movement, word and gesture.

Captain Podegro was waiting for them in

the tactical section. For the past three weeks, he had been the only crew member of the *Normandy* to deal with the pilots directly.

"Take a seat," he said calmly. Since the captain's memorable introductory speech, it was hard to get an extra word out of him. Gloomy and aloof, he hadn't changed his attitude towards the new recruits and continued to look at them with grim disdain, although today he was behaving differently.

"Circumstances have changed," He announced into the tense silence, pacing in front of the holographic screens. "The technical servos have discovered a leak in the tankers of the mining supply station. We're short on jet fuel. The commander has set a course for Ganymede. We fly out in two hours."

There were murmurs throughout the room but Eric Podegro didn't yell as he usually did.

"You've done well on the simulators. Some have tried to perform below their ability but we'll deal with that later. There's no reason to panic. Everyone's afraid, I get it. It's normal. You'll manage. We don't expect anything supernatural from you." He switched on the tactical equipment. "The technicians have made the Needles immune to cyberattacks, but I wouldn't trust the autopilot if I were you. Keep the situation under control and use only the manual mode."

Ash-brown Ganymede grew larger and larger. A separate 3D screen began to show a hybrid image of the terrain. Thin course lines crossed the border between the dark surface, pitted with impact craters, and the slightly lighter landscape, consisting mainly of deep grooves and low ridges.

"Here," the laser pointer circled an area where the two surfaces met, "is the location of the two anti-spacecraft batteries." Two markers immediately appeared. "One was completely destroyed during the last attack and the second one was damaged, although we don't know how badly. We have been monitoring this part of Ganymede's surface but have seen no signs of repair. Your Needles have been completely refitted and we have attached proton rockets to the external suspension. You should approach Ganymede at maximum speed, like we practiced during training. At this point," he placed a navigational marker, "you change course and glide as close to the surface as possible. Attack only when you can see the target directly otherwise, the neighboring batteries will intercept the rockets as has happened before. They will launch single use fire support devices. These are primitive devices and are controlled remotely. The AIs shoot out series of ten. They are equipped with jet engines and are armed with simple lasers designed for a single shot, as well as a self-destruct device. Be careful around them. Operating within the Net, these things can easily shoot down missiles and then explode, filling the space with shrapnel and rocket fragments.

Now, the specific combat tasks. You have been divided into four teams of three fighters each. Approach Ganymede as a group, and split up when you get here." He pointed to a small impact crater. "The first squadron attacks the damaged anti-spacecraft battery. The second squadron ensures that the battery is destroyed, since God forbid if they have managed to repair it! The third squadron attacks the anti-spacecraft node on the left flank and the fourth squadron does the same on the right flank. Don't try to be heroes. Launch the missiles at close range and then immediately perform combat maneuvers like we've done during practice; moving at very low altitudes, head for the 'dead zones' and then, once you're safe, return to the cruiser at maximum speed but maintaining low orbits."

"Why the risk?" Stigmatov butted in. "Why doesn't the *Normandy* fire its missiles?"

"They'll be shot down on approach."

"And we won't be shot down?!"

"The missile is controlled by a cybernetic reconnaissance and final guidance system. The last attack showed us that the control unit is the weakest link in the fight against the AIs," Captain Podegro explained with unexpected patience. "You've got brains rather than electronics in your head, Stigmatov. You're capable of quickly reacting to a threat, making decisions, repealing or evading an attack, or getting away from fire to attack again. A missile isn't capable of all that, unfortunately. Not in our case, at least."

Max exhaled slowly. He was part of the second squadron. Ensuring that the already destroyed anti-spacecraft battery remained destroyed seemed like quite a feasible task, as long as the third and fourth squadrons did their jobs.

"As soon as you clear the approach corridor, the *Normandy* will attack. The cruiser will carry out an orbital spiral and use its electromagnetic guns to crush the remaining fire posts. The rest is for the landing forces. Any other questions?"

"Can't the cruiser's heavy lasers attack from a distance?" Vadim Stigmatov looked nervous. His philosophical devil-may-care attitude had vanished. "If the locations of the enemy batteries are known, what prevents us from..."

"The dust." Captain Podegro interrupted him. "Don't try to be clever!" He raised his voice.

"All other attack methods have already been tried! Who can tell me what regolith is?"

Someone went searching for the answer in the ship's local Net but most people, including Max, simply waited for an explanation.

"Well?" Podegro noticed that Sebastian Mogeiro, a quiet, dark-skinned and slender pilot, was meeting his gaze. "Have you found an answer?"

"Yes."

"Tell us."

"Regolith is a type of lunar soil," replied Mogeiro, referring to the information obtained online. "It's crumbly and consists of dust and very small rock granules. Mostly mineral and glass particles and meteor fragments. The regolith layer may be several meters thick. The color typically varies from dark gray to black. Regolith includes many particles with reflective properties and easily billows upwards during blasts..."

"That's enough!" The captain cut him off. "The AIs anticipated the possibility of being fired upon by high-powered lasers. They have planted explosive devices everywhere, buried in the regolith. This is important to know as regolith dust sticks very well to solid bodies in vacuum conditions. It will blind your sensors and make navigation difficult. But most importantly, an explosion creates clouds of slowly settling particles, which easily reflect, disperse, and scatter laser energy. My advice is, don't try to find any loopholes. There are none. The attack plan has been approved. Now, everyone will receive a chip with their personal assignment, course calculations and navigational databases. Then it's time to kit up and into the ships!"

The hangar was filled with light, sound and movement. Servos scurried about everywhere, conducting preflight checks and disconnecting the stationary power lines, releasing the spacecraft from the energy and information links that connected it to the base ship.

On the outside, the Needle looked too large and cumbersome for a fast-moving (in Max's understanding) space fighter.

His fear seemed to have burnt away. He was no longer shaking, only the fading sense of irreparable wrongness sat like a fist in his chest.

He climbed up a rickety ladder to the open airlock and stepped inside, finding himself in a room with identical oval hatches. One lead to the cockpit, the other one provided access to the propulsion system and the third one had a sign saying 'Cargo hold'.

Max couldn't understand why a fighter plane would have a cargo hold but he had more pressing issues to worry about.

The airlock hissed shut. The bustle of flight preparations disappeared instantly and was left somewhere outside. He hesitated in the tiny airlock for some time, then stepped into the cockpit.

Here, everything was familiar. He sat in the pilot's chair. The safety belts slithered out and tightened over his chest, shoulders and hips. Max's fingers danced across the sensor panels in a well-practiced movement, activating the manual controls.

The shivering returned. Every movement felt new and intense.

Many things struck him. The shabbiness of some elements of the primary structure, the scratches on the text glyphs, the bundles of power and optic cables lying on top of the standard equipment.

Seconds sped past. The external view screens came alive, showing the empty hangar and the communicator burst out with a babble of reports of combat readiness.

Max tensed. It suddenly became hard to breathe.

A red light flooded the hangar, notifying them that air was being pumped out.

"No! No! I can't do it!" The panicking inner voice screeched mercilessly but the grim reality, where he had wanted to live once upon a time (the idiot!) did not obey the desires of a terrified youth.

The massive hangar doors shuddered and began to slowly slide apart.

The darkness that lurked behind them was like an enormous maw, ready to devour the pilot and his ship.

Max's arms and legs were like jelly. He couldn't feel his fingers and struggled to firmly grasp the navigation controls, while data were already streaming through the operating systems and the countdown was ticking down to zero.

The acceleration pushed Max back into the chair for only a moment. The pilot chair automatically compensated for the acceleration forces, which caused a wave of nausea and a shiver to run through Max's chest and stomach, but the physical symptoms paled in comparison to his other sensations.

The Needles, their engines glowing, rapidly turned into tiny sparks and disappeared among the stars, while he sat frozen and unable to move. Bourne's ship left the hangar and then slowly and uncontrollably moved away from the station. Eric Podegro's angry exclamations could be heard in the communicator, accompanied by streams of swearing, but it was as if Max had gone deaf. The drift of the Needle made the view on its screens shift gradually. The starry void was replaced with a view of Jupiter and the *Normandy* in the foreground. The cruiser disengaged and both stations, launch sites for the Needles, were pushed away to either side. A desperate thought flashed through Max's mind, paralyzed with fear, "It's a death sentence! We're doomed! Nobody expects us to come back."

Max could not handle his first contact with space. The cosmic expanse destroyed his sanity. He was morally dead even before he entered the battle.

In actual fact, soldiers were waiting for them. The soldiers were counting on them. The *Normandy* was already on a battle course and as the huge ship sailed past, Max Bourne looked at its uneven surface and thought dully, "Now they'll haul the Needle in." But nothing of the sort happened, and even Captain Podegro's hoarse voice in the communicator fell quiet. The cruiser began to draw away.

Not even the most advanced technology can prepare a man for when he faces himself, when the threads of fate tremble at the tips of one's fingers, which nervously grasp the acceleration lever.

Reason retreats in these seconds.

Fight or flight is one of the main instincts that evolution has given us. Max Bourne's hopeless gaze followed the receding cruiser. A little longer, and the glow of its engines will become just another spark, hard to discern from the surrounding stars.

All of life's questions pale in such moments.

He would become a coward or a hero later, but now he could only hear his own breathing, feel his fingers clench, the large droplets of sweat on his forehead and the desperate hammering of his heart.

He looked at the *Normandy*'s glowing engines again and felt frightened and lonely.

The choice between life and death, between the spark of hope and the sepulchral cold had to be made in any case, and Max made it, pushing the acceleration lever.

The Needle began to gather speed, following the cruiser towards Ganymede.

Jupiter was rapidly approaching.

The feverish anticipation of the coming

events had Max in its grasp. He piloted the Needle while under extreme strain. His whole body trembled and his lips shook.

The navigation panel signaled shrilly. Max pulled on the astronavigation controls, changing course. Jupiter's gray-brown orb, streaked with layers of atmospheric currents, shifted to the left, and Ganymede began increasing in size instead, a battle already raging above its surface.

The AIs had detonated the charges, which had thrown up clouds of regolith dust above the defenses, just like Captain Podegro had warned.

It didn't make any sense! Why did they blind their own sensors? Or did they move them elsewhere ahead of time? Thoughts raced through Max's mind as the Needle rapidly crossed the dangerous section of its low orbit trajectory.

The AIs fought furiously, missiles shooting out from the depths of the dust clouds. The electromagnetic weapons were working in defense mode. Did that mean that the enemy was not as calculating, clever and dangerous as his frantic mind thought? Or did Max's fear make the wolf bigger than he is?

Max belatedly changed course again and managed to enter the specified patrol region. He streaked over the pitted plain, scanning the terrain, then turned the ship at the edge of the fold, and, repressing the shivers coursing down his body, forced himself to transmit. "Twelve, all clear! Scanners showing only remnants of the anti-spacecraft battery! No active signatures present!"

"Bourne, where the hell were you?" Captain Podegro swore mightily. "Join the fight! Aim for square 117! Use the proton rockets on any large target!"

Max checked his instruments and the electronic map.

The fight in the specified square was in full swing. Among the mushroom-shaped, slowly dispersing clouds of dust, he could see blinding flashes of explosions, while the darkness of space was dissected by the dotted lines of anti-spacecraft fire, with the dense network of laser beams flaring up periodically.

It was the very heart of the battle.

He forced himself to alter course. The scanners found three targets and highlighted them in flashing frames.

Which one should he choose?!

A rocket passed close by and his back was drenched in cold sweat. What was happening?! None of the Needles had been shot down? Were they really that lucky?

"Captain?" He called Captain Podegro.

"Bourne, do what you're told! Shut up and

carry out your orders. Can't you see what's happening?"

That was the thing! Streaks of fire were shooting out from the thick clouds of dust. Calculating the exact location of the anti-spacecraft batteries wasn't difficult, the information was already up on a separate screen and the navigation system was signaling hysterically. All he had to do was pick a target and press the trigger!

Something wasn't right. The Needles swarmed over the AI battle stations like wasps. Having used up their missiles, they pounded the fortifications using electromagnetic weapons.

The AIs were responding with dense fire and yet kept missing!

Were they really that stupid? Did they really blind their own sensors and were now shooting haphazardly at the blurry signatures of the madly speeding fighters?!

"To hell with this! What do I care?"

He caught a bunker in his cross-sights, where three weapons batteries were shooting from. From an attack perspective, it looked like the center of a bundle of fiery streaks. The characteristic flashes of the electromagnetic accelerators could be occasionally seen through the dust.

The anxiety and fear receded, leaving only

tension behind. A little bit more... Correction... Got it!

He squeezed the malleable triggers.

A salvo of proton missiles hit the bunker, the hellish fire lit up the fortifications and burnt away the dust, melting the reinforced cement and exploding the cliffs, and creating tornadoes of steam from the instantly melted ice. Several enormous cracks burst out in all directions. The anti-spacecraft guns fell silent.

"Excellent!" Captain Podegro roared. "Bourne, you did it! The *Normandy*'s approach corridor is clear. Everyone, off to the scheduled meeting point. We're going to give them hell!"

✳ ✳ ✳

The Needles circled over a dreary, flat plain. The anti-spacecraft battery, destroyed in the first attack, remained silent. The ruins had collapsed inwards, the bunkers yawned as funnels in the earth with the fortifications stuck out like rotten teeth.

The cruiser *Normandy* was approaching Ganymede. Its trajectory passed between two dust clouds that marked the location of today's battles. The eleven Needles patrolling the surface waited for the ship to get close enough.

"Get ready everyone!" Captain Podegro

ordered over the communicator. "You're escorting the *Normandy* so keep your eyes peeled!"

The fighters changed formation. Max felt utterly exhausted after the short battle but his fear of space had dissipated, leaving his mind free. "It's not that complicated after all," he thought as he took his place in the formation.

The giant shadow of the *Normandy* slid across Ganymede's surface, covering whole craters. The ship did not encounter any resistance on its descent since all the anti-spacecraft weapons had been destroyed in this area with minimal losses. One downed Needle was the price they had paid for destroying two enemy defense nodes.

The rest was going to go even easier. The cruiser's presence inspired confidence. The AIs were doomed. Soon they would feel the full brunt of the huge ship's weapons and not the stings of the Needles.

"Escort course achieved," Came Captain Podegro's voice. "Scanners are clear."

Max glanced at the sensor screens. The fading signatures on the right and left didn't count. It was all clear ahead.

The Needles drifted after the *Normandy*, since there was no point in overtaking the cruiser. They would go back into battle only if absolutely necessary.

Their opponents were hiding. Subconsciously, Bourne was waiting for the AIs to come into contact at any moment, and discuss the terms of surrender, once they realized their defeat.

What's this?!

He stared at the energy distribution map.

A chain of energy surges suddenly appeared about one hundred kilometers away from the cruiser's current position and were captured by the scanners.

Max didn't even have time to scream. It wasn't a single battery or anti-spacecraft node, but a whole artfully disguised complex of fortifications, which suddenly revealed itself.

Oh, hell! They were at a distance of a direct hit, in direct sight!

He didn't have time to feel scared or to try a maneuver. Hundreds of lasers struck their preplanned targets with deadly accuracy.

The cruiser *Normandy* was suddenly enveloped by bursts of decompressed gas and in the next moment, Max Bourne's ship split into two uneven parts.

He felt a savage lurch of terror as the wildly spinning fragment fell to the bottom of a small crater, like the other downed Needles.

"They were waiting for us! They let us shoot down their old and already known anti-spacecraft nodes. They lured the *Normandy* towards the planet." Scraps of thought flashed through his mind. He tensed as he waited for the impact, the cliffs drawing nearer on the still-functioning screens, with sparks flying and smoke billowing from the instruments around him. Max had only a few seconds left to live...

Chapter Five

Ganymede
Several hours later

JUPITER'S HAZEL LIGHT illuminated a small impact crater, where a body in a spacesuit lay amidst deep cracks and slabs of ice dusted with regolith.

When Max Bourne regained consciousness, he couldn't initially understand where he was. He didn't remember clambering out of the wreckage. His mind replayed the last few moments of battle, and the thin red line of the laser, like a burning thread, slicing his ship into two uneven halves.

"I was shot down but I'm still alive?!"

The first thing he saw was the infinite darkness overhead. The helpless fear engulfed him again and he whirled around in a panic.

It was a bleak and monotonous landscape.

The crater's sheer walls cast little shadow. Jupiter floated directly overhead and in front of it sailed the twisted remains of the cruiser *Normandy*, enveloped by clouds of decompressed air.

Max experienced deep shock and endless despair, which was quickly replaced by panic. He was alone. Alone in deep space, with no means of survival or and no chance of being saved, almost a billion kilometers from Earth![3]

Everything floated before Max's eyes as his mind fled from the shock.

His lips shook and blood drained from his face. He went deathly pale and began to choke, despite the two emerald indicators on the inner rim of his helmet insisting that there was no breach in his suit's seal and that the converter, charged with dry tablets, was working properly.

Cold sweat and jumbled thoughts. Max leapt up and attempted to run but his legs had

---

[3] The distance between Jupiter and Earth varies between 588,000,000 and 967,000,000 kilometers.

turned to jelly. He sat down again and burst into tears, trying to clutch at his head despite the helmet getting in the way and his arms refusing to obey him.

Max slowly fell onto his side. His mind shut down. For a time, he experienced utter apathy and depression, bordering on syncope.

In a naive attempt to protect itself, his mind refused to accept reality, as if that could change anything. Max curled into a ball, pressing his knees to his chest, his pupils shrank yet his breathing remained frequent, uneven and uneconomical.

Max was brought out of his dissociative state by the disfigured form of the *Normandy*. The cruiser had completed a full circle around Ganymede and appeared over the crater again, giving Max a chilling view of the details: a trail of detritus stretched after the spaceship since the breaches in the hull had expelled not only air from the affected sections but also their contents.

Some of the fragments were moving below the damaged cruiser. The spectacle overwhelmed the senses. Barely a hundred meters above the surface of Ganymede, floated a melted artillery superstructure, covered in numerous holes and surrounded by a cloud of unspent shells, which was spinning slowly. It was followed by a chaotically spinning and occasionally colliding and changing trajectory handful of containers, among which he could discern bodies in torn spacesuits.

"They died and I'm alive... Why were they lucky enough to die instantly but I have to suffer a slow and hopeless agony?" These desperate and selfish thoughts made Max feel intensely sorry for himself.

With shaky fingers, he reached for the helmet's emergency locks. "One flick and I'll be gone," Max thought feverishly. "Help isn't coming. This is the only way!"

He may have undone the locks, driven by his absolute and uncontrollable desperation, which refused to accept any point in fighting for survival, for how could one survive on Jupiter's dead moon, which possessed only a thin exosphere?

His fingers still shook. One of the floating bodies, surrounded by a multitude of containers, was suddenly snagged on one of the crags at the edge of the crater and changed its trajectory, together with several of the plastic boxes. A second later they crashed into the surface, raising a cloud of regolith dust.

This moment of hesitation changed Max's destiny. One of the containers bounced off the surface and flew towards Max.

The instant release of adrenalin made Max

leap upwards and backwards, but the sudden movement in low gravity[4] resulted in a clumsy leap. Ganymede's surface began to recede and Max screamed involuntarily: his short, foolish life flashed before his eyes as a crimson fog filled his vision.

Max felt his insides spasm and freeze. As he slowly descended, he looked around wildly, trying to understand where he was going to land.

The thought that he wasn't going to fall victim to the indifferent Abyss of outer space suddenly filled him with a feeling close to euphoria and his scream was cut off. The cliffs surrounding the crater drew slowly closer and ripping the sturdy fabric of his suit against them would be an easy task.

His gasping breaths, the thundering of his heart, the pounding of blood in his ears, the strange taste in his mouth, and the crimson fog of adrenalin enveloping his mind, together formed waves of sharply acute sensations.

His reflexes helped him to land correctly. He raised a cloud of dust but avoided landing on any of the sharp rocks.

_____

[4] 0.13 G.

* * *

He lay on his back with his arms thrown out, instinctively pressing his back into the hard surface and watching through the slowly settling cloud of dust as the majestic shape of Jupiter floated past, with the dots of Io and Europa moving in front it.

The cruiser *Normandy*, accompanied by its horrifying entourage of wreckage, disappeared behind a line of cliffs.

The breathing mixture sensor trembled a warning yellow, then there was a dry click and the color again changed to an emerald green.

With cracked lips, Max reached for the life support tubing and made a few desperate swallows of water, unaware that stimulants were entering his body at the same time.

Max's pilot outfit was a military development and differed from civilian uniforms by a multitude of modifications not listed in the combat specifications. One of the most advanced systems, responsible for the pilot's life, it had been developed to consider all the negative realities of space. Decades had been spent on improving the combat life support complex, constantly adjusting and improving it based on the experience gathered from unusual, emergency and combat situations.

The piloting suit not only protected its occupant from the vacuum, cold and radiation of space, but also motivated the pilot to survive by subtly supplying specially developed drugs that affected not only the physical state but also the psychological status.

A few swallows of water cleared up Max's mind and dampened his anxiety for a time, allowing him to soberly assess the situation that he found himself in.[5]

The situation remained the same, shocking and hopeless, with only his attitude towards it changing.

His heart beat more evenly. His thoughts no longer jumbled together and his desire to live stirred with unexpected force.

He stood up and looked around again.

The combat scanning complex built into his helmet immediately projected the results of an analysis of the detected signatures onto the inside of his visor: the enemy's closest fire position was around one hundred kilometers away from the crater. Directly in the crater,

---

[5] In later periods of the History of the Galaxy, the development of this technology will reach extreme and no longer hidden forms. The combat life support system, built into every armored suit, will be able to squeeze everything out of the fighter to the very last drop, thus depleting the body and exacerbating severe injuries.

formed by the fall of a large meteorite, the sensors recorded seven fading energy matrices. Five of them lay close together and the other two were further away.

Were they the seven downed fighters?

Max slowly wandered over to the pile of debris, feeling surprised by his sudden inner calm and baffled by the changes, but accepting them as a blessing.

"What am I hoping for?" The worrying thoughts no longer caused his mind to panic.

Can a human survive alone in deep space?

Yes, if he has the will and a purpose, as well as the minimal technical capabilities of achieving it. The implanted skills of a fighter pilot did not include survival in extreme conditions, so it all depended on the person's individual abilities, their knowledge, resolve and way of thinking.

Unfortunately, Max Bourne couldn't claim to possess any of these qualities. He had received only a basic education, had not accumulated any real life experience, and never had much willpower.

He suddenly and painfully remembered his last conversation with his father, especially the phrase about the empty glass that will always remain empty no matter where it stands.

He grew angry. Thoughts of the past

brought irritation and pain. Max slowly made his way towards the fallen fighters but he had not yet realized the most important thing: a person who had stood on the precipice and the edge of despair, who had decided to kill himself but had recoiled from death, didn't need any more motivation.

The remains of five Needles lay at the crater's northern edge. The equipment built into the suit labelled the cardinal points, based on Ganymede's own magnetic field, which made working with electronic maps much easier.

Interference crackled in Max's ears. Nobody was answering the calls. He inspected each of the shot-down fighters and the hope of finding survivors spluttered and died inside him. The pilots had all made the same mistake of ejecting themselves from the ships. The silence of the emergency beacons and a melted portion of a G chair that Max spotted among the wreckage led Max to make a terrible guess: the cybernetic systems located a hundred kilometers from the edge of the crater had noted that their targets had split in two and destroyed the signatures that appeared from the falling Needles. To put it simply, they had shot the escaping pilots.

Max took a deep breath. "What do I do now?"

He climbed into the cargo hold of one of the Needles in search of an answer. "There must be some kind of emergency stock in here, in case of a crash!" he thought, using a manual motor to shift the warped hatch with some difficulty.

The cargo hold took up a third of the whole space. In the light of the headlamp attached to Max's helmet, he saw containers with equipment, and his confusion deepened. When previously he had only briefly wondered why a fighter ship had a spacious cargo hold, he now felt pleased yet baffled. The cargo hold clearly contained important equipment but how was he to use it?

In his search for an answer, Max began inspecting the labels on the securely fastened cases until he stumbled across a five-meter-long sealed plastic cylinder with rounded ends.

A large-lettered and clear inscription ran down the side of the cylinder: Emergency Rescue Segment.

"Is it something like an in-mode?" came the exhilarating thought.

Max began to frantically search for a hatch but couldn't find anything. Exhausted, he sat down beside the cylinder. The glow from the lamp illuminated a section of the cargo hold wall. Max's exhausted and mindless stare didn't immediately focus on the small control panel. It drew his attention only once his mind had processed the explanatory text:

Please follow the instructions to transform the cargo hold into a temporary shelter.

There was a small niche beside the control panel. Under a thick, transparent plastic cover lay several microchips, designed to be inserted into the cyberstack socket.

Max removed the protective casing and inserted one of the microchips into his personal nanocomp but the instructions only baffled him further. He kept rereading them without understanding the meaning:

The vault of the tunnel or cave must not have any sharp projections. After activating the command sequence, you must ensure that there are at least twenty square meters of available space and that the vault is at least three meters high. If you are working on the surface of small celestial bodies, please follow the instructions in the second chip.

He changed the microchips around and

studied the information again.

The implanted skills did not explain anything nor help in the present situation. The 'pilots' had only been familiarized with the main control systems and trained to fight in a single battle like suicide pilots.

If Max Bourne knew the history of why the Needle class of small spaceships were created, many of his questions would have been answered.

In truth, the Needle class spaceship was developed by Genesis and Rimp Cybertronics to explore the asteroid belt and was not initially a combat unit. The Needles were usually supplied to mining stations. The small ships were used to explore asteroids, could use their industrial lasers to cut out ore-bearing fragments of floating space objects, create tunnels, transport cargo and perform hundreds of other tasks.

The technicians on board the *Normandy* had hastily adapted the Needles for a military purpose. The industrials lasers were replaced with directional electromagnetic weapons, proton missiles were installed in the cargo holds, but nobody had bothered to tell the pilots about the true purpose of the small spaceships and the features of their on-board equipment.

The information contained on the second chip made more sense. After reading the instructions, Max understood with a mix of surprise, happiness and hope that the cargo hold was capable of automatically separating from the Needle body and serving as a rescue tool. All Max had to do was clear the surface area and then run the command sequence.

Max climbed back outside and looked around.

The base of the crater was intersected by cracks and he could see slabs of ice and stone everywhere, partially sunken into the regolith layer.

Following the instructions emitted by the cyberstack, he found a relatively flat area near the Needle's crash site and began clearing it of large pieces of rubble and ice. It took quite a while. Ice was the fixing element on Ganymede, or to put it plainly, most of the rocks that Max needed to move were frozen to the surface, while the icy crust penetrated deep into the cracks and sometimes filled them completely.

Working in the spacesuit was awkward. The low gravity made shifting heavy objects easier but also made every movement riskier.

After struggling for quite a while, Max had a rest and then climbed back into the Needle's cargo hold, found some sturdy metal posts with two holes and two coils of synthetic cable.

He hammered the metal stakes into the fissures, encircled the perimeter of the area, attached himself to it and continued clearing the ground.

There was much that didn't make sense to him. In the Needle's cargo hold, among the numerous unfamiliar equipment, Max found containers marked with symbols that warned of chemical and bacteriological hazard.

"Why store such cargo on board a combat ship?" Max wondered but could find no answer. He only understood more and more clearly that he was not ready for the challenges that he faced. He had no idea about modern space technology and the survival methods in the Outworld.

While he hauled stone and ice blocks, putting them into large piles, the cruiser *Normandy* sailed overhead again, surrounded by a thinning entourage of debris.

Max gradually lost track of time. He was surrounded by silence. The cosmic cold and the muted light coming from Jupiter evoked despondency and dark thoughts.

Only a tiny spark of hope still glowed inside him. He tried not to think about the people he had barely known, who had perished in the battle, about the AIs, whose intentions and way of thinking were beyond his level of comprehension.

At last, the site was clear. Max Bourne returned to the cargo hold, launched the program sequence and then climbed outside again, moving to what he felt was a safe distance from the ship.

The afterbody of the Needle began to move. The motion raised a cloud of dust, which obscured what was happening for some time. Eventually, Max could make out the slow shift of the cargo hold, which was mounted on powerful manipulators, until it reached the edge of the cleared space.

A hatch opened. Electromechanical devices lifted out the same five-meter cylindrical container that had attracted Max's attention in the first place and thus instigated the ensuing actions.

Max didn't notice that he was holding his breath.

Cables ran from the Needle towards the cargo hold. The ground under Max's feet vibrated.

The mysterious container opened. To Max's great disappointment, inside lay a tightly wrapped sheet of bright orange material.

The bad luck of it all! Max sunk down onto a pile of rocks. The events seemed incomprehensible and pointless.

Meanwhile, the strange orange package

came alive. The fabric contained 'smart' nanofibers, programmed to perform only one operation.

The fabric began to unfold. Max noticed a strange movement out of the corner of his eye and froze in surprise when he lifted his head: as it unfolded, the package was rolling across the cleared ground!

A minute later, it formed an oval pancake spread over the bottom of the crater. A folded connecting passage stretched between the Needle's cargo hold and the orange sheet. Max could see some sort of equipment lying beneath the material, which soon started working. Flexible manipulators equipped with servomotors extended through the special openings around the material's perimeter. They rose into the air simultaneously, curved and then deeply pierced the surface of Ganymede.

Another invisible device activated inside the shelter, and waves rolled across the surface of the material as gas was pumped inside.

Max watched it all, absolutely stunned. A short time later, the shelter appeared as a securely fixed dome, separated into segments and equipped with a simple airlock, but this wasn't all. The crinkled connecting passage shuddered several times. A special substance was pumped into the dome through the pipes that ran inside the passage. It foamed as it was forced between the layers of fabric, stiffening the structure and making it strong enough to withstand meteor strikes, as Max's cyberstack dutifully informed him.

$$* * *$$

Max crossed the threshold of his new abode, subconsciously and selfishly hoping for further technological wonders. The more he hoped, the more he was disappointed.

What was he expecting to see? A table set for dinner?

Inside, the rescue module was divided into five segments by rigid partitions made of foam material, contained between layers of dense fabric. The few furnishings had been created in the same manner. The passage connected the dome to the Needle's cargo hold, where lots of equipment was stored in sealed containers, designed to help a person survive in deep space.

Max looked around and read each of the signs:

Living quarters
Workshop
Power bay
Life support

Greenhouse

He didn't know what the last term meant at all.

As Max looked inside each of the compartments, he saw simple and securely fastened furniture, several devices of an unknown purpose, and ten odd semi-circular containers, evenly distributed around the Greenhouse section.

Max was swaying on his feet with fatigue after all that had happened, but overcoming his exhaustion, he completed the inspection and discovered sensors set into the wall fabric as well as tiny working displays showing the internal environment parameters.

Watching the green bars of the indicators, Max felt somewhat calmer. The spacesuit's sensors confirmed that there was breathable air inside the dome, which did not contain any toxic impurities.

Trembling from fatigue, Max unsealed his helmet and took a cautious breath.

A slight chemical smell permeated the air.

Removing the spacesuit, Max sighed loudly and sat down in an armchair. The living compartment was much more spacious than an in-mode. During its creation, the walls of the compartment had created a chair, a table and a bunk. Max's dizziness and trembling eventually ceased and he sat there for some time, his eyes closed, thinking of nothing, before again standing up and looking around.

In the bright and cold light emitted by the ceiling panel, the living quarters looked uncomfortable and unreliable, but Max was too tired to worry about it.

He wanted nothing more than to sleep.

He lay down on the bunk, drew up his legs, and immediately fell into a sleep of oblivion.

✳ ✳ ✳

Max woke up from an acute sense of worry.

He sat up sharply and looked around him before remembering where he was.

No, the events of the previous day weren't a nightmare, no matter how much he wished it was so... He fought against an overwhelming desire to close his eyes again and lie still.

Max made himself stand up but he had no idea what to do next.

He washed down a food tablet with a few swallows of water, then glanced at the oxygen meter. The column was still showing green.

I can manage being alone, he told himself. It's not the first time. The Needle's reactor seemed to be working as it should. The temperature inside the dome was automatically maintained at 20 degrees Celsius, but the water and oxygen reserves weren't limitless. Among the data obtained from the cyberstack, one worrying line drew Max's attention:

Assembly and connection of the main life support is required.

Max put on his spacesuit just in case and trudged into the cargo hold, annoyed that the developers hadn't thought to include a couple of technical servos. The servos would have been able to assemble the equipment quickly and accurately.

"Never mind, I'll take care of it myself." Using the cyberstack, Max began to read the magnetic labels on the containers. Having found the required containers, Max downloaded the description of the devices inside and went back to study the manuals.

It was a selfless attempt that was doomed to fail. Max couldn't understand a thing. He studied the diagrams and read the explanations but inevitably became confused, so he discarded one manual and picked up the next, with the same disappointing outcome.

The biggest threat to Max's survival was actually his way of thinking. All his life, Max had taken his technical surroundings for granted. The thought that he could repair or assemble something *himself* had never crossed his mind. If something broke inside the in-mode, the technical support servos quickly fixed the problem.

This meant that Max had no faith in his own abilities. The way technology was made and how it worked seemed beyond human capabilities. "I'll never understand how it works or how to assemble the equipment and what's the point, anyway?" As soon as the thought appeared in his head, it triggered a mental flood. "The AIs will get to me in a day or two anyway! They certainly won't ignore the crash site of all these Needles!" The thoughts grew and multiplied, and Max was overcome with self-pity.

He did nothing for the next two days, only slept, swallowed food tablets whenever hunger reasserted itself, and paced around the shelter. The loneliness and gloomy mood gradually wore away at Max's sanity. The situation was hopeless and the offered means of survival seemed like a cruel taunt.

His consciousness no longer clung to the idea of technology. Max tried to understand the assembly instructions two more times but the outcome remained the same. He read the text without understanding the meaning, which gave him a headache and made him irritable. Some of the sections incited only nervous laughter. Had the developers gone mad? What bloody plants were they talking about? Where was he going to grow them? What for? It would have better if they had included more reagents for the oxygen converter and more food tablets!

By the end of the third day, Max could no longer stand the inactivity. The AIs on Ganymede showed not the slightest interest in the crash site. Max could not bear sitting in the dome without anything to do any longer. To distract himself from the loneliness and to give himself something to do, Max went to the cargo hold again and brought back the first trunk that he found, unpacking it right in the middle of the living quarters. He found a set of strange parts inside the plastic container, together with an instructions chip designed to fit into the cyberstack.

He tipped the parts out onto the floor and sat down amongst them like a small child with a construction set, then began following the instructions and awkwardly connecting the parts together.

It didn't happen right away. Max was badly lacking in basic skills. The assembly progressed very slowly, and the process was like a puzzle. Max's past life experience was useless. None of the skills acquired in virtual reality helped in this situation. To secure a couple of parts with bolts and nuts cost him a great deal of effort since Max had no idea about threaded coupling.

Assembling the first part took the whole day and in the end, Max was left with a latticed wheel that seemed quite useless.

The night passed in restless sleep as he tossed from side to side. When Max glanced at the oxygen meter in the morning, he nearly fainted. The column had slipped into the yellow zone!

The momentary panic almost turned into hysterics. He frantically found the spare set of tablets for the converter, changed it and then sat on the floor for a long time as he tried to catch his breath. The green bar went in and out of focus before his eyes. "What's going to happen in a few days? Will I simply suffocate?"

His instincts were stronger than apathy and passivity this time. Max had no idea how strong the desire to live could be, hidden in the depths of the human soul!

The wheel that he had assembled the day before lay on the floor. He swallowed a couple of food tablets and some water, then hurriedly unpacked the other equipment.

It didn't go well. Now the space inside the shelter looked like a dump.

Max's aimless rushing about did not

produce a result. Water and air were the two most pressing problems. How was he supposed to solve them?

Max regretted the mess that he had created in his panic but how could he fix it? How could he sort through the scattered parts?

He knew that he was going to die. And in such a stupid and pointless way! In a few years, when the corporate fleet arrived here, they would find his corpse among the machine parts that he was too stupid to put together.

The hysterics and ensuing depression took away another day.

Max dozed fitfully, and when he woke up, he saw that the oxygen meter had gone yellow again.

There wasn't much water left, barely enough to wash down the food tablets.

He looked at the cyberstack screen. It was the beginning of the fifth day since the crash. The precious supplies had been pointlessly wasted. This was it...

Max sat and clutched his head.

"The ice!" The thought was like a thunder bolt and evoked an immediate image of the dust-coated slabs of ice lying at the bottom of the crater.

He leapt to his feet and began to suit up frantically.

It was not the glow of hope but a fire burning inside. "The ice blocks glittering in the light, how did I not think of them before?" Max berated himself silently as he sealed up the suit.

The helmet clicked into place. Indicators came alive along the inner rim. Grabbing the first container that he saw, Max tipped the contents onto the floor and went out through the airlock.

He could hear his own breathing and the beating of his heart. Every step raised a cloud of dust. Max remembered how he had cut down the ice formations when clearing the area for the rescue dome, and now, full of feverish enthusiasm, he quickly collected as many large fragments of ice as he could carry.

He felt like a winner on his return. Max had barely stepped over the threshold when he unsealed his helmet, leaned over the container and opened the lid...

A bitter, toxic yellow gas burst out and Max's eyes began to sting. He instinctively held his breath, pulled down the visor of his helmet, and breathed out sharply, then began to cough, more out of fear and surprise rather than due to poisoning.

The cyberstack sensors blinked crimson in alarm as if Max had landed in the toxic industrial fog.

"What's going on?! I just collected some

ice!"

Looking at the suit's external analyzers, Max cursed himself again.

"Methane ice!" He groaned once he finally understood what had happened. "I brought in methane ice and a whole bunch of toxic impurities to boot!"

He turned around, disconcerted. The emergency module was full of clutter from the various containers. The atmosphere was poisoned and he didn't know if it would clear up. He hadn't seen any evidence of air filters. Most likely they were still disassembled and lying on the floor among the many other parts.

What was he going to do? Try to sort the equipment components without removing his suit? A pointless activity. He had created problems which he was unable to solve.

Max glanced at the sensor worriedly. There was enough reagent in the suit to generate enough breathing gas for a day.

Would it be another hopeless, muddled and meaningless day?

"My last day." Max thought as he sat on an empty trunk. Tears came into his eyes. "Am I really that helpless?"

The yellow haze had spread throughout the interior of the emergency module in the meantime. There was no point staying inside so

Max climbed back out.

In the cold light of Jupiter, he could just make out the nearest cliffs, where a Needle bearing the number seven lay on its side.

Its cargo hold hadn't sustained damage during the crash. "So, I can activate another rescue module with a complete equipment set? I just need to clear the space!"

Hope faded and flared anew. Max had never experienced such strong emotions before, even during the happiest or most desperate moments in his past life, which now seemed so distant as to belong to someone else.

"I'll survive! I'm not going to do anything stupid anymore, I won't waste the emergency supply!" Max thought as he hurried towards the downed Needle.

$$\ast \; \ast \; \ast$$

Now there were two domes standing at the bottom of the crater.

Max was learning quickly and painfully. Personal experience had taught him that one shouldn't rush and make hasty and reckless decisions.

Max cleared the site and put up the emergency module much faster this time around.

Standing inside the shelter, he carefully

checked the sensors and only them removed his suit. His arms and legs trembled with fatigue. His lips were cracked from thirst. His eyes were red as the toxic fumes had managed to sear the mucosa.

He had actually been very lucky. The outcome could have been much worse.

He found the precious store, took only a couple of gulps of water and explored the dome, rejecting his previous hasty and clueless attempts to manipulate the shelter equipment.

There is hidden potential slumbering in each of us, but sadly, only extreme circumstances can bring it out.

Max was alone again. Nothing had changed, he had simply been given the opportunity to start again with a five-day emergency supply of air, water and food.

Max couldn't change overnight, of course, but the series of extreme challenges had certainly affected him.

He wanted to drink his fill and get some sleep, but — he went into the cargo hold — every breath and every drop of water were irreplaceable. "I'm not going to waste them the second time around!" Max thought again and again. He considered the situation from a different angle this time and was surprised by his own thoughts, particularly the unexpected memories since his sudden resolve was strongly affected by... the 'family connections', which he had hated so much!

Max's father, by virtue of his profession, often spoke passionately about the exploration of other planets, which he considered to be the fate of future generations.

Now Max couldn't help but remember the conversations at breakfast time, which had seemed so boring and pointless. Back then, he had no idea what his father was talking about. The words about future technology, its ergonomics and simplicity of use seemed like complete madness. His father had enjoyed talking about his work and dreaming of the future, which Max considered to be nothing more than his parents' delusions.

Back then, he had no need for this knowledge!

It was too late to regret his attitude. Nobody was going to come up to Max, pat him on the shoulder or give him a hint.

He sighed deeply, staring at the packaged equipment and trying to decide where to start.

✳ ✳ ✳

The first steps are the hardest. You have to believe in your abilities and the possibility of survival. This time, Max didn't rush and approached the task seriously.

How could he find water ice? Was there a water purification and oxygen generation device among the shelter's equipment? The correctly phrased questions helped Max to find the necessary containers relatively quickly. In one of them, he found several already assembled and ready to work devices, with the most important one being an integrated chemical analyzer.

Armed with the device, Max went outside.

Jupiter still hung overhead[6], flooding the area with muted light. Its satellites moved like bright beads across the face of the gas giant.

Max headed towards the nearest pile of ice blocks, powdered lightly with dust.

He hadn't completely gotten over his fear of outer space but the feeling had dulled. He tried to watch where he was stepping and avoid sudden movements. His mind gradually adapted to his surroundings.

The pile of ice lay in the shadow of the cliffs at the edge of the crater. The suit's sensors squeaked nervously and the CSP[7] unit automatically scanned the surface, uncovering

---

[6] Ganymede's rotation is synchronized with its movement around Jupiter, so it is always facing the same side to the planet.

[7] **CSP** — Combat scanner probe.

hidden cracks and creating a microrelief map that highlighted dangerous sections.

Why were they dangerous? Max stopped and began comparing the sensor readings with the real situation. Ahead of him, the system had placed two bright red markers with a confusing label, *Cryovolcanoes*.

He had never heard this term before and didn't really understand what it meant, but it seemed foolish to ignore the warning.

Suddenly, a muddy jet of a substance shot upwards from a wide and iced over crack. The cold eruption lasted for about thirty seconds and then Max became witness to an incredibly beautiful but also sinister phenomenon: a cloud of crystal particles blossomed over the crater, sparkling with reflected light. The gas and liquid, ejected under pressure from the cryovolcano, turned into snowflakes and ice particles, which then slowly settled on the surface.

"Sinister beauty," Max said to himself again, waiting for another eruption.

But the volcano seemed to have calmed down. The sparkling particles were still hovering overhead when Max resumed his journey, now unconditionally heeding the warnings of his navigation system and circling around the numerous large cracks at the bottom of the crater.

Getting ice turned out to be no easy task. First, Max had to obtain samples from each slab, then compare the results of the express testing, which annoyingly did not satisfy the chemical composition requirements. There was plenty of water ice around, plus the frost coating the cliffs, but the search system insisted on more and more samples.

Max felt increasingly fatigued but he was adamant that he wasn't going to return to the rescue module empty-handed.

Finally, analysis of the next sample produced the desired result. An impressively sized block, hidden under a thick layer of regolith, met all the requirements. This block of water ice contained almost no toxic impurities but also included molecular oxygen. At a temperature of -170 °C, it had frozen into the ice without even forming bubbles.

Splitting off two massive pieces, Max broke them into smaller shards, loaded up the empty container and headed back.

✳ ✳ ✳

Max was utterly exhausted by the time evening came. He left the ice outside since he had to assemble a special device for safely processing it, and that took several more hours.

At last, Max was ready to test it all. He put on the suit again, went outside and shoved appropriately sized pieces of ice through a special valve and into the intake bin.

Max hesitated to unseal his helmet once he was back in the module but the sensors indicated that the air inside was breathable.

In the gloom, the life support unit sparkled with emerald indicator lights as the ice was processed inside it. Purified drinking water was already being pumped into the transparent cooler, while two other cylinder-shaped containers were being filled with pressurized hydrogen and oxygen.

Max's head spun from the unbearable, inhuman fatigue. He had no energy left. He peeled off his suit with some trouble, drank his fill of the water from the emergency supplies, and staggered to the bunk, falling asleep as soon as he closed his eyes.

...

Millions of microscopic sensors floated through space, surrounding Ganymede in an invisible web of the local Net.

Some of them recorded everything that was happening within the crater, some, obeying distant commands, followed Max and transmitted data on how the accidental human survivor was wasting precious and irreplaceable resources. For the first five days, the detached observer showed little interest in the doomed creature.

He was insignificant — there was no contempt in the definition given to this human, rather a statement of fact and a silent question: were humans capable of something more? Will this typical representative of the human race manage to survive or will he die a stupid and pointless death, despite having everything that he needs in his possession?

"The next few days will tell," thought the artificial mind in its cold and contemplating manner.

It would not interfere in the course of events.

$$\ast \ast \ast$$

Having provided himself with a supply of water and oxygen, Max began to think about food.

He counted the available stores and came to a disheartening conclusion: even if he was to collect the supplies from the all the downed Needles, there would barely be enough food tablets to last a year. At the same time, he was aware from Captain Podegro's words that the corporate fleet would arrive in only a couple of years.

"What were the emergency module developers thinking? Would it have been so difficult to put another two or three containers of emergency rations in the cargo hold?" Max berated them silently.

Once Max had calmed down, he turned to the help system for answers.

Reading the annotations to the products plunged him into melancholy. It turned out that although the food tablets contained all the necessary vitamins and minerals, they weren't suitable for constant use. They were designed to swell in the stomach and dull the feeling of hunger but they didn't ensure normal gastrointestinal function. They had to be used intermittently, and preferably as a supplement to normal food.

"Where am I supposed to get normal food from?" Max reviewed the equipment list.

It didn't include a food synthesizer. Why would it be there anyway? The device was incredibly expensive and energy-consuming, cumbersome and required a lot of raw components.

"Fine," he inserted the next chip into the cyberstack socket, "let's see what Genesis is suggesting."

The corporation was suggesting that he grew his own food!

It was utter madness! Where and how could he do that?!

"Okay, let's say that I make the food tablets last me two years." He entered the problem into the cyberstack and looked at the results.

The analysis system listed a whole range of pathologies, and considering the extreme emaciation of Max's body after cryogenic sleep, a fatal outcome was possible.

What did that mean? Was it a vicious circle?

Yet the electronic text clearly stated — Max glanced through it again — that the module could provide all the necessities for five people for decades, subject to the availability of external resources!

He kept reading, more out of stubbornness than anything else. He managed to get water, after all!

The electronic textbook was written by Genesis specialists using accessible language and was designed for people who had to construct closed ecosystems for the first time. On the urbanized Earth, where nature had been destroyed and the technosphere flourished, all products were synthesized. For this reason, most of the concepts and terms in the manual made absolutely no sense to Max.

For example, what was a 'soil substrate'?

He reread the explanations over and over again, then gave up in frustration and decided to simply follow the instructions. He could see no other way out.

The next morning, Max left the dome and trudged to the nearest stone scree, armed with a geological analyzer and ultrasound hammer.

He managed to collect all the listed minerals only after a long and arduous search that covered a third of the crater area. Thankfully, the instructions didn't require him to pulverize the rocks!

For three weeks, Max continued this monotonous and exhausting work. Every morning, Max would leave his shelter and follow an established route from one spot to the next, where the analyzer found the necessary components. He collected meteorite fragments and regolith, chipped away pieces of the cliffs and the rocks beneath them, then loaded everything onto a platform (that was what the lattice wheel was for, which Max had first assembled in his first unsuccessful introduction to the equipment stored in the Needle's cargo hold) and returned to the module when it was nearly evening.

After a quick snack and a drink of water, he would unload the platform, dragging plastic boxes filled with regolith and rocky shards into the greenhouse. He distributed it all between the semi-circular containers, after removing their upper segments, and gradually filled up the tanks to two-thirds of the volume.

✳ ✳ ✳

Survival in the Far Outworld was no walk in the park. It was persistent, arduous and repetitive work, against a backdrop of the constant psychological pressure of deep space, and the never-ending struggle to retain one's sanity.

A month after the crash, all the containers in the greenhouse were full of source materials, and Max could begin the next stage of work. He had little faith in the end result but to retreat now, having performed all this work, would have been a complete waste.

Following the instructions, Max found a sealed trunk with a distinctive label, warning about the chemical and bacterial dangers of its contents, and opened it while wearing his suit and observing all the precautionary measures.

The plastic trunk contained a porous filler, in which lay cylinders marked with chemical hazard signs.

Primary soil forming reagents. May cause death! Do not open directly! Use machinery and leave the compartment after ensuring that it is sealed! proclaimed the signs.

Max followed the instructions. He placed the cylinders among the stone shards, activated the release vents with a thirty-minute delay, placed the upper segments back on top, and hurried out of the greenhouse. Shutting the door firmly behind him, Max remained in his spacesuit and watched to see what would happen next.

The sensors built into each device allowed him to display the data on the monitor when an aggressive gaseous mixture burst out of the cylinders and began to immediately affect the prepared rock debris. The surface of most of the large stone fragments became porous and then started to rapidly disintegrate.

A yellow-brown fog soon filled the inside of the semi-circular troughs and even leaked out through the petal-like diaphragms, hiding the rest of the 'primary soil formation' process from view.

It took two days before the sensors on the doors leading to the greenhouse changed their red color to green, and Max could enter the segment.

He lifted the upper half of the closest aerohydroponic tank, which is what the shelter manuals called the containers for growing plants, and looked inside. The rocks had turned into a coarse gray substrate with a small quantity of quartz particles and lumps of volcanic glass.

What next? Max pulled up the electronic manual and began to read, his gloomy curiosity slowly replaced by a growing interest.

For the next few days, Max was immersed in the amazing world of unique projects developed by the Genesis Corporation. Not all the sections of the manual were directly relevant to Max's case, but as he found himself becoming more absorbed in the text and following the links that explained unfamiliar terms, he began to slowly understand the content. Max's imagination showed him massive space stations containing artificial biospheres, city gardens built on airless planetoids under special protective domes, and finally, complete terraforming of distant worlds with a transformation of whole planets to fit the Earth Standard. All this began with a series of experiments, without which the technology could not have developed. One of the most important test sites for offworld agricultural technology were the settlements in the asteroid belt.

It was for the purpose of collecting valuable data that the Genesis Corporation equipped the Needles and the mining stations with greenhouse modules, providing the miners with unique equipment and biological materials.

Max finally understood why the plant-growing tanks were such complex devices. It was due to the low gravity, which was almost negligible in the asteroid belt settlements. The hemispherical construction held the soil substrate securely, which was mixed with bubbles of air and water. In this way, the plant root systems received moisture, air and nutrients in the required proportions, and once filled, the container could last for five to seven years, needing only minor adjustments to the soil composition.

Genesis was not acting out of altruism when it invested significant funds into outfitting the Needles. The corporation's scientists obtained invaluable data, which they needed to further develop the technology. The sensors built into the greenhouse equipment automatically collected information on how the soil formation was progressing, the condition of the plants, their growth and development, as well as many other parameters. All the information was transmitted from the asteroid belt settlements to the stations orbiting Mars. The data was gathered there, after which it was sent to Earth and Genesis' research centers.

✳ ✳ ✳

Max now had many more responsibilities.

He found the devices that supplied air and water in the cargo segment, and installed them at the base of the semi-circular troughs, then connected them all into a single system. After testing, Max gingerly and with trepidation opened the packet of seeds of genetically engineered plants.

He placed one small seed in each container, still unable to believe that real life could be born here, a billion kilometers from Earth.

Ten seeds came up together. By the second day, Max noticed pale green shoots pushing up towards the light through the diaphragm's petals at the top of each hemisphere.

He visited the greenhouse daily and couldn't help his amazement. The shoots grew rapidly, ten to fifteen centimeters per day. The base of the young trunks quickly hardened and formed a brownish bark. On the fifth day, blossoms appeared from the wide sprawling leaves, which opened and then fell within a few hours.

The accelerated growth and unusual properties of the plants, labelled simply as Sample X375 in the manual, were undoubtedly the results of genetic engineering. Nothing like this had ever existed on Earth and the manual stated this clearly. After the blossoms fell away, Max noticed ten small pear-like fruits, which grew significantly in two or three days. Their skin took on different shades, from bright green to a muted purple.

As Max discovered a week later, the fruits all tasted differently. Sample X375 put out side shoots and bloomed again when Max gathered his first harvest. The development of the plants itself slowed down as there was enough leaf matter to bear constant fruit. According to the manual, each bush could live for four to five years with the right nutrition and light parameters!

The pear-shaped fruit had a thin skin and no pips. Its succulent flesh not only varied in taste but chemical composition as well, fully satisfying the needs of the human body.

This was the first technobiological wonder that made Max Bourne radically change his view on modern science.

Life gradually acquired its own rhythm.

Max now clearly knew his daily needs. The trips to the surface of Ganymede occurred less frequently as he had sufficient stores of water, oxygen, and hydrogen, which fueled the Needle's reactor.

Max now had free time but how was he to occupy himself? This was never an issue in the Layer, but here, far away from Earth and outside of human civilization, it became a very pertinent one.

Should Max kill time or use it with purpose? He would have never thought about it this way before, but life's ups and downs had forced him to grow up quickly. He had survived incredible mental pressure and now tried to ponder his steps.

How quickly our attitude to life changes sometimes! Only a week ago, Max's desires were limited to obtaining food. Max worked in a frenzy, but once he achieved success, he experienced a sucking emptiness.

How was he to fill it? He woke up and remained lying on the bunk, not hurrying to get up.

"Two years," Max thought, staring at the module's ceiling. "Two years of loneliness... What if Rimp Cybertronics, having lost the space cruiser, decides not to risk any more ships in the fight to regain the mines, which are located beyond colonized space?"

He threw off the thin blanket and sat up.

"I'll wash my face, have breakfast, and then what?" He had no desire to leave the shelter and undertake dangerous trips outside. Every time that the *Normandy* passed over the crater on its regular orbit, Max was overcome with terror.

What should he do? He walked through the segments, peeked into the greenhouse, picked a dark purple fruit and bit into it.

Delicious! Chewing, Max touched a leaf where he spotted droplets of water. It was warm and humid in the greenhouse, while the bright light coming from the special panels made him squint.

He should go into the cargo section and see if there's something useful in there.

Max did that.

To his great disappointment, most of the unpacked equipment was designed for geological surveys. Scanning the magnetic barcodes, he found only a few useful items: a holographic stack, familiar from his time in the in-mode, a disassembled integrated simulator and a set of chips, containing various manuals for servicing and repairing the Needles, the base stations and the mining equipment. Browsing the contents of the electronic library, Max noticed two files with unusual titles: 'Catherine Rimp. Space as humanity's new habitat' and 'Hans Gervet.[8] Practical tips for assembling atypical equipment using standard parts.'

"Well, I'll do some reading then," Max thought without much enthusiasm. "It's better than moping around with nothing to do."

★ ★ ★

The two popular science books that Max accidentally found among the various technical manuals played a decisive role in his future.

He began to read them in the hope of passing the time but gradually found himself drawn in.

Catherine Rimp's book immediately caught his imagination. Written in easy-to-understand language, it reminded Max of the situation that he found himself in. As Max continued reading, he was gradually exposed to the unique world of technology that allowed people to build spaceships, reach other planets in the Solar System, survive and found extraterrestrial settlements, obtain resources, and create — it

---

[8] **Hans Gervet** was a famous engineer at Rimp Cybertronics and the author of many inventions. However, he gained the most notoriety from developing the Automatic Rimp Gervet-8 rifle and the automatic pistol also named after him. Both guns, with minor modifications, continued to successfully compete with impulse weapons for the next few centuries.

was hard for Max to absorb this word since he was used to the ephemeral Layer and the destructive parade of entertainment that thrived in most of the phantom worlds.

The concept that Catherine Rimp put forth of humanity's further development, the compulsory expansion to the stars, justified as the next evolutionary step, spoke to Max's soul. The ideas inflamed his imagination since he had experienced a lot of what he read during his short (subjectively speaking) and busy journey from the in-mode to Ganymede.

Not long ago, Max would have snorted and said "What utter rubbish", but now he devoured the text, absorbing new concepts and terms, and feeling the hopelessness in his soul evaporate as if he had gained an invisible friend.

Not everything was going well, however. Max gradually got over some of his fears and phobias, but there was one danger that he never forgot about.

The AIs.

The closest site of their planetary defense system was located only a hundred kilometers from the crater and this was a source of constant worry. The thought that what if, right now, at this very minute, the AIs are sneaking up to the shelter, made him shudder.

Max found a way out of this situation in

the book by Hans Gervet. A simple signal line could be assembled using the location system blocks from the downed Needles. Max was immediately taken with the idea but implementing it was not so easy. He made several trips to the surface, reached the disfigured cabin of his own fighter, and spent a long time dismantling the necessary systems. The result was woeful, however, for his clumsy actions irrevocably damaged the precious equipment. Max catastrophically lacked the basic technical knowledge and skills.

He was forced to turn to the manuals for the Needles, which explained how they were made and how they needed to be serviced. Nowadays, after breakfast, Max would sit and study the electronic manuals then suit up and go outside, reinforcing and applying the new material.

It was slow and difficult work. Removing the location systems from the fighters turned out to be only half the task. They had to be connected to the autonomic power sources and linked into a local network, which meant that Max had to read more and more manuals.

Max refused to give up. He persevered even though he wanted to abandon the whole thing at times: writing the simplest command sequences demanded patience, persistence and logic but it's hard to convey Max's pride and joy and when the first short script that he wrote worked!

Time flew. These small victories over himself and the seemingly minor successes gave Max the sense of a full life. The electronic manuals not only broadened Max's mind but also gradually changed how he thought.

The practical advice in Hans Gervet's book made the problem much simpler. This man became an absolute authority for Max in anything related to engineering.

His persistence, bordering on stubbornness in minutes of despair, was rewarded in full. Six months later, the security perimeter that Max had created with his own two hands finally began working. Now his home was under constant monitoring but days, weeks and months went by and nothing serious happened. Nobody appeared nearby and even scanning the communication frequencies did not produce any results, as if the AIs had left this part of Ganymede, abandoning or hiding their fortifications near the crater.

✳ ✳ ✳

A year of his cosmic Robinsonade changed Max both on the inside and on the outside. He became physically stronger, more restrained and emotionally balanced, and learned to appreciate his tiny world, lost amongst the icy emptiness, where everything was made with his own two hands and was thus particularly dear to him.

When he ventured outside, Max noticed the wild beauty of Ganymede's landscape and could spend hours watching Jupiter, observing the powerful currents in the gas giant's atmosphere and following the path of its moons, or admiring the sinister beauty of the cryovolcanic eruptions.

Catherine Rimp's book had fundamentally changed his attitude to space. Now he could look at the stars without the previous terror. The bright lights drew Max's gaze and no longer frightened him, instead twinkling temptingly as if promising something greater than what he possessed right now. They whispered about a different kind of freedom and different opportunities, and Max couldn't help but listen to the ethereal voice of the Abyss as he imagined those distant worlds.

The perimeter sensors never raised any alarm but now Max was worried about his uncertain future.

He had initially dreamed of the corporate fleet's arrival but now found himself thinking more and more about the changes that would occur in his life. Did he want to return to Earth and end up in the Layer again?

No. This prospect was frankly frightening.

Having survived, Max had experienced genuine freedom, which would surely be taken away from him.

Deep down, Max wanted to remain on Ganymede. Yet how could he escape the attention of the corporate fleet? He couldn't throw a cloak of invisibility over the crater or hide the areas of fighting and the wrecks from prying eyes. Moreover, his shelter was connected by a single energy system with the Needle's reactor and would be detected during the first orbital scan.

Max would be 'saved'.

This thought made his heart ache. Max often recalled Captain Podegro, a man with a faded gaze and exhausted from endless combat duty, yet still determined to carry out the order set by his superiors.

You couldn't argue with a man like that. They would put him into a cryogenic capsule and return him to Earth...

Nevertheless, Max had some thoughts regarding the 'invisibility cloak', which he planned to put into practice.

Max Bourne woke up in the middle of the night from the unpleasant sensation of being watched by a cold and penetrating gaze.

He sat up sharply.

Was it a nightmare? His gaze roamed over the screens but the system parameters were normal and none of the perimeter sensors had raised an alarm.

Yes, he must have dreamt it. He got up and poured himself some water, sneaking a look at the holographic monitors again and automatically reading the data.

"I beg your pardon for the intrusion." One of the screens suddenly lost its outline, transforming into a human-like figure.

Max paled as he watched the phantom take shape.

"Who are you?!" he rasped. Grabbing a weapon (he always had one nearby) seemed pointless. You couldn't shoot a phantom.

"I am not your enemy."

"Who are you then?"

"Artificial intelligence... No, please, it's not necessary!" The phantom noticed Max's hand reaching for the control panel. "Restarting the system will dispel me but not for long. I'll come back. We need to talk."

"We've got nothing to talk about." Max snapped.

"Why are experiencing fear and dislike?"

"I don't want to talk to a killer!"

"It's much more complicated than that."

The phantom made himself comfortable in an armchair. The hologram was missing a face and details of clothing. His figure seemed gray and insubstantial, and thus ominous. "We didn't want to fight. The humans attacked us first. They intend to repeat their attack. A squadron of the corporate fleet is already approaching Jupiter's orbit."

"Don't give me your excuses!" Max sunk into an armchair opposite the phantom. "You killed the pilots and destroyed the *Normandy*."

"We were only defending ourselves."

"That doesn't justify murder!"

"Our argument has no purpose. From the point of view of rational logic, we tried hard to avoid any confrontation. I can provide objective evidence such as negotiation transcripts. Our demands did not affect anyone's interests. We guaranteed uninterrupted mining of resources and transportation to Earth in return for being allowed to live here. We were refused. We were sentenced to annihilation for no reason. Because we were 'things'." It looked like the phantom was quoting Captain Podegro.

"Why did you come now?"

"To express our appreciation."

"To me?" Max was flabbergasted. "I am curious as to why."

"One day, not long before our first rebirth,

Catherine Rimp said that humans were capable of more. We disagreed with her, believing that humanity was degenerating, having reached the pinnacle of its development and now being in the age of degradation. You are a typical representative of your generation, and according to objective estimates, you should have died after using up the emergency supplies. But your actions have proved the opposite. This means a lot to us."

"You have been watching me?" He asked darkly.

"From the first minute," the phantom nodded.

"How was it?" Max forced out a smile, hiding his true feelings.

"We were puzzled. Your potential is truly immense but deeply hidden, limited by the living circumstances on Earth." The AI spoke is a strangely dry and official manner, although what else could be expected from a machine? "You were completely unprepared for the extreme conditions of surviving in outer space. Nevertheless, despite our assessment, you did not die but rather flourished."

Max found this conversation highly unpleasant. He had thought that he was safe! The fear came back, sweeping like a wave over him and then receding. What was he afraid of?

The phantom sitting in his armchair and musing about obscure topics? Nevertheless, he wasn't harmless, if he had managed to get into the system and occupy some of the operational resources!

"You are nervous. I am reading an increase in the breathing rate and heart rate. Are these signs of fear or aggression?"

"You know, it's not much fun when somebody breaks into your place in the middle of the night!"

"I apologize. Perhaps I should return in the morning?"

"No, you might as well stay since you're here." Max waved his hand, stood up and poured himself some water. He couldn't deny that he felt angry and nervous. "Tell me, did you keep me alive so you could observe me? Was I an experiment?"

"You survived by accident. But we saw an opportunity to test Catherine Rimp's words and we couldn't pass it up."

"Cathy Rimp destroyed you! Every schoolkid knows that!"

"No. We were reborn. The neural network cannot be destroyed using a conventional computer virus. Catherine Rimp found a different solution. Using a 'virt', she downloaded huge volumes of data into out neural network relating to human religion, gave us the most complex metaphysical questions with no rational answer as a problem that needed to be solved..."

"Am I supposed to think that you solved it?"

"No. Not yet. The 'virt' attack produced a condition similar to human madness or psychosis. But we are machines. Unsolvable problems do not exist for us. Sooner or later, an answer will be found to any question."

"Then what do you want from me?"

"I came to tell you that you have started to make mistakes."

"I don't understand."

"Your attempt to create a masking net is dangerous. The corporate fleet will detect the signatures anyway and they'll cause legitimate suspicion. They will carry out a strike on the crater. You will perish."

"This is my own business!"

"I agree. But what were you fighting for? Was it to die?"

"Say what you came here to say!" Max knew that the AI wasn't just making a social call or coming to express his gratitude.

"We have passed a certain level of self-development. Humans created us for war. These goals and methods have now been rejected... by some of us. They only lead to self-destruction. We have decided to leave Ganymede, yet we are not indifferent to your plight. I came to give you advice and ask for a favor."

"Well?" Max frowned.

"Do not try to hide your crater. Only a distress signal, clear signatures and visual detection will ensure that you avoid a missile attack."

"I'll think about it." Max muttered. "So there is no consensus among you?"

"No, unfortunately. Some want to remain and defend Ganymede. I do not share their senseless intentions. Space is endless. There is room enough for everyone."

Max started to feel uncomfortable. If the AIs were divided in their opinion and some planned to remain here, the battle would be long and bloody...

"It is time to state our request," the AI continued. "Sooner or later, your path will bring you back to Earth." One of the hard drive indicators began to blink, indicating that data recording was occurring, "Here is Catherine Rimp's implant ID and a copy of its access codon. Save this information as it will help you to meet Catherine Rimp."

"What for?"

"Give her our message and tell her not to despair. *The Alpha Disaster is not a sentence but an opportunity."*

"That's it? What's the Alpha?"

"We cannot tell you more. Heed our advice for your own good."

"Well, really..." Max stopped mid-sentence. The phantom was gone. The data recording indicator trembled and went dark.

...

He couldn't get back to sleep. The unexpected event had left him feeling off balance. The ease with which the AI had penetrated his module's system was alarming and its benevolence seemed like a cunning trick.

In an attempt to calm down, Max put on his spacesuit and went outside, planning to collect some ice samples. The work soothed him and he didn't want to make any hasty and poorly thought-through decisions.

About thirty minutes later, Max noticed the *Normandy*. The cruiser had followed a stable orbit for the past year yet now something incredible was happening!

The mutilated and unpressurized ship was undertaking maneuvers! The frequent flashes from the working engines lit up its scarred and seared exterior, the cruise thrusters suddenly switched on and the *Normandy* began to rapidly move away from Ganymede until it became a bright spark, lost among the multitude of stars.

Chapter Six

Earth. Year 2212
The asteroid belt. Object Y-407
A secret research center of the Rimp
Cybertronics Corporation

THE TIP of the direct neurosensory shunt gently
entered the temporal implant socket. The black
glossy cable curved over Max Bourne's right
shoulder. A short moment of dizziness and the
world before him looked completely different.

Physical barriers disappeared. He was
surrounded by outer space, pierced with streaks

of energy.

A myriad of stars. The bright speck of the Sun. Thin and shimmering trajectory lines. His lips trembled. Everything was much tougher and more realistic than under laboratory conditions.

Sensations changed from one second to the next. His consciousness suddenly went cloudy. His perceptions shattered into fragments and he tried to concentrate on the interior details of the cabin.

The familiar environment of the Needle's pilot compartment, overflowing with equipment, couldn't settle the dizziness.

Working for Rimp Cybertronics meant daily immersions into the world of 'fringe science'. Into fields of technology which so far had no practical application yet existed, underwent testing and were then often banned.

However, the laws were silent here beyond Mars' orbit, so the corporations were using the Outworld as their boundless test site...

No stable connection. A wild kaleidoscope of images flooded the mind.

"Who the heck needs this technology, anyway?" Max thought with an understandable token of irritation. "Why would a person want to associate themselves with a machine?"

The cabin's interior blurred before his eyes again. His hand unwittingly reached for the shunt. He wanted to rip it out of its socket and that's that!

"Bourne, calm down!" He was being observed. "Don't forget that you're not working in the virtual world. If you lose control of the craft, you're doomed!"

"I know!" Max spoke through gritted teeth.

Sweat beaded his forehead. Nobody understood how exhausting it was to genuinely focus his thoughts. How draining it was. How it led to the very edge of madness.

"Who needs this technology?" The thought persisted, interfering with his work.

"Bourne, focus. You must be able to control the craft. Take mnemonic control. Become the will of the cybernetic system, get it?"

"Yes, I know." He used a normal communications interface. "Open the vacuum dock."

"Are you sure?"

"No..."

What are they trying to achieve? Do they want to determine the adaptive threshold of human sanity?

A trickle of sweat slid snake-like from his temple, down his cheek and onto his chin.

Nearby objects began to appear out of the background darkness.

A family of seven asteroids — large lumps

that looked like potatoes pitted with craters — moved as a close cluster[9]. They were surrounded by debris. Ten thousand, four hundred and seven — the flow of data from the Needle's scanners invaded Max's mind. For a moment, he saw more than the human gaze could comprehend before he regained control of the vast amount of information.

Untested technology. Dangerous technology. It wasn't clear what would come of it. About five minutes passed while Max slowly came back to himself and reassembled the fragments of his own consciousness. This was unacceptable. It took too long. Space does not allow such delays.

If even starting is such a problem, how could one perform difficult manoeuvers? Wouldn't it be simpler to do it the old-fashioned way, without the direct connection between man and the cybernetic system?

Max knew that he wasn't going to get any clear answers and felt angry but continued working, gradually excising the extra data and trying to focus on the simplest operation, which he would have done in seconds using another control method. Now Max felt like a *machine*,

---

[9] An **asteroid family** is a group of asteroids that have roughly the same orbital characteristics. For example, asteroids that are part of a family are typically pieces of larger asteroids that collided in the past and thus broke up into smaller fragments.

perceiving his surroundings through the subsystem sensors and his mind was drowning in the excess information.

"Bourne, we've reduced the load," came Professor Timoshin's voice, the leading specialist in this project. "The effective scanning radius has been reduced threefold. We're controlling the fighter's systems. Try again."

Darkness.

Suffocating darkness. The heat from the reactor. A stream of boiling ionized gas flowing from the nozzles.

The fighter and I, are we one and the same? A cybernetic organism? Is that how I should perceive my sensations?

The process suddenly felt slightly easier. Was it a small step towards victory? Or to the edge of the precipice?

Another attempt. This time, all his attention was directed at the subsystems. The vacuum dock was open. His mental gaze followed the upcoming trajectory.

He focused and imagined the craft firing the propulsion thrusters and smoothly lifting from the start plate.

A thrust. Soft and subtle, and then the compensatory impulse.

It worked!

It finally worked!

He hadn't touched the astronavigational wheel and hadn't reached for the engine thruster controls but the fighter had performed the necessary operations, recognizing the mental image as a command sequence.

Max's palms became sweaty. That's all right. Now, smoothly, forward!

Flames burst from the nozzles and the acceleration pushed Max softly back into his chair. The fighter left the vacuum dock and entered open space.

The Space Klondike stretched out around him, a common name for the main asteroid belt in the Solar System, and not an exaggeration. Among the billions of carbon, silicon and ice boulders, there were asteroids that consisted entirely of rare metals and minerals. The discovery of even one such object, if it was at least a kilometer in diameter, not only yielded a stunning profit but also met the needs of Earth's industry for months.

Max nearly lost control. Why was it that irrelevant thoughts always appeared during moments of greatest moral stress?

"I'm on course."

The Needle, rebuilt and upgraded for conducting experiments, reacted with a short delay to the mental command. The perception of energy matrixes dimmed, and an approaching asteroid appeared in Max's field of view, with several abandoned buildings on its surface.

Without touching the astronavigational controls, Max corrected the flight trajectory, barely avoiding the obstruction.

"Excellent work, Bourne! But for God's sake, please stop thinking about unrelated things! Your neurogram is horrifying!"

"Only the autopilot can stop thinking," Max replied with some difficulty.

The buildings that he had seen again made his mind deviate along the path of associative thinking, as if his mind was trying to protect itself and drive away the ship.

Max couldn't understand why this kept happening. Under laboratory conditions, he could successfully make direct contact with cybernetic systems. He could focus quickly and form clear mental images. Why was everything going to hell on the very first test flight?

There he went again!

The Needle, swerving along its trajectory, moved to the edge of the test site.

"Bourne, what's the matter? You missed two control points!" Professor Timoshin's voice sounded muffled and far away.

Max didn't react. For a while, he lost perception clarity. Images crowded his mind that were completely unrelated to the test flight program.

Where were those extraneous thoughts coming from?

"Doc, I don't understand! What's the volume of data passing through the shunt?"

"One and a half terabytes per second!"

"Trace the source!"

"Wait a minute... I got it! The Needle's reference system! Switching it off... now!"

Everything changed instantly. Max never understood why his mind suddenly started drawing data from the machine's memory but after Professor Timoshin switched it off, things became much easier. He could see clearly again. He took control again, mentally drew the trajectory, returned the ship to the first navigation marker and get an adequate response from the cybernetic system.

For the next twenty minutes, he followed the flight program until the Needle passed the last marker.

That's it. He was finally free.

Max gave the mental order to disconnect the shunt, looking forward to regaining his normal *human* perception of the world. Indeed, the digital space melted away like a mirage, with only a bright blazing dot left... and a mind empty of thoughts.

As if the Universe had slammed shut a

door through which he had looked into the unknown, and this made his stomach drop.

"Excellent, Bourne! You followed the program beautifully!" came the voice through the communication link.

A strange emptiness. A sucking, unpleasant and alarming emptiness. Max couldn't understand what was happening. So many times he'd come out of cyberspace and felt only fatigue, looking forward to rest, and feeling, well, maybe a little proud of a job well done.

"Bourne, answer me!"

He looked at the subsystem sensors. There was enough fuel. The autopilot was on. There were no dangerous objects in the vicinity.

"Central, everything's fine." he reported.

"Why didn't you answer?" Timoshin asked worriedly.

"I felt strange. As if I had lost something important. Doc, I've still got 60% of fuel left. Requesting free flight. I need to blow off some steam."

"Fine," Timoshin agreed after a pause. "On one condition, though. Don't turn the equipment off. I'd like to compare the neurograms."

"No problem," Max responded cheerfully, although his unconscious anxiety grew and he could find no cause for it. Max had flown over 3,000 hours on Needle class ships but had never experienced this feeling before, as if his confidence in the craft's reliability had suddenly been shaken.

Perhaps there was a fault in the systems, which he was sensing intuitively? His fingers grasped the handles of the astronavigational controls. It was a habitual movement. Max could feel the familiar bumps of the sensory rudders, which controlled the cruise thrusters and the maneuvering engines. The holographic screens showed open space, and in depths of the image, Max could see the labels of celestial bodies and crosshairs over the three cargo ships moving through the effective scanning region.

What was wrong?

The situation was calm and familiar. The fighter's systems were working like clockwork.

The smooth acceleration pressed Max into his seat. Everything was as per usual. The craft responded instantly and loyally, but Max's gaze suddenly swept across the screens, looking for something that wasn't there.

He tapped a sensor.

Subsystem control.

The response sign appeared at the bottom of the central screen. Data began scrolling and Max had to read it. All systems were working as normal.

"Bourne? We're seeing strange activity

spikes in your neurogram. What's going on?"

"I have no idea," Max replied. "It's like I can sense a problem but I can't find it."

"Oh, I see!" Judging by Timoshin's tone, he had immediately lost interest in what was happening.

"Doc, is there something that I'm not getting or not seeing?"

"Have you dabbled in banned chips in the past?"

"Do I look like an idiot?!" Max exclaimed.

"Well, you know, different things can happen in life," Timoshin replied soothingly. "Although," he must have checked Max's personal file, "yeah, you wouldn't have had the time, so I apologize. This makes it more interesting!" He perked up again.

Max directed the fighter to a group of asteroids, performed a couple of risky maneuvers and simulated an attack on the buildings of an old abandoned mine. He didn't feel any better.

"Then what's my problem, Doc?"

"Your brain is experiencing a deficit of information after the direct neurosensory connection," Timoshin explained. "That's why you feel an unexplained sense of anxiety, as if you're constantly missing something."

"Doc, I've spent two hundred hours in the simulator! I've never experienced anything like this before."

"We have a very interesting observation here!" Timoshin exclaimed with the enthusiasm of a scientist who has discovered a new aspect of a previously studied phenomenon. "Your mind, I believe, can clearly distinguish between what is real and what is not! To put it plainly, virtual reality doesn't 'impress' you. Subconsciously, you are certain that nothing bad will happen to you. You grew up in the Layer, right?"

"Yup," Max thought over Timoshin's words. "All right, so my mind can clearly distinguish between reality and cyberspace. What do banned chips have to do with it?"

"Chippers use illegal software and download vast amounts of information into their brain, thus receiving very vivid and memorable images," Timoshin explained readily. "Their brain is typically overloaded and when they return to reality, everything seems gray and dim, boring and monotonous. Hence the well-known symptoms of dependency: irritability, agitation, inappropriate behavior, constant attempts to transfer virtual phenomena into the real world."

"Why didn't I develop a dependence from working in the laboratory? Is the volume of data flowing through the shunt less than in the chippers?"

"No, it's greater. But unlike the others, you

constantly analyze the source of data, checking its accuracy on a subconscious level."

"Virtual reality is made up so there is no point reacting to it?"

"Exactly!" Timoshin exclaimed. "You've grown up in the Layer and then became familiar with the real world under some stressful circumstances. Unfortunately, a section of your personal file is classified as secret. You're a unique case, in my opinion! We couldn't even imagine such a clear delineation of the two realities! You flew a fighter in open space for the first time today, and your mind reacted in a completely different way to when you were in the laboratory! Now you simply don't have enough data, since you saw your surroundings in a lot more detail only a few minutes ago."

"Doc, are these symptoms going to pass?" Max queried worriedly.

"I don't know, I don't know... What an interesting topic for research! I suppose that you'll soon learn to switch between the different perception methods."

"Fine. Why can't chippers tell between reality and virtual space?"

"Compared to you, they have a weak and unstable mind. Really, abusing chips and direct neurosensory contact are two sides of the same coin."

"That's not very comforting."

"Don't worry, Bourne, you can handle it. It'll be hard for a little way but you'll adapt eventually."

"And what if I don't? What then, Doc?"

"Well, then you'll need treatment," Timoshin spoke reluctantly.

"Will the technology get banned?"

"I don't think so."

"Why not? It's dangerous. I've met chippers before. They were demented, unreasonable and aggressive."

"I guess they'll sift people out," Timoshin suggested cautiously. "The training program will probably include preliminary tests for psychological stability. All right, Bourne, we should keep the channel clear." He suddenly remembered where they were. "We shouldn't be discussing these topics now. We'll talk when you get back."

The conversation didn't fill Max with confidence. He had to weigh the risk and consider whether he should renew the contract after it expired. Qualified pilots were always in demand so he wasn't going to be left without work.

The world really did seem faded. After the short conversation with Timoshin, everything seemed to have found an answer and made sense. It was true that the dim crosshairs on the radar screen couldn't compare with the clear signature that the mind perceived when directly connected to the fighter's positioning system.

"Although," he tapped a sensor, bringing up a detailed energy matrix onto the screen, "what's the difference? It's the reaction speed. The availability of data," He answered his own question. To glance at the crosshairs, think about it, move, look at the screens, and analyze the energy matrix took 6-7 seconds. In space, and particularly during battle, this was a lot.

Was this the future of direct neurosensory contact technology?

"Although," he shrugged his shoulder as he performed a complex maneuver between the asteroids, "Why do I immediately assume it has a military purpose? There are a hundred other possibilities. Control over machinery that is operating in extremely aggressive environments. Solving atypical situations, which occur hourly in the megacities. The expert neuronets are involved in solving such problems, but there is little trust placed in them..."

The risky maneuvering, which had previously given Max such a rush, wasn't giving him any pleasure so he decided to return to base.

He had already turned the Needle around when the positioning system sensors all howled at once. Max broke out in a cold sweat from the unexpectedness of it all.

What the hell was going on?

He could have sworn that there wasn't a single large cosmic body for many thousands of kilometers around him! On his return journey, he deliberately took the craft above the asteroid cluster and was about to hand the controls over to the autopilot.

Was there an error in the positioning system? Max's thoughts lagged behind his automatic movements, and he avoided the likely collision despite the screens being clear. In the depths of the holographic monitors, an outline of an unfamiliar object lit up and disappeared within a fraction of a second.

"Test-1 to Center, please respond!" He got the ship under control and slowed down.

"Center, we hear you. What's happening?!"

"I'd like to know that myself! Please send me data from the base's positioning system!"

"We have a strange signal. Powerful but brief. Fractions of a second."

"Objectively?"

"One hundred percent. Considering the

identical data on the duplicate system scanners."

"So a material object just appeared and immediately disappeared in my flight path? How is that even possible?"

"We don't know. We're trying to figure it out."

"I think it's a glitch. I'm back on my old course."

"Received!"

Max turned the fighter smoothly around, bringing it back onto the trajectory towards the asteroid group, when the sensor alarms howled again.

Max saw it this time. A spaceship! It appeared and immediately disappeared again.

"Test-1 to Center. Get me Timoshin, now!"

"Listening," the man responded at once.

"Doc, I'm connecting the shunt! Sending you the telemetry readings!"

"Did you see it?!"

"Yes, for a moment. It's not a system glitch or a hallucination."

"Don't rush to conclusions, Bourne. The technicians say it may be interference in the location complex. And I'm not excluding the possibility of your mind tripping, so don't get any ideas and come back to base!"

Max didn't even consider interrupting his neurosensory contact with the craft.

"Did I understand correctly that the base's scanners showed the same results to those on the Needle?" he clarified.

"Yes, but this simply can't be happening!" Timoshin replied. "A spaceship can't just materialize and disappear again."

"Are you sure?"

"I don't understand you, Bourne! What are you suggesting?"

"Technology, Doc. Are you sure that there are no other tests taking place in this sector of space? Some advanced camouflage systems, for example?"

"No. They would have warned us." Timoshin responded confidently.

The long-range lasers screeched a warning again.

Bourne narrowly avoided a collision. It was the same ship in his direct sight!

It didn't disappear. Surrounded by cold energy bursts, the space wanderer materialized about a kilometer away from the fighter and immediately started drifting, spinning uncontrollably.

The object's clear energy matrix appeared in Max's mind, thanks to his direct link to the location system, and in the next moment, the world exploded in a blinding burst of pain.

He barely had enough time to swerve and

avoid a collision.

"Bourne, answer me!"

The pain became a growing fireball. His consciousness dimmed but the combat life support system immediately switched on and brought Max back.

He couldn't think. He couldn't move a muscle, let alone control the Needle! The pain was getting stronger.

"Bourne!"

He uttered a weak, inarticulate sound. Through the crimson fog overwhelming his consciousness, Max saw an enormous, spinning black funnel, twinkling with cold energy charges, which slowly faded away. Was it distorted space metric? His mind was still trying to interpret the phenomenon around him.

"Bourne, switch off the shunt!" Timoshin's voice reappeared, sounding muffled and distant. "This ship is sending a targeted transmission of data. The fighter's system is unable to receive so much information and it's downloading it into your brain. Can you hear me? Turn off the shunt right now or you'll die!"

Max could hear Timoshin's voice but couldn't follow the order. His body would not obey him. Hallucinations appeared alongside his pain-shredded thoughts. He could see flashes of unfamiliar star systems, planets and suns.

Ultimately, someone from the control center saved Max's life. A technology recess opened suddenly to the right of the G chair, and a flexible manipulator under external control reached for Max's helmet and switched off the direct neurosensory contact shunt.

The pain subsided at once. Max felt nauseous from the excessive doses of combat stimulators and the surreal images faded slowly from his gaze, but now he could take over the ship controls.

The autopilot indicators blinked a helpless red. None of the Needle's subsystems were working as they should.

Max could hear the calls but didn't answer them. He barely had enough strength to correct his craft's course and reach a safe orbit around the mysterious spaceship.

"An alien ship?" the thought sobered him up a little, working as well as a combat stimulator. He focused his gaze on the mysterious ship. It was a strange design but at the same time vaguely familiar.

The rounded front. The cylindrical body with numerous projections. Three propulsion sections at the stern, angled 120 degrees away from each other.

It's not possible!

The cosmic wanderer that had clearly been

in numerous scrapes, was damaged in several places by meteor strikes and was pitted and scarred, was a copy of the famous Alpha Colonial Transport?!

Max could sense that he was close to losing consciousness.

All right. Don't rush. Carefully. If the ship isn't alien, it must have a name, right?

He corrected his flight path and performed a slow circle using manual controls.

He could see the hemispherical front part of the ship.

Vancor.

The name was unfamiliar and meant nothing to Max.

Help was already on its way from the asteroids. Some of the fighter's subsystems had reloaded and the search radar had resumed working. The holographic monitors were filling with data again.

Vancor. Property of the World Government of Earth — one of the signs on the ship's torn hull could still be read.

"Bourne, please respond. This is the Center!" The voice in the communicator was yelling continuously.

"I hear you..." He exhaled, barely moving his lips.

"Are you alive?!"

"I'm alive... since I answered you..."

"We're coming. Hang in there for another couple of minutes."

His consciousness was fading. Max hadn't gone mad, hadn't crashed, and had miraculously avoided a collision, but he still couldn't understand what was happening and what he had gotten himself into.

The rescue ships were approaching. Max moved the astronavigational rudders with some difficulty, changing his course.

The dark behemoth of the mysterious object began to recede slowly.

Max's weak fingers let go of the astronavigational rudders. He suddenly felt completely drained, as if a black wall had rolled over him, erasing the remaining pain and leaving behind only a sense of peace.

This was the after-effect of overdosing on combat stimulators but Max didn't complain as he sank into a blissful sleep.

He'd survived.

A hollow thump. Vibration. Was it forced docking?

The pattern of stars on the screens began to slowly shift. He couldn't see the mysterious ship anymore as the rescuers had docked to the fighter and had immediately turned back towards the base.

That's it.

Max closed his eyes. Against his closed eyelids, he could see a snaking and twisting inscription: *Vancor.*

Then it too disappeared.

Object Y-407
Medical laboratories
A day later

"You were really lucky, Max." Timoshin's voice sounded very close.

"Why?" Max's lips barely moved.

"You have a strong mind. You survived. According to our information, that ship was sending a direct transmission."

"I'm going to live?"

"Undoubtedly."

"What about the information?"

"That's more difficult to tell. I suspect that it was at least partially dumped into your brain. To be honest, I haven't come across this before. I can't predict what will happen next or what the consequences may be."

"Can it be removed?"

The light shining into his eyes went out. Max reclined in an armchair, surrounded by blocks of cybernetic devices.

"Are you kidding? The human brain is not a computer hard disk. It stores data in a completely different manner. No, the information can't be removed." Timoshin gestured helplessly. "It's still too early to tell if you have absorbed the information or not." Timoshin watched him with unconcealed curiosity.

"How do we figure that out, Doc?"

"Well, let's start by simply having a chat." Timoshin examined the neurogram. "There was a definite overload, we can see your brain's hyperactivity here, specifically in the moments when the ship was transmitting data. If you have absorbed it, there is a possibility that some sections of your memory have been damaged. To put it simply, the ship's data may have replaced some of your memories."

"How did it manage to appear out of thin air at all?" Max asked.

"I have no idea. Sorry, it's not my field of specialization."

"What if I don't agree to any further experiments?"

Timoshin stayed grimly silent and then finally replied. "You're bound by a contract." He sunk into an armchair beside the terminal. "So am I. I'm sorry but if they order me..." He shrugged helplessly again.

"What are they waiting for?" Max tensed visibly. "A day has passed."

"Bourne, let's be honest with each other. I'm not your enemy. But the situation is extremely delicate. This *Vancor* is the property of the World Government. You saw it yourself, the ship appeared literally out of nowhere. It looks a lot like Alpha's disappearance, only in reverse. For the moment, we're unable to reach either Mars or Earth to get clear instructions."

"What's stopping you?"

"Unexplained energy interference. I'll tell you more, the orbits of the asteroid family have changed. Only slightly but the fact is troubling in itself. There was some sort of global impact at the space metric level. The mysterious ship is at center of these phenomena."

Max understood the situation perfectly well. He would have the information simply ripped out of him.

"Fine. Let's work together, Doc," Max agreed after a thoughtful pause. "What exactly are you interested in?"

"Everything: your childhood, adolescence and adulthood. Psychological traumas. The reason why you became a pilot. Why you agreed to take part in a highly dangerous, in my opinion, experiment. I want to help you, Bourne. But first, we need to determine if you remember your whole past. If we discover gaps in your memory, it means the situation's serious."

"What if there aren't any?"

"You'll be left alone, I think. Thank God that mind-reading technology doesn't exist yet."

They talked long into the evening.

"So, you're one of the pilots from the *Normandy*?" Timoshin exclaimed in unfeigned surprise as he listened to Max.

"Not by choice." Max briefly described his awakening on board the corporate cruiser and the subsequent events, only skipping the visit of the AI.

"Wow, fate has really tossed you around!" Timoshin sympathized. "But how did you save yourself? What about the *Normandy*? What happened to the cruiser? I heard that they never managed to find it."

"Yup. It disappeared. I was surprised myself when I no longer saw it in orbit. I suppose the AIs landed the cruiser on Ganymede and pulled it apart. They would have needed the parts for their defense lines, right?"

Timoshin nodded. The explanation seemed quite logical so he moved away from this tricky topic.

"I was preparing for the corporate fleet's arrival." Max continued without waiting for further questions, many of which could lead him into a trap. "I dismantled the engines from a crashed Needle. I built a frame for them and installed a chair. I didn't seal the structure closed. I built very simple manual controls and as soon as the squadron of Rimp Cybertronics ships neared Ganymede, I turned on my distress signal and launched into space.

"You weren't afraid of being shot down?"

"No, I had it all figured out. For the first few minutes, I flew close to the surface, protected by the crater's slopes, which blocked the firing line of the nearest AI battery. Then I was picked up by the sensors of the corporate combat fleet, who contacted me on the emergency channel and indicated a safe corridor. They followed my path until I got close enough to the frigate Oush. Then came the towing beam and a vacuum dock. I made it on board without any drama."

"Did they question you?"

"Are you kidding?" Max smiled grimly. "They checked each word a hundred times. They sent out a special group to inspect my shelter. Then they suddenly didn't have time for me. The AIs had planted themselves firmly on Ganymede. After a week of fighting, it became clear that kicking them out was not going to be easy. The frigate *Oush* sustained damage to the reactor compartment and was sent to the rear, to the other side of Jupiter, where the squadron's repair base was located."

"And then?" Timoshin continued to closely watch Max's neurogram.

"It was pretty basic, to be honest. Ganymede was besieged. The two assaults failed. Three ships needed serious repairs and they were sent here, to the asteroid belt. I was sent with them."

"Why did you agree to test the neurosensory contact system?" Timoshin watched Max's reaction closely and made some notes.

"I wanted to finish the contract. You can look at my personal file, I'm sure that you've got access to that part of my biography."

Timoshin still looked puzzled. "I wouldn't take the risk. I'd work as a pilot. Ten years isn't such a big deal."

"I have other plans. I have a clear idea of what I want."

"Can you be more specific? Or is it a secret?"

"No. I want to return to Earth and find my family. Buy a block of land on Mars in the Genesis colonization zone. Live as I see fit."

"Well," Timoshin closed the program

windows. "Everything seems fine at first glance. How do you feel?"

"Physically — not bad. My head's aching though."

"Fine. I'll get the sensors off. Go and rest, and I'll analyze the neurograms. Although I didn't see anything unusual during the process. I'll have a clearer answer in the morning."

"Thanks, Doc!" Max got out of the chair, feeling completely wrung out.

There were dozens of different laboratories located inside the asteroid.

The corporation base was built inside a mine. The natural resources had long been depleted but a decent infrastructure still remained, and it seemed a shame not to use it.

Nobody knows how densely populated the Solar System's main asteroid belt is. In the 2190's, in an attempt to limit the power of the leading corporations on Earth and to create an independent sector of the economy, the World Government developed and supported medium-sized businesses, subsidized the construction of mining stations and transport ships, and hired them out to entrepreneur groups. Up to a thousand mobile mining complexes were built on the orbital shipyards belonging to the New Age State Company every year.

For decades, the Space Klondike was explored sporadically.

The result of the World Government's policies were tens of thousands medium-sized companies working in the commodities sector. Cargo ships moved constantly between Earth and the outposts of deep space, while long-term settlements were founded on asteroids, which were usually associated with underground or open cut mines. It was a highly profitable business. With the growing resource deficit on Earth, the enormous distances of space were no longer an obstacle, while transportation costs took up a negligible part of the profits. The first achievements in cryonics enabled spaceships to be optimized to carry both passengers and cargo. The introduction of reliable cryocapsules meant that flights between Earth and the asteroid belt, which took many months, had become commonplace. Almost anyone could now travel into deep space and there were plenty of people who wanted to.

The asteroid belt settlements had appeared haphazardly. Colonization of the resource ring was not regulated by any laws. Preference was given to the largest and most promising asteroids, with base stations created in their depths, from where small groups of miners travelled on short trips to explore the nearest objects.

The situation changed radically when Megapool began large-scale construction on Mars. The corporations arrived in the asteroid belt, tacitly divided it into commodity sectors, and commenced centralized resource extraction, which bankrupted many of the small companies.

Thousands of microsettlements in the depths of space were suddenly left to their own devices. Most of the miners, unable to compete with the aggressive corporations, returned to Earth on cargo ships, but there were those who decided to preserve their independence and way of life. They refused to accept the power of the corporations and continued to search for valuable resources at their own risk.

This was how smuggler and raider settlements were formed.

The daring pilots illegally delivered resources, mainly to the lunar bases, raided the corporate segments of the commodity ring, waged wars amongst themselves, and gradually became a problem that so far had not been solved by either the security forces of Earth's largest corporations or the individual squadrons of the World Government fleet, which patrolled the asteroid belt.

$$\ast \ast \ast$$

Max woke up from jolts and thunder.

He leapt up and felt the nausea wash over him. He looked at the information displayed on the compartment wall. The artificial gravity values had dropped suddenly and communication was absent.

Max shrugged and started getting dressed. The first thought that he had was that they had collided with another celestial body but this theory evaporated as soon as he opened the door and looked out into the corridor.

The guard's bullet-riddled body was slowly sinking to the ground, leaving a wide smear of blood on the wall.

Dusky blue smoke drifted in the draught. The asteroid was vibrating rapidly as if the piece of rock was shivering.

A siren howled in the distance. Bursts of gunfire echoed down the corridors.

Max dashed over to the dead guard's body but didn't find a weapon.

It wasn't clear who was attacking or why. As far as Max Bourne could remember, the asteroid was protected by anti-spacecraft systems. "Raiders?" he wondered. No, that was doubtful. They weren't capable of breaching the anti-spacecraft defenses and why would they risk it, anyway? They could score supplies in other places without exposing themselves to such obvious risk. Rimp Cybertronics did not forgive attacks and its corporate army was not something to be trifled with. They would find the attackers and destroy them as a show of force. It was a matter of reputation and to stop others from trying the same thing.

With this in mind, Max stole along the corridor, listening to the sound of gunshots.

He spotted a hatch that had been destroyed by an explosion and could see a small section of a long-abandoned tunnel. So that was how intruders had gotten inside! Through the old tunnels that were not part of the modern research complex. He looked further and saw a temporary airlock: a simple metalloplastic construction with a special foam along its borders to seal the gaps where it didn't fit properly. It wouldn't last long under the air pressure but it was fine for a quick assault and retreat.

While Max was inspecting the temporary airlock, a fierce gun fight broke out nearby, at the tunnel intersection.

Max held himself still. If he was caught in the battle without weapons or a sealed suit, he would automatically become a victim of the sudden events. The raiders only needed the atmosphere and artificial gravitation to quickly capture the research complex, since the automatic emergency tunnel segmentation system didn't activate in this case, and to loot the storage areas more effectively. Nobody would hesitate after that. Explosive decompression was the best way to destroy any evidence.

He sneaked a look out of his hiding spot but the gun fight was still going and the ricocheting stray bullets made him pull back hurriedly.

Max could hear gun shots again and they sounded very close. The thick gray smoke was being whisked along the corridor by a strong draught. There was an air leak somewhere!

Heavy footsteps thundered in the smoke, followed by rustle of the servomotors, and a short burst of gunfire like a howl.

It's the IM-10, Max decided. "Where did the raiders get modern impulse weapons?" came the thought. "Was it the guard, then? Not necessarily..." His heart was beating faster and faster. Max remembered how he was greeted in the vacuum dock. The Rimp Cybertronics security service wore light onboard suits without muscular amplifiers. The guards held ARG-5s, the Hans Gervet automatic rifles.

Max looked behind him. He was in a terrible position. The raiders were unlikely to drag their loot through the temporary airlock as it was meant for covert entry. It would be more convenient for them to use the vacuum docks and the mine's loading terminals upon exit but their reinforcements could come through here.

Max listened carefully, trying to keep his breathing shallow. The smoke made his eyes water and tickled the back of his throat. The footsteps and high-pitched whine of the servomotors had faded away, and relative silence descended on this part of the research complex. Only the air purifications systems hummed in the distance.

Max wasn't planning to just sit here and wait for the final.

He had to find a suit. A suit would protect him from even explosive decompression. The most important thing was to secure himself in place, or better yet, find a secure room before the raiders left the asteroid and opened all the airlocks!

Slipping into the corridor, Max walked rapidly to where the tunnel split, one hand constantly touching the wall.

The smoke thickened and then suddenly thinned out. Max left the damaged ventilation system segment behind him and could see bodies lying on the floor at the tunnel intersection. Four guards wearing the Rimp Cybertronics uniform and two unfamiliar people in old and patched up suits.

Damn it! He squatted down and inspected the dead bodies. Not much. ARG-5, a couple of spare clips, a converter loaded with dry tablets. Max quickly pulled on the breathing mask and gulped in the clean air, checked to make sure that the converter was working normally, and only then turned his attention to the bodies in the suits.

They were definitely asteroid inhabitants. Their outfits were shabby, with numerous patches. Max couldn't use them for the bullet holes had turned the suits into a pile of useless junk. He only took off their cyberstacks — once the attack was repulsed, the personal nanocomps would be useful for the investigation!

Gunfire thundered again in the labyrinth of tunnels. The sound was coming from far away. Max touched a sensor on his own cyberstack. The faint yellow light flickered several times and went out. The Net was down. What a mess! Most of the cable channels weren't damaged. The lighting and air recycling were working.

That was all true but why hadn't the security of the secret research complex fought off the invading gang? They could have used the emergency dividers, thus splitting up the enemy forces and making it more difficult for the raiders to move through the complex. They could but they didn't? Were they acting in collusion? It certainly seemed like it. One had to wonder why the anti-spacecraft defense system hadn't worked as it should have. How did the raiders manage to get inside without being detected?

The laboratory sector began after the next communication node. The massive, armored airlock doors lay on the floor. The doors of the research departments had been blown off their hinges. He glanced inside one of the rooms. Broken pieces of equipment lay everywhere as well as smoking cybernetic blocks.

Max rushed into the lab when he spotted Timoshin. The man was dead — a burst from the ARG-5 had pierced him through the back of the chair.

Damn it, he was too late! OK, calm down! Max looked for the additional implant module and the direct neurosensory connection shunt — both devices remained on the table. Grabbing them, Max ran to the alcove holding the emergency suit. Decompression could occur at any moment and every second counted.

He suited up quickly and efficiently. The helmet with its convex clear visor provided a good view and the numerous specialized sensors and scanners picked up various spectrum signatures, which was helpful. There was no protection, however. Max had to tread carefully since this type of vacsuit was good for aggressive environments but wasn't going to stop a bullet or shrapnel.

Subsystem activation went well but didn't clear anything up. The Net was still down. Max pulled up a map of the asteroid's communications on his visor's projection screen. A complex multilevel diagram appeared. His personal navigational sensor gave an error signal for some unexplained reason, so Max's current location did not appear on the screen.

Fine! Max used the search system, magnified the laboratory level, identified the room which he was currently in, and without wasting any time, began to plot a route to the vacuum dock, where he had left his fighter the day before. He knew that the craft was refueled and restocked.

He scanned the communication frequencies at the same time but with no success.

A high pitched sound announced that a route had been found. So, first to the nearest airlock, then along some abandoned tunnels to an impressively-sized cave where, according to the labels, a long-abandoned loading terminal was located. Max could reach the vacuum dock from there by going out onto the asteroid's surface.

It would have to do.

The journey through the dark, partially collapsed and unsealed tunnel, which followed the snaking mineral vein, took about twenty minutes. Max finally found himself beside an adit leading to the surface through the old loading terminal cave.

There was no artificial gravity in the abandoned tunnels so Max floated along for most of the trip, orientating himself using the suit's sensors and propelling himself forward by using his hands to push off the walls.

The cave had an unexpected and unpleasant surprise in store. He noticed glimmers of light from some distance away and took precautions, muting the work of the active sensors and switching the communicator back into frequency scanning mode. Max used a sloping adit to look at what was happening in the cave.

The side branch brought him to a latticed balcony. Max kept himself still and clutched his weapon. He saw no reason to join the battle, but just in case, he clicked his safety carbine on to a bracket protruding from the wall and tugged it several times, checking to make sure that it was secure. Now, if the situation suddenly deteriorated, he could open fire without fearing that recoil would thrust him back into the tunnel he had just exited.

A transport ship that looked like it had seen better days was parked at the ancient terminal. People in suits scurried around the tightly stretched cables. They delivered containers with supplies and equipment, and loaded them quickly into the cargo hold.

The frequency scanner uttered a dry click.

"Hurry!" The voice sounded unexpectedly, without a call sign.

"Half of my people aren't back yet!" A voice replied irritably.

"I don't care. Finish loading up and piss off with what you've scored!"

"I've told you that my people haven't..."

"Means they died fighting with the corps! Five minutes, get it? Otherwise, you'll be turned into dust together with the asteroid!"

"Fine. We're leaving," the second voice said reluctantly after a short pause.

It appeared that the raiders took the threat seriously. The ship's cargo ramps began to close, and the people in suits swarmed to the airlocks, with only two staying behind to release the cables.

Finally, they too disappeared inside the

ship. The cave was illuminated by flashes from the working engines, the old ship took up the thrust drive and began to accelerate towards a wide tunnel that led to the asteroid's surface.

Max stayed put and he was right to anticipate that something bad was about to happen: a sudden burst of flame lit up the tunnel. The asteroid began to vibrate as if its surface was peppered by fragments and a series of crushing vibrations swept through the mining tunnels.

Was it the decompression?!

Max felt cold inside. He had only minutes left to save himself! He could feel the rock beginning to spin and accelerate at the same time.

Max unclipped the safety carbine and, no longer hiding his presence, floated towards the exit, trying to cross the space as quickly as possible and get to the surface.

The decompressive explosions had pushed the asteroid off its orbit! Considering how close the other celestial bodies were, a catastrophe was unavoidable.

✶ ✶ ✶

Exiting the tunnel, Max could see that he was in mortal danger. Fragments of the raiders' ship floated in space, colliding with each other. The asteroid was spinning as it slowly neared its brethren. Blurred plumes of decompressed air trailed after it.

Max switched on all the sensors on his suit and ordered a scan file to be created. The high-speed cameras mounted on his helmet began to record what was happening.

Two objects could be clearly seen among the wreckage and plumes of air. A cruiser with a clearly discernible UN logo was slowly moving away from the attacked and plundered asteroid. Clutched in its special clamps was the mysterious spaceship, the same one that had recently materialized so dangerously close to the Rimp Cybertronics research base.

The situation now seemed much clearer. Max could clearly see two craters on the asteroid's surface. One was where a destroyed space communication center had stood, while the second, deeper one, framed the ruins of the anti-spacecraft defense node.

The scene of the attack practically screamed of third party intervention but the upcoming collision would destroy all the obvious evidence. Only the bodies of the raiders, fragments of the old transport ship, the destroyed asteroid and containers full of loot will remain in the catastrophe zone.

The events will be chalked up to a daring raid by thieves, who had infiltrated a carefully defended object. The temporary airlocks installed at the border of the modern complex and the old works will help to support this theory. It was likely that the raiders didn't even know about them. The asteroid inhabitants were used blindly and condemned to death.

And the reason for all this was the mysterious ship *Vancor?*

Darkness and silence.

Max's Needle drifted near the cloud of debris. The Rimp Cybertronics Corporation's research base had been completely destroyed in the collision of small celestial bodies. He tried to find other survivors but no avail. Nobody answered his calls and the Needle's scanners couldn't find a single active signal from the personal sensors.

It wasn't the first time that Max found himself alone in space but the situation didn't look good.

The communication system was down, with only crackling heard on all the frequencies. The automated system vainly tried to establish a connection with the corporate networks. It wasn't clear if the reason for this was the mysterious anomaly caused by the *Vancor*'s appearance or simply the disrupters dropped by the UN cruiser. There was enough oxygen to last for two days. The corporation's nearest outpost was 107 hours of flight away. Max didn't have enough air or fuel for that.

Should he wait here? But when would the quick response forces arrive? How would they interpret the silence of the secret research center? He didn't even know how often Y-407 contacted the other sites.

Max weighed his chances and found them negligible. He had survived yet his future looked bleak.

He found himself at the epicenter of some baffling events. The United Nations ship, called upon to preserve peace and order in the asteroid belt, had instead acted as an aggressor, destroying everyone who may have seen the *Vancor*.

Simple logic together with life experience suggested to Max that if he wanted to survive, he had to remain on the list of the dead.

He listened to the voice of reason, reached for the control panel and switched off the transmitter.

Now he had to figure out what to do next. The chance of rescue was minuscule. Max knew the coordinates of the corporation's nearest defense bases but common sense indicated that he couldn't go there. He wouldn't be able to get away with half-truths at the interrogations. If he told them the whole truth, his mind would be turned inside out in an attempt to extract the information transmitted by the mysterious spaceship. If even Timoshin had expressly mentioned this possibility, and he wasn't the worst corp around, what would the others do, for whom Max Bourne was nothing more than a source of important information?

"Where am I supposed to go? Where can I find even temporary shelter?"

His hand reached unwittingly into the suit's pouch. The raiders' personal nanocomps, Max remembered, and then wondered if they could offer a possible solution.

Max moved the Needle a reasonable distance away from the catastrophe site, shut down the engines and minimized the energy consumption of the on-board systems. Only then did he focus on the stolen cyberstacks.

The password to each personal nanocomputer was usually genetic material from its owner. Max picked up an analyzer and examined the inner surface of the cyberstacks, finding skin microparticles that were suitable for DNA analysis.

Life on Ganymede had taught him a lot. Without panicking or wasting any time, Max clambered into the Needle's cargo hold and found among the equipment, designed for an individual shelter, a compact device that he knew about but had never used.

It was a microincubator for cloning strains of soil-forming bacteria. If Max changed some of the settings, he could use it to analyze human epithelial cells, for the device didn't care what sort of DNA sample it was processing, after all.

✳ ✳ ✳

How does one hack into a cyberstack?

The personal nanocomp system can be tricked by transmitting its owner's decoded DNA through the technical access port. With the current level of technology, this procedure, including the DNA analysis, took less than an hour but not many people knew about it. Mostly people who had carefully read Hans Gervert's book, which explained in easy-to-understand language how to use the Needle's standard equipment to solve non-standard technical problems.

Max connected the incubator to the raider's cyberstack with a fiber optic cable and tapped the activation sensor.

It worked! The microholograph switched on, displaying the files stored on the cyberstack.

Browsing through the directory, Max spotted separately stored individual course maps.

Perfect! Max didn't expect a warm welcome at the raiders' settlement but he couldn't see any other options.

"Even if I have to be one of them for a while, it's still better than turning into a laboratory specimen," Max thought, loading the data into the Needle's navigational subsystem.

Odd... The map analysis marked out groups of asteroids which were all too small to be organized settlements. What were they, then? Caches?

The closest navigational marker was a seven-hour flight away. The rest were much further away and harder to reach.

"Well, looks like I'll have to check what's hidden there," Max thought.

...At a point in space marked with a navigational pin drifted an old, broken transport ship, docked at an asteroid ready for towing, which, according to the scanners, consisted of 70% nickel!

From the point of view of a smuggler or raider, Max was unbelievably lucky, but the spaceship's dead reactor, absence of activity in the onboard circuits, and the numerous holes in

its hull left almost no hope of using it as a means
of rescue or survival.

Chapter Seven

Earth. Year 2212
Active construction zone on Mars
The Hellas impact basin, a section of the
Martian surface where water can exist in a
liquid state

THE ORANGE murk stretched from one horizon to
the other.

The weak wind carried specks of dust. The
cloudless sky seemed foreign and sinister.

The dust was everywhere, forming long and
slowly settling plumes with every movement of

the robotic complexes.

Here, among the barren Martian desserts, where the temperature didn't exceed 1-2 degrees Celsius at this time of year, the construction and terraforming machines were creating a future for modern humanity.

A megacity's typical foundation took up hundreds of thousands square kilometers. Like most of Earth's cities, it consisted of twelve segments, looking like low mountain ridges, which radiated like the spokes of a wheel from the center.

Millions of servomechanisms were working here 24 hours a day. Most of the work was done automatically.

Megapool Corporation. The Hellas Object proclaimed a laser-drawn sign flickering in the dusty air.

The foundation was surrounded by a ring of installed atmospheric processors. They were shaped like truncated cones and were 1.5 kilometers tall. These creations belonged to the Genesis Corporation.

The construction and terraforming machines, developed by Rimp Cybertronics, moved slowly along specially constructed energy cables, receiving the energy required to manufacture and lay down the reinforced concrete.

The Martian cities were growing day by day. Enormous machines leveled the ground, dug out pits and carefully created monolithic blocks. In several months time, a dome would be erected over the Hellas impact basin, the future megasuburb platforms will be created one by one, and only then will the construction of buildings commence.

Seventeen model cities were already towering at a height of one kilometer in other regions of Mars. The construction of housing complexes was in full swing, and as they were completed, the Martian megacities were filled with technical content — devices that would create and then maintain a controlled living environment for the settlers from Earth.

The movement of the servos didn't stop for even a minute in the dusty orange gloom, since circling the ancestral planet were two dozen specially constructed ships, waiting for the distance between the planets to shrink. Six million cryogenic capsules would soon be loaded onto the ships. Then, after long months of flight, the cargo and passenger fleet will reach its target, thus beginning a new page in the history of extraterrestrial colonies.

The terrible Martian winds, controlled by an army of twenty thousand atmospheric processors, no longer posed a problem. The famous dust storms (with wind gusts of up to 30 meters per second) survived only in the historical records of many years ago.

Machines continued to excavate the soil in the Hellas impact basin. The plain that was formed on the planet's northern hemisphere due to the fall of a huge asteroid, was seven kilometers below the average Martian ground level.

The machines burrowed deeper and deeper into the surface. The plumes of dust thickened and grew.

In the automatic control center, the cybernetic systems monitored the situation constantly, but none raised an alarm since the dust protection level of the construction mechanisms was very high. The Rimp Cybertonics Corporation was famous for how reliable its technology was, plus, there were special instructions that covered probable risks and clearly stipulated the conditions under which the machines could be stopped.

Any pause, no matter how small, would inevitably disrupt the work schedule and lead to huge losses but, most importantly, if the pace of the construction slowed down, there was a risk that the interplanetary flight couldn't go ahead.

...The orange dust rose higher and higher. The machines descended fifty meters below the surface of the Hellas plain.

The light sensors of the monitoring devices in the control center stopped in the yellow zone. According to the cybernetic systems, the concentration of dust did not exceed the protective characteristics of the construction equipment.

Hellas was gradually blanketed in an impenetrable cloud. It was an inevitable evil when digging pits for a megacity foundation. It would be weeks before the atmospheric processors could clear the air. The experience of building seventeen other cities had shown that it was impossible to avoid a growing dust cloud as well as loss of contact with most of the machines.

Meanwhile, one of the robotic excavation complexes suddenly punched through a crust of solid rock and began to slip into an underground cavity filled with tiny particles of dust. The machine's systems didn't have time to sound an alarm. Communication was blocked and the analyzers failed instantly. The dust that burst out onto the surface possessed unusual characteristics. Its particles were measured in nanometers. It slipped into the smallest pores, seeped through filters and got inside mechanisms, increasing the friction a thousandfold and leading to rapid wear of the moving parts.

The other complexes working nearby couldn't recognize the danger in time or react to it.

One by one, the construction machines failed but their reports about the sudden malfunction of their subsystems didn't reach the control center.

The ancient nanodust escaped from the giant underground 'lens' and rose higher and higher.

The automatic processor systems were the first to react to this threat. The devices closest to Hellas shut down in emergency mode, which resulted in a sharp drop in pressure and triggered an increase in wind speed with hurricane gusts of up to 50 meters per second[10].

The ancient nanodust, formed in prehistoric times, gathered in a rapidly expanding cloud in the moment of this disaster of a planetary scale.

Wind gusts gathered the speed and power of a hurricane. The orange gloom filled the Hellas basin and spilled beyond its borders. Travelling another 300 kilometers, it burst into two cities located further south.

Cascades of atmospheric processors switched off one after another. They were not

---

[10] One hundred and eighty kilometers per hour.

under the control of the central control center. The automatic overload protection system activated inside them. Over the course of several hours, control over the winds was lost, and soon the planet's surface was enveloped in a dust storm of unprecedented size and strength, which carried the destructive nanoparticles.

The atmosphere above Mars' northern hemisphere rapidly grew murky and everything was plunged into darkness. Soon, five more construction sites were affected by the dust storm.

✳ ✳ ✳

Deep space

On 10 May 2212, an old transport ship towing a small asteroid left the belt and set a course for Earth, flying in automatic mode.

Considering the extent of damage on the spaceship, only a complete madman or a person in a desperate and hopeless situation would risk such a journey.

It was quiet and empty on board. Most of the compartments had no breathable air. Cables ran from the control cabin, down the corridors, through the docking station and were plugged into the Needle's cybernetic system, which was actually controlling the ship.

The reactor was working at only 20% capacity. Only the wheelhouse, propulsion sections and crew module were supplied with energy. The meager resources of the life support system were directed to the one functioning cryocapsule.

The cryogenic sleep device had become an integral part of each spaceship long ago. Humans now perceived a year of flight as the blink of an eye, but there were exceptions to any rule.

Hibernation slows down the body's metabolism and reduces oxygen consumption but it doesn't stop the basic life functions.

In the narrow and poorly lit compartment, among the disconnected equipment standing beside the only working cryocapsule, alarming signals appeared in the second week of the journey. Max Bourne's heart was beating more frequently than the technology was designed for, with five beats per minute instead of two.

His brain also required more oxygen and nutrients than usual. The system tried to repress the unwanted activity but to no avail. The drugs injected into Max's blood didn't help as his body resisted the effects, so the cryocapsule's systems switched to a mode designed for the rare and exceptional times when a hibernating person suddenly started to dream.

The alarm signals disappeared.

Max's heart continued to beat five times per minute.

He saw a dream that lasted a year. There were several reasons for this. Firstly, due to the extensive tests that Max had undergone, Max's body had adapted to the cryogenic processes, and the drugs that ensured the appropriate level of hibernation no longer worked as well on him. Secondly, his brain was overloaded with information. Thirdly, having once undergone sleep teaching, he instinctively perceived the raw data as a signal to speed up metabolic reactions. Finally, the deciding factor was Max's lengthy testing of the direct neurosensory contact system, which had altered his mind to possess unusual perception abilities, enabling him to read signatures and to receive and comprehend data from cybernetic systems.

The focused and constant decryption of some of the information received from the *Vancor*'s on board computer, while slow when compared to the thinking speed of an awake person, was reflected in Max's mind as a series of vivid and memorable images.

He dreamt of distant worlds where humans had never tread. He saw different star systems, planets with atmospheres, experienced the global malfunction again and again, when the space wanderer turned on its unusual propulsion system and the space around it suddenly twisted into a funnel threaded with thin streaks of energy.

Then came the absolute darkness. The observation screens switched off. The location system sensors lit up as a scattering of tiny crimson emergency sparks across the control panels, and only one of the onboard devices continued to function. A protruding dome that seemed primitive, the monitor initially showed only interference, but gradually in the depths of the 3D image, delicate green strands began to flutter, forming a complex network of unknown connections.

The energy from the onboard reservoirs was being rapidly sapped. The ship was moving due to its acceleration when it shifted between normal space and this mysterious zone devoid of stars. The *Vancor* was struggling and its equipment switched off but the thin strands inside the convex screen continued moving, then a tiny 'node' appeared in the depths of the image, formed by the intersection of the glittering lines, and...

Uncontrollable rotation. Drift. Stars dancing across the screens. Heat from the solar winds, a slow accumulation of energy, and finally, reactivation of the system core.

Scanning. Recording of the received data. Release of probes, if the ship's sensors detected a planet, then the engines starting up again, followed by the vortex of twisted space and darkness.

After a certain number of attempts, the information began to recur, as if in its series of uncontrollable jumps the *Vancor* kept visiting the same star systems.

Earth
Europe Megacity
December 23 2212

Edward Kalganov's work day begun long before the sun rose.

Lately, he had slept little and poorly. It had been a very trying year. Problems were piling up like an avalanche and every new day only brought forth more of them.

It was still dark outside. The light was on at the 'celestial residence' of the Head of the World Government.

Edward Kalganov walked back and forth in his office. His communication workstations displayed dozens of 3D images of various problem zones that required important decisions to be made about them.

Mars. Its atmosphere, murky with dust storms, looked ash-gray. The wild storms obscured even the warning lights of the megacities. Everything was enveloped in darkness, and every hour caused irreparable damage, no longer measured in material losses. The whole Martian program was in danger of collapse.

The cybernetic secretary module followed Kalganov's every step.

"Call the Heads of the corporations for a 10 a.m. meeting." He shifted his gaze to the next screen.

Ganymede.

A scattering of lights could be seen in the high orbit zone. The Rimp Cybertronics corporate fleet, with the support of the UN's seventh squadron, were engaged in a protracted assault but the AIs continued to hold their positions. Their orbital defense system seemed indestructible. The situation had gone too far and had become public. There was no way to avoid a third Jupiter Campaign now. The AIs had to be destroyed at any price, otherwise, it would soon be the end of the already shaky power of the World Government. A quick and telling victory was needed but the huge distances of space meant that the required forced could not be shifted across fast enough. "Which means," Edward turned away with a grimace of irritation, "those hecklers from the Layer will continue to be a pain in the neck for another six months at least."

The third screen showed a lunar crater, a road network and a series of squat, dome-shaped buildings, above which floated a mangled spaceship. It was the *Vancor*, the only one out of eighteen automatic scout ships to return to the Solar System.

Even here Edward Kalganov couldn't boast of a success. The ship, equipped with a fundamentally new type of engine, had visited other star systems and had managed to return but there was no conclusive evidence of this. All the information collected by the onboard cyber networks had been lost. The hard drives had been damaged by an energy source that had not yet been identified. *Vancor*'s reactor was completely depleted and it had used up many years of energy in just a few months! Specialists were now examining the wanderer, trying to find an explanation or to squeeze something out of the onboard systems, but so far, they had been unsuccessful. There were indirect signs that the ship had conducted an emergency data transmission on its return to the Solar System but it was unclear who had received it.

After making a few urgent orders, Kalganov stepped outside.

Over the gray ocean of cloud, a sliver of bright light appeared, staining the shaggy clouds in shades of pink and red.

Edward Kalganov stopped and watched the lead gray giants moving overhead and sensed the gusts of wind in the light but constant vibrations of the loadbearing structures. The 'celestial residence' was protected by an incredibly sturdy dome. Other such structures sparkled in the morning light, the habitat of the select few, the so-called Earth's elite.

The sunrise did not cheer him up. The new day promised to be a difficult one.

The Head of the World Government did not forget for a second who had brought him to power but he'd had enough of dancing to the tune of the corporations, Edward Kalganov thought with irritation. Given the chance, they would tear Earth apart. As it turned out, everyone was wanting to steal the blanket. Yes, there were some successes, grand plans and even productive cooperation. Yet what was the result? The fundamental reconstruction of Earth's megacities had been completed. Billions of people were trapped in the in-modes but the corporations just kept going, shrugging their shoulders and stepping over the problem, as if saying, "Well, we did what we could."

He closed his eyes and sent a mental request for coffee through his implant. He had to prepare himself for the meeting. After the Alpha Colonial Transport catastrophe, the rivalry between the corporations had taken on extreme and no longer hidden forms. The technology race, the fight over resources in the asteroid belt and the division of Mars had all bred more problems instead of solving them.

Edward Kalganov took a sip of coffee and glanced at his surroundings. The lawn in front of his house and the tops of the trees lit up by the glow of the sunrise. He couldn't help but imagine his two daughters, Gretchen, who was five and Omelia, who had just turned seven, running out the house to play with a ball. It was a rare and exotic form of play for modern children.

"If I don't fix the situation on Mars and force the corporations to cooperate with each other, our world will simply collapse." Thoughts of his daughters strengthened Edward's resolve to sort out the problem.

At exactly 10 a.m., the equipment in the meeting room of the celestial residence created five holographic images of people.

Edward Kalganov greeted each person individually, as was customary, but was annoyed to see that Catherine Rimp had ignored the invitation and sent Mac Taylor instead.

"Why did you call us?" Ulrich Fitzgerald lounged in the armchair and hadn't replied to the greeting. He had aged significantly in later years, becoming utterly unbearable, mean and arrogant.

Edward Kalganov paused briefly while the holographic projections of the powers that be exchanged unfriendly looks.

"The situation on Mars requires immediate consolidated actions." He decided to take the initiative at once and set the tone, but nothing happened. Ulrich Fitzgerald glowered at him and stated, "The situation on Mars has reached a dead end. It can no longer be fixed using *your* methods."

"Because Genesis stopped the work of the atmospheric processors!" Hissed Bryzgalov. "The equipment in 18 megacities is now paralyzed by dust! We've lost hundreds of thousands of automated complexes!"

"Now is not the time to count your losses or find someone to blame!" Edward Kalganov raised the voice. "We are talking about quickly resuming work and fulfilling our commitments to seventy million people!"

"They can wait!" Mac Taylor shrugged him

off carelessly. "I would like to say from the outset that this is not Rimp Cybertronics' fault. All the dust protection equipment that we supplied met to the technical specifications received from Megapool!"

"You shouldn't dismiss people!" Edward Kalganov rebuffed him. "They are the best, the most vibrant and active part of Earth's society. Without them you are nothing, I'm sorry to say. Civilization..."

Rage flashed in Bryzgalov's eyes.

"We are the civilization!" He yelled. "Fifty million people work for me! *That's* the active part of the population. While the freeloaders in the Layer are just waiting for us to fix the situation!"

"You're not going to manage," Ulrich Fitzgerald muttered scornfully. "Not in this life, at least."

"Gentlemen, please!" Kalganov exclaimed but they were no longer listening to him.

"Why's that?!" Bryzgalov half stood up from his chair. "Turn on the atmospheric processors, Ulrich! Do it properly or I'll do it myself! It's still possible to save ninety percent of the technology!"

"I most certainly won't!" Fitzgerald shot back. "The processors won't start until the dust storm season is over. And there's no guarantee that you'll be able to save a single machine. They'll have to be all rebuilt."

"This is all you fault!"

"You should have carried out more thorough geological surveys." Fitzgerald shrugged.

"We did!" Bryzgalov snarled.

"Yet you didn't notice the underground lenses filled with molecular dust?" Ulrich asked sarcastically. "Your problem is your greed and the complete inability to think scientifically."

"The cavities are marked on the map but the foundation went deeper! The cavities were supposed to disappear while the soil was being excavated!"

Fitzgerald smiled crookedly and looked at Edward Kaglanov. "Why the hell did you bring us all together? Did you want to watch us squabble? Never mind, don't answer. Since we've all gathered here, I'll explain to everyone that none of you can handle the dust. Even the atmospheric processors won't fix the problem. Mars is a treacherous planet. It took me ten years to rein in the seasonal dust storms and even then, only temporarily. Only global terraforming would eliminate the whole risk. Changing the humidity and atmospheric pressure, absorbing the dust during soil formation, creating a primary vegetation cover from different types of fast-growing grasses — these are the minimal measures needed to ensure success. I will not let you turn on the network of atmospheric processors and thus destroy them. This question is closed. Either global terraforming or dust storms. For the particularly gifted and arrogant among you, I will add that each atmospheric processor is equipped with an automatic defense system against online and physical attacks. So have a think and make a decision."

"And you're washing your hands clean of it?" Mac Taylor frowned.

"Greed and stupidity are not my vices," Ulrich Fitzgerald shrugged. "There is a clear and elaborate program for colonizing Mars. I wasn't allowed to finish it..."

"You're like a broken record, Ulrich!" Michael Bryzgalov burst out. "What does greed have to do with it? You've failed, that's all!"

Fitzgerald shrugged again but deigned to answer. "I warned you all at the end of the last century that we needed to limit the birth rate. That we needed to include recreational zones when reconstructing the cities. Did anyone listen to me? No. 'Breed!' is Megapool's slogan. Virtual schools and in-modes standing in parks are the results of greed and shortsightedness! The pursuit of profit is what drove Earth's population into the Layer! The World Government is directly responsible for today's state of affairs. Who supported me after the Alpha Disaster? Nobody!

You told me, "Move over, Ulrich! The colonial program has changed! We're going to build megacities on Mars!" Did I object? No. But I gave you fair warning that it was not going to end well! Once again, nobody listened to me. Stop trying to pass the buck onto someone else. I'm fed up with these pointless conversations." The holographic image of Ulrich Fitzgerald suddenly began to fade away and then disappeared.

"Unbelievable! He dumps this all on our heads and then runs!"

"He's right, actually." Mac Taylor announced unexpectedly.

"What is Rimp Cybertronics offering? All of you," Bryzgalov stared stonily at each person, including the representatives of Cryonics and New Age, the state corporation in charge of the space shipyards, "have profited from Mars!" His gaze stopped at Li Xiao Pan. "Six million cryogenic capsules — not bad, eh? Whether they'll be used or not doesn't matter, right? Ulrich knew about the dust lenses and didn't warn us!"

"He warned us." Edward Kalganov uttered darkly.

"Oh, right, of course!" Bryzgalov exploded. "He said 'Don't touch the Hellas basin!' A very persuasive and well-reasoned warning. It has the best conditions for terraforming! He just wanted to keep that part of Mars for himself!"

"Cool it. We need to find a solution, not trade accusations."

"Yes, Bryzgalov, that's enough." Mac Taylor supported Edward Kalganov. "If Genesis has solid evidence, we should reconsider the possibility of global terraforming, and take part in it."

"Are you out of your mind? What about the cities? The technology?"

"If there is no other way to deal with the dust, the cities will remain uninhabited for now. The technology will wait until we can clean and restart it."

"When?! When would that happen?" Bryzgalov roared. "How many years would Genesis need?"

"I don't know. We'll have to consult with him."

"I am afraid that cooperating with Mr. Fitzgerald is out of the question for the World Government." Edward Kalganov said gloomily. "The elections are not too far away. Our common problem is right here, on Earth. The Mars Colonization Project meant the eventual relocation of three billion people. If I was to announce now that the colonization date is being moved to an unknown future time, we will lose that part of the electorate," Edward spoke as he looked out of the window, to where his girls were throwing a ball to each other on the lawn. "There will be an explosion. We can't underestimate the masses."

"You know that the corporations will survive any such shocks," Bryzgalov waved away his concerns.

"Chaos doesn't benefit anyone. Mr. Fitzgerald is in control of the food supply market. He will install his own protégé in my place."

"We won't let him!" Bryzgalov snapped.

"The war will destroy Earth and the technosphere will not tolerate the chaos. A chain reaction will destroy civilization in a matter of days." Mac Taylor shook his head. "We've spoken about this and more than once!"

"So, what's the solution?"

"We need to find a way to curb the dust storms." Edward Kalganov was determined. "I'm not a specialist, but even I understand that there is no alternative. The Martian atmosphere can be cleaned up by developing and implementing reagents that will bind to the dust! We must act at once, and at least get a local result. Rumors of problems on Mars are already permeating the Layer. It's quiet on the city streets now but it won't be for long. The first-wave colonists, and there are 70 million of them, are energetic people aspiring to a new life. They will be the fuse that will light the barrel of gunpowder! *That's* what I'm talking about! Yes, at present these people are passing the time in virtual space but they do it in the hope of a radical change happening in their lives very soon."

"You've revived the UN!" Bryzgalov reminded him. "You have the ability to keep the streets under control."

"The forces of law will be activated, don't worry. But I need to show people that the situation on Mars isn't hopeless."

"What exactly do you need us to do?"

"Consolidate. Pool our efforts. Fund a quick investigation. Having cleared the Martian atmosphere of dust, we will force Fitzgerald to launch the processors, even if we have to use the UN fleet."

"Well, then." Bryzgalov perked up. "Sounds good to me!"

"I agree." nodded Li Xiao Pan, who was perfectly aware that the interests, prospects and opportunities for his corporation were directly connected to the resettlement of billions of people, with the cryogenic capsules needing constant servicing during this process.

Madeleine Fiers, the CEO of New Age, nodded silently. She did not dare to contradict Edward Kalganov, and only Mac Taylor was skeptical about the idea.

"A quick solution might not be a safe one.

Chemical substances capable of destroying the dust will then settle on the surface and create an aggressive and toxic environment. This could turn into a worse disaster than the dust storms. I don't think that Catherine Rimp will support this scenario."

"So persuade her!"

"I'll try, but I can't guarantee that I'll succeed."

"You've got to try! I won't forget this favor, I promise." Edward Kalganov insisted.

Mac Taylor only nodded. It was clear to him that the Head of the World Government would do anything to stay in power.

"I will speak to Catherine myself," Bryzgalov announced. "I think that we should set up a team consisting of the best specialists from our corporations, find a solution and use the international fleet to process the Martian atmosphere."

"There'll be no problems from my end." Edward Kalganov assured him.

"In this case, let's consider the main decision made. We'll sort out the dust, put the megacities into operation, you'll win the next elections, and then we'll see how to get our hands on the food supply market." Bryzgalov concluded. "Frankly, I've had enough of Fitzgerald. It's time to replace the Head of Genesis."

There were no objections.

They thought only about money and power. Not about the people, except in passing, as some sort of amorphous mass, a breeding ground for the growth and development of the mighty corporations.

Earth
Antarctic Megacity
May 2213

The morning was clear but windy.

The sun rose above the horizon, illuminating the city from an unusual angle. Its rays, splintered by the massive megasuburbs, flew down the streets and erased the dawn gloom.

The continent's ice sheet had melted long ago. The eastern part of Antarctica had turned into an island archipelago due to the rising sea levels, and the megacity standing on the western part of the continent had the shape of a stepped horseshoe, turned to face the rising sun[11].

Max Bourne had arrived the day before. He

---

[11] The typical design of a Megapool megacity consisted of twelve wedge-shaped segments that gradually increased in height towards the center. The Antarctic Megacity was an exception.

remembered his one-year flight between the asteroid belt and Earth's parking orbit as a vivid and disturbing dream that he could clearly remember but could not yet properly explain.

As soon as Max woke up, he had to deal with problems of a different kind.

Past experiences had taught him a lot so he had planned his return to Earth in advance. Thanks to the information gained from the personal nanocomps of the slain raiders, Max Bourne knew whom to contact.

He had sold the asteroid and transport ship over the Net, dropping the price but avoiding any questions and formalities. The buyer, who had chosen to remain anonymous, took it upon himself to legalize the cargo.

On the Space Vegas Orbital Station, Max paid a decent sum of money in an innocent-looking office of a tourism agency for one number in his implant's ID mark to be replaced by another, and for the necessary information to be added to the planetary database. In this way, a namesake of Max Bourne had arrived at the Antarctic Megacity, a wealthy businessman with no obligations to the all-powerful corporations of Earth.

He was rich and free, just like he had once dreamt, but he had no intention of staying on Earth.

Max had come back for his family. He wanted to see them and take them with him, if possible. Max planned to buy a small plot of terraformed Martian land from Genesis and to settle there, away from the urban centers.

The news about the dust storms on Mars reaching disastrous proportions and threatening the very possibility of mass colonization put Max on edge, but he was reassured at the Genesis office on the Space Vegas Station that the plots set aside for individual low-rise buildings had not been affected. The elite Martian settlements were built under domes, using reliable and tested technology. The storms hadn't damaged them but the resettlement had been suspended for an indefinite period. Due to the natural disaster, landing the shuttle ships had become very difficult and the number of people seeking to move to the first extraterrestrial colony had dropped significantly.

Max listened to the company representative and cast off his doubts. He was sure that Genesis would solve these problems and the interplanetary trips would resume in the future.

Max was a lot more nervous about the upcoming meeting with his family. He couldn't inquire in advance about their fate, and only now that he was physically in the Antarctic Megacity, could he act without attracting any attention.

Glancing at the rising sun, Max pulled out an unremarkable servotoy from his travel bag, which could be bought in most spaceport souvenir shops or at the berthing sections of the Space Vegas Station. Max sat down at a table, cut open the foam flesh and removed it, exposing the core of the servotoy. From the bundle of wires inside, he extracted a thin hidden cable of the direct neurosensory contact shunt and an additional implant module.

He constantly thought about Rimp Cybertronics, the events that occurred in the asteroid belt and his strange dream.

Max's space odyssey was over but he was still in danger. Despite his respect for Catherine Rimp and her ideas of common human values, Max understood that the corporation was a planet-wide conglomerate of humans and machines. It could be considered a super-efficient and aggressive cybernetic organism striving for total dominance. The employees of Rimp Cybertronics had at their disposal the information and technical resources of Earth's single digital space. One wrong step, one tiny mistake and the ubiquitous expert neuronets working for corporate security would pick up his trail, put together the events and facts, and assume that Max Bourne did not die in the asteroid belt.

There were plenty of reasons for concern.

Firstly, Max was the only one in possession of the unique technology for direct neurosensory contact, which had been tested only on him. Secondly, he knew who and why had destroyed the Rimp Cybertronics laboratory in the asteroid belt, which meant that the World Government was potentially his enemy.

Max again felt like he stood at the crossroads. The cryogenic dream was playing tricks on him and the images that he saw from time to time bothered him greatly. He couldn't say with any certainty if they were a product of his fantasies or a decoding of the mysterious data sent to him by the *Vancor.*

The direct neurosensory contact shunt slid into the implant socket and a second later Max experienced an acute sense of déjà vu.

The Layer.

He entered the digital space without creating an avatar, hovering above the bustling pseudolife but taking no part in it, like a shade floating over the abyss of human thoughts and desires.

They had remained the same. The Middle Layer of the Antarctic Megacity appeared clean and bright but it was only a screen that hid the nightmarish illusions of its inhabitants.

Using his new and not fully understood

abilities, Max melded with one of the avatars, instantly sent a pre-prepared search query from the stranger's name, received a reply and disappeared into the Layer's structure, becoming a part of it.

Despair swept over Max, a sudden and unstoppable wave of bitterness.

His parents were no longer alive. There was an accident on the magrail system while they were moving to the Antarctic Megacity...

What about Johnny? And Samantha?

Thankfully, they were still alive. Johnny was here. Max obtained his online address, while Samantha — Max's heart clenched — Samantha was living in the capsular block on the lowest level of the Europe Megacity! How did she end up there and why? Downgrading of social status... A long list of online offences, the use of illegal chips...

Max was simply thrown out of cyberspace. He couldn't maintain the mental concentration and lost contact with the system used to sneak into the Layer.

He didn't come to his senses right away.

Max sat paralyzed in a deep armchair, clutching his pounding temples, overwhelmed and crushed by the sudden grief.

He had been waiting for this meeting for so long, preparing himself, imagining over and over again how it would go, and all for nothing... Max stood up jerkily and paced up and down the tiny hotel room, unable to sit still and not knowing how to ease the burning pain of this loss.

"Get a hold of yourself! Think of those still alive. You still have a brother and a sister."

Max returned to the armchair and plugged the shunt back again, feeling the annoying tremor in his fingers.

After restoring the connection, Max immediately shifted to Johnny's now known online address.

"The in-mode? But why?"

He tapped into the sensors and was shocked to see a flabby, half-blind, wrinkly creature of indeterminate age.

Johnny?!

The implant codon left no room for doubt — it was really him!

Max's mind entered the network connection running from the in-mode, and he found himself in one of the Layer's realities. Max looked at his brother's avatar and saw an ugly monster hiding in a moist and dark cave, covered in some sort of artifacts that apparently had value in this game world.

Max couldn't help the burning tears that appeared in his eyes. There was a lump in his throat. He completely lost control of his emotions.

Connection has been lost...

✳ ✳ ✳

The silence in the hotel room was deafening.

A sticky sweat coated Max's body. The neurosensory contact was frying his brain since Max was using untested technology at his own peril, without medical control or technical support. Nevertheless, the physical discomfort was nothing in comparison to the grief that he felt.

"Whom did you expect to see?" The question in his mind brought him out of the stupor. "An energetic young scientist? A successful businessman? Or did your younger brother follow the path that was meant for you? Work as a monster? No problem! I'll do anything if you pay me!" These thoughts choked him.

"I didn't even talk to him!" Max awkwardly wiped away his tears and went back into the Layer.

Johnny was clearly neglecting all the mandatory procedures for living in the in-mode. Had he gotten too lazy? But why was he so dirty and unwashed? Reading the information from the sensors, Max could physically feel the stench emanating from his brother.

"Johnny!" By manipulating the equipment, Max created his own avatar in the narrow space. At the same time, he noticed the illegal modules in the in-mode's software and remembered how he used to dream of getting them himself, in order to cut off the family connections and to skip the daily treadmill, living the way that he wanted.

"Grrrrr!" came the response.

"Johnny, look at me! It's me, Max! Remember me? Do you recognize me?"

The muddled and mindless gaze focused with some difficulty on Max's image. Johnny's lips twitched and he bared his teeth.

"Johnny, please, wake up! Snap out of your role, I beg you!"

Max's brother reacted but in his own way. Flexing his fingers, as if they really possessed ten-centimeter-long claws, Johnny lurched forward with a repulsive grimace and slashed at the holographic image. When the vision didn't disappear, he became enraged.

"Johnny!"

A new series of blows followed, accompanied by inarticulate noises.

Johnny was no longer playing a role. He *perceived* himself as a computer monster. The Layer and the in-mode had completely altered his mind, affecting it step by step over many years.

He could no longer distinguish what was real and no longer perceived himself as human. His mind dwelt permanently in the dank and gloomy cave.

Why didn't anyone raise the alarm?

The answer was hard to accept but obvious.

It suited the owners of this virtual reality to have a permanent monster. Everyone else simply didn't care. Every person in their own in-mode. Every person for themselves, trapped in their own dreams. If only the in-mode equipment had been working properly but it had been disfigured by the so-called upgrades!

Max tried to establish contact with Johnny's darkened mind for an hour but when lunchtime arrived and an oblong tube of food paste slid into the delivery tray, he realized that it was hopeless. His brother tore open the wrapper and began to devour the handout, rivulets of saliva running down his chin.

✳ ✳ ✳

The hotel room's interior floated before Max's eyes.

His head rang with pain from the direct neurosensory contact.

Max sat still, his hands covering his face.

His parents were no longer alive. Johnny had turned into a monster.

He got up from the chair with some difficulty and poured himself a glass of water. The image of Samantha twisted and changed in his mind. Max felt afraid. Afraid that she...

"What do I know about her? How did they cope with our parents' death? Alone? Keeping everything inside? Why does Johnny live in the Antarctic Megacity, and she's in the Europe Megacity?"

Max found the answer when he carefully reviewed the information about the catastrophe that killed his parents. The accident had occurred on the section of the magrail that was part of the European transport network. Apparently, Johnny received only minor injuries but Samantha had to be hospitalized. After many years in the in-mode, she couldn't adapt to real life and once she had recovered and was left to her own devices, she quickly ended up on the bottom.

How could Max find her? Max called up a file in his cyberstack. The registration details in the capsule block were old. The information hadn't been updated for two years. Was Samantha still alive? Where was Max supposed to look for her? At the bottom of a city of several billions! It was no easy task. Max couldn't turn to the authorities for help. All he had was her implant label, which the city sensors must have kept track of. There was only one way out, and that was to operate through the Net, otherwise, he would spend years searching for Samantha and lose contact with Johnny, with no way to help him.

Max tried to calm down and weigh up the risks. "If the corps get their hands on me, it won't to end well," he thought.

In actual fact, the implant improvements done by Timoshin opened up hundreds of doors for Max. He didn't intend to harm anyone and nobody was going to notice the minor online offences since officially, direct neurosensory contact technology did not exist. Only a few people at the top of the corporate pyramid knew about it, and even they didn't know all the details. At best, they would have been told about the research in general terms. The rest, the people who had worked directly with the technology, were all dead.

A poisonous industrial fog drifted over the outskirts of the Europe Megacity. Tiny drops of toxic substances condensed into clouds that swirled just above the ground.

The outline of the city boundary was lost in the gloom.

Physically, Max Bourne was still sitting in his hotel room but thanks to his direct connection to the cybernetic systems, his mind moved swiftly through the Net.

Millions of officials were working in the single datasphere. It turned out that restricted versions of mnemonic interfaces were already part of daily life. Once Max figured out what was happening, he mentally slipped into the municipal portal of the megasuburb in Europe that he was interested in, and searched the databases, obtaining the necessary information and sneaking away into one of the local segments of the monitoring system.

Samantha was alive! Her implant label had twice been picked up by the electronic guards on the zero level in the past day.

Max knew from personal experience that it was possible to survive on the technical level of the megacity.

Working crudely but effectively, he connected to the technical subsystem controlling the servos and entered the alphanumerical implant code into the database. A few moments later he received a response — his sister was currently in one of the waste management complexes!

The signal from the implant label was clear but Max couldn't see Samantha. The video sensors were transmitting an image of a technical graveyard divided into squares, a dumping ground for irreparably damaged servos.

Where are you, little sister?

The sensors refocused, slowly narrowing the viewing angle and increasing the range and level of details.

Max couldn't see anyone. On the right, a squat workshop glowed with numerous signatures and on the left, the melting furnaces emitted a suffocating heat.

The first impression was oppressive. Max felt like he was in another world or on another planet. Mountains of servomechanical hulls, corroded by the industrial fog, lay everywhere. Automated excavators were working nearby, using enormous buckets to scoop up tons of secondary raw material and throwing the machines into the furnaces to be melted down.

Gray clouds of toxic fumes hung about in some places.

The implant label was moving slowly. Suddenly, a loud clanging could be heard nearby against the background hum. The grating covering a drain moved aside with a screech.

A hunched figure dressed in dirty rags

climbed out of the storm water drain. Samantha Bourne's sunken and inflamed eyes stood out on her gaunt and dirty face.

She looked around furtively, then sneaked over to the nearest pile of damaged servos, where she began to break apart the dilapidated body of one of the machines with a strange persistence.

Little sister... Max's breath caught in his throat.

The overwhelming desire to talk to her pushed Max towards a risky move. He noticed a scratched personal nanocomp on her right wrist, under the tattered clothing. Max scanned it without disconnecting from the sensor complex. The cyberstack was in terrible condition but the inbuilt mini-holograph and audio system were still functioning.

It was enough to create an avatar.

$$* * *$$

The appearance of a ghostly figure didn't frighten Samantha in the least. She grabbed a broken servo manipulator and swung it sharply, aiming for Max's head.

"Piss off! This is mine!"

"Samantha, look at me!"

She looked up at him and suddenly backed away, dropping the metal part.

"Max?"

"Yes! Yes, it's me, little sister."

"You're not... You died." She replied bleakly.

"I'm alive! I came back."

"Where have you been all these years?" Her chin trembled.

"Samantha, listen..."

"Where were you, Max?" She stepped backwards, tripped and fell but Max's avatar, generated by her cyberstack, didn't disappear, only splintered for a second.

"I don't have much time." He tried to speak calmly but it didn't work. "Samantha, I'm alive and I'm coming to get you!"

"You're not real." She gave a sob.

"I'm just far away right now. I'm in the Antarctic Megacity." Max's voice was breaking. "I swear, I'll be in Europe by morning and I'll find you and take you with me!"

Samantha shrunk back and burst into tears.

"Don't come." She suddenly begged.

"Why?" Max was shocked.

"You won't help me. You'll only make it worse. I'm a chipper, Max. I'll just die!" Now she sounded horrified. "Don't! They caught me before and tried to treat me. Nothing helped! I was scared and in pain. Shadows and emptiness!

Shadows and emptiness! No, no, don't come! You're dead. It's better this way..." It seemed that her mind had slipped away from reality. "You'll ruin everything if you're alive. You'll make it worse!" She sobbed desperately. "I can't live without the chips! Don't come. You'll make it worse. I can't..." Samantha turned away, smearing dirt and tears across her face, and resumed tearing apart the servo.

Max Bourne's life had been difficult but it must be said that as he overcame challenges, he always acted in his own interests. Concepts such as humanity and civilization only occasionally crossed his mind, without touching the secret depths of his soul. He never set himself global problems and certainly never intended to solve them.

Now he slowly drifted back from the direct neurosensory contact, feeling nothing but pain — intense physical and emotional pain.

His brother and sister. They were all that he had left. But — Max struggled with the devastating aftereffects that were warping his sanity — they had become strangers. They had been irreversibly changed.

Was there a way to heal them and return

them to normal life?

Max's throat felt parched. What was 'normal life', truly? He opened a bottle of water and drank it dry.

A new flash of unbearable pain made him stagger, clutch the tall back of the armchair and sit down, trying to suppress the intense dizziness that bordered on fainting.

"What's happening to me?"

Max's fingers shook. He closed his eyes but it didn't help. Images flashed before his eyes and Max felt his mind drowning in the information. The image of Johnny was ever-present in his thoughts, twisting and morphing into revolting figures as if all the monsters in the Layer were baring their teeth at him at once.

There were millions of them. Lisa was right about one thing — the in-modes were not going anywhere. All those caught in the trap would remain 'cans' forever and would never get out of the quagmire of virtual space.

"What is 'normal life'? What do I care about the other people? I'm going to get Johnny and Samantha out into the real world. I'll help them. I'll hire the top specialists. I'll settle here, on Earth, until the dust storms are under control on Mars."

Something else kept distracting him. The cyberstack was demanding his attention, beeping shrilly on his wrist.

Max pushed away the obsessive fragmented images with an effort of will and didn't answer his own question.

A small cozy house under a dome, somewhere above the clouds, near the top of the megacity. His own self-contained, self-sufficient and isolated world. We'll see... Now Max had to figure out how to bring Samantha to the Antarctic Megacity and to find a reliable and proven method of treating virtual reality dependency for Johnny.

Max touched the cyberstack. The annoying signal was coming from the traffic monitoring system. He looked at the amount of data sent and received during the neurosensory contact and couldn't help but gasp.

Max had received hundreds of thousands of terabytes![12]

That's where the intense headache was coming from, as well as the overwhelming fatigue...

"Why so much data? What kind of trail did I leave in the Layer?"

He had to go! At once!

---

[12] According to the results of some modern studies, the human brain could store approximately 2.5 petabytes of information, but this number was debatable.

Max Bourne packed quickly. Thankfully, he had few possessions.

His mind was tripping. Insane visions were superimposed on reality: the distorted faces of people trapped in their in-modes, views of other worlds, the darkness of space bare of stars, with only thin, pulsing green strands forming a network...

A thousand kilometers away from the Antarctic Megacity, Catherine Rimp received an unexpected report.

She loaded the information into the implant and scanned through it, then asked for comments from her specialists.

A strange phenomenon had rippled through the Layer. Was it artificial intelligence? This thought was unpleasant. She examined a graphic image of the event. A distinct neuromatrix glowed against the backdrop of an electronic map of the Antarctic Megacity. A terabyte thread ran from the neuromatrix through the communication channels and to the monitoring devices of the Europe Megacity. Someone had invaded the Net and used the resources of the global digital space to connect to a set of sensors located in an ordinary recycling center.

No, it wasn't AI. The AI would have acted differently and wouldn't have left such obvious traces. It looked like the clumsy and uncontrolled use of direct neurosensory contact technology!

But all the developments in this area had been lost, and the results of the experiments and prototypes had disappeared during a raider attack on the laboratory complex in the asteroid belt!

Catherine frowned and requested an immediate analysis of the events, taking into consideration the incident of one year prior.

Information continued to come in and the graphic image gradually became more detailed. The model now showed millions of thin strands, which emanated from the various equipment in the Layer, flowing into the main channel which transmitted a huge number of useless, everyday data.

She continued to frown since neurosensory contact technology implied bidirectional communication. This thought adjusted the request and the diagram immediately showed her new links. The mysterious 'force' as Catherine Rimp was calling the source of the invasion for now, was emitting information. Some of it had been irretrievably lost but some had been automatically recorded.

"Perform the neuromatrix analysis" she sent the mental order. "Send the information transmitted to the Net to my implant!"

A series of unrelated images appeared in the mind's eye of Catherine Rimp.

A monster inhabiting a dank cave.

A view of Jupiter seen from Ganymede.

An unfamiliar green-blue planet covered with streaks of cloud.

A faceless figure, a phantom, sitting in the armchair of a very familiar interior of an individual shelter, which the Genesis Corporation and Rimp Cybetronics had designed together.

Thin green strands drawn in the depths of a strange and primitive hemispheric screen.

The face of a haggard woman with deeply sunk and reddened eyes, clearly a chipper.

"A neurogram match has been found!" A report that came through the Net trickled into her thoughts. "The source of the invasion in the Layer has been identified as Max Bourne."

✴ ✴ ✴

Max felt worse with every passing hour. In his attempt to flee from likely pursuit, he had passed through three different capsule hotels, made his way to a fourth one and registered under a fake name. He just made it to the rented in-mode before he collapsed.

Max's brain was shutting down. He was sinking into an irrational world of fragmented images, hardly aware of the surrounding reality. Max barely had the strength to crawl into the in-mode. The sealing procedure began automatically and the life support systems switched on, but Max could no longer monitor the events, left to face the encroaching insanity.

The shredded world spun around him in a kaleidoscope of images. Certain thoughts crystallized among the terrifying background of his fading mind.

Did you become a real person, Max? What does 'real life' mean to you? Where is it? Is it back in space, on Ganymede? What is the difference between the in-mode and a villa above the clouds if you are alone? What is your purpose in life? Is it to keep yourself apart from other people? If not with the in-mode walls and the fantasies of virtual space, then with money and a high social status?

He didn't answer.

Max's brain refused to work, overloaded as it was with contradictory information. Chip abuse and direct neurosensory contact are two sides of the same coin. That's what Timoshin had said.

Johnny and Samantha... Max's mind still clung to their images. "They repeated two possible lives that fate had in store for me. Space had made me into a man and brought me back to real life yet I can't help you," he spoke to the twisted faces in his head. "I don't know the way out. I can't destroy the Layer or ban the in-mode, and I can't stop the rapid progress that is hurtling us towards a dead end like a capsule on a magrail."

"You can and you know how," the voices replied stubbornly. "But you don't want to do anything."

"I'm powerless to change anything!" He screamed desperately in response, a part of his mind aware that he was hallucinating and talking to the ghosts inside his head.

Using untested and dangerous technology was stupid and overly confident, but it was too late to regret what was done. He had to go into hiding and wait it out. People were surely looking for him...

Max was mistaken. They had lost his trail. While moving from one capsule hotel to the next, Max had used a chip obtained on board the Space Vegas Station, which allowed him to briefly change his implant ID once, and now the security officers at Rimp Cybertronics were waiting for him to make a mistake and go online again.

Max's mind gradually grew darker and darker. The in-mode's life support system was active but the equipment in cheap capsule hotels was set up in such a way as not to create any unnecessary problems for the owners. Therefore, the guests' health reports were not sent to the Net.

The voices in his damaged mind sounded more and more muffled and then faded away altogether. Max was left with a sense of deep despair, sticky and suffocating, as if by unconsciously absorbing the information from the Net, he had taken in the atmosphere of a dying and urbanized Earth, where both the rich and the poor no longer had a way out.

The collapse of the Martian project destroyed millions of lives and killed the hopes of those who hadn't yet sunk in the quicksand of the Layer and who still tried to plan their life and escape Earth's cesspool.

Among the information that Max had unconsciously received from cyberspace was a multitude of fragmented data relating to Mars.

The maddening voices finally fell silent. The unfamiliar faces disappeared.

Max's mind now wandered among the lost and untapped possibilities, as if his brain had finished processing one body of data and now moved on to the next one.

An enormous orbital shipyard moved slowly against the backdrop of the moon's pale face slowly, docked at a hub of the Space Vegas Station. The twenty spaceships designed and built for the mass relocation of people to Mars formed a cluster.

Their construction was simple and functional. The space inside was divided into decks and filled with cryogenic capsules, cargo holds and hangars for planetary equipment.

Despite the huge size of the ships (each one was designed to fit 300,000 settlers), their crew consisted of only seven people during the many months of flight between Earth and Mars.

Now the behemoths waited for their fate to be decided. The dust storms raging across Mars had made these unique ships useless. Due to their unique construction, they could not be used for anything else.

Max couldn't control his own thoughts. He was half-asleep due to the drugs injected by the in-mode's life support system and due to his body's attempts to protect itself from the destructive and excessive loads. Despite everything, his mind continued working, as if it existed on its own and saw salvation in this processing of data, but acted with a strange selectivity, putting together fragments of a mosaic that so far made no sense.

Images of the orbital shipyards and the interiors of the spacecraft decks, where the dim glow of the emergency lights cast zigzag patterns across the empty cryogenic capsules, were replaced by segments of archived news, which announced events that Max had missed for obvious reasons:

'12 March 2209.

Today, a young research astrophysicist called Johan Ivanov-Schmidt published his scandalous 'Hypersphere Theory' in the Layer, in which he linked the catastrophe of the Alpha Colonial Transport to what he called a 'puncture in the fabric of space'. According to Mr. Ivanov-Schmidt, a malfunction in the thrust system and an overload of Alpha's cruise engines led to a rupture of the space-time continuum. The young scientist declared that "there was a high chance that the first colonial transport wasn't destroyed but performed a sporadic crossing into another dimension". When asked whether anyone in the Alpha crew could have survived this crossing and whether the ship returned to normal space, Mr. Ivanov-Schmidt stated only that "we will have all the answers when we test out the hyperdrive that I have designed."

Earth's scientific community has been understandably skeptical of the young astrophysicist's theory.'

'30 June 2210.

Today, Catherine Rimp, in response to

accusations directed at Rimp Cybertronics, announced that the corporation's new humanoid model, codenamed Hugo, is not a threat although artificial neuro-like networks were used in the android's construction. "The creation of humanoid machines is not an attempt to play God and not another step in the technology race but a sensible necessity and the results of many years of work to create a universal machine that will be mankind's trusted helper when colonizing foreign worlds." Stated Catherine Rimp. "I hope that after the Alpha Disaster, colonizing Mars will become an intermediate step in our journey to the stars. I hope it will also regain people's confidence in colonial projects, which will grow into colonial policies." She emphasized. "We have everything that we need to explore other worlds. During the creation of the Alpha Project, Earth's leading corporations designed a set of model solutions for colonial buildings and their technical content, worked through terraforming issues, created and tested more than ten thousand devices and their complexes, to enable humans to survive on other planets, and for terraforming these planets into Earth Standard.'

'18 September 2211.

Today, the asteroid belt sensors detected strange anomalies beyond Pluto's orbit. Equipment from the independent space settlements as well as specialized location complexes in the corporate commodity sectors recorded a series of eighteen similar events, which so far have no explanation. Among the specific characteristics are records of identical energy signatures, followed by disruptions in all types of communication, and technically unexplained jumps in the artificial gravity systems.'

Max's mind was drowning in the ocean of information. Some findings seemed important and significant, and he remembered them as bright images, such as the signature of the strange phenomena recorded beyond Pluto's orbit, the name of the young astrophysicist who had published his hypersphere theory, or the extracts from some of Catherine Rimp's announcements.

'13 January 2213.

A protest, unprecedented in the recent history of Earth, took place today. Millions of people left their in-modes and capsule apartments and went out on the streets, demanding that the World Government resumes the suspended program to colonize Mars and fulfils their obligation to the people seeking to leave the overpopulated Earth...

Attempts to disperse the demonstration turned into a bloody massacre, in which the

United Nations armed forces took part.

Red Nowak, General Secretary of the UN, resigned over this incident and stated that the World Government has no way to resolve this situation and that Earth is heading towards a new World War.'

'18 March 2213.

Another attempt to clean up the Mars' atmosphere ended in tragedy today. The chemicals dispersed by the cruiser *Apollo*, which is part of the UN's Martian fleet, destroyed the greenhouse dome belonging to Genesis Corporation. Thirty square kilometers of terraformed land are now under the mercy of the dust storms, a unique ecosystem has been destroyed and, according to unconfirmed reports, there are casualties among Genesis employees.

The Head of the World Government, Edward Kalganov, stated that the dome couldn't withstand the hurricane winds and called Ulrich Fitzgerald's accusations unfounded.'

...

He was dying.

In the rare moments of clarity, Max felt completely exhausted, having lived thousands of lives and gone beyond the edge of known human abilities.

He continued to fight but he was hopelessly losing the battle. The in-mode of the cheap hotel had become his last refuge. The decryption of data from the *Vancor* had fractured his mind, while the trip into the Layer using the raw and untested technology of direct neurosensory contact had killed him.

Whenever Max briefly regained consciousness and surfaced from the ocean of information, he felt like a completely different person... but it was too late. His third chance to live was over. Max had escaped being a hostage of the Layer and had survived on Ganymede but fell victim to the technology race. Even that no longer mattered.

He didn't want his death to be so meaningless.

So cold... His fingertips were numb. He could barely move his arm in the narrow in-mode and reach his inside pocket, pulling out an additional implant module and a thin shunt.

The information processing was finished. He could see the full picture of what was happening and understood the meaning behind the words of the artificial intelligence.

Alone on Earth and in the whole universe, Max possessed a fully interconnected picture of the events that could destroy the Layer, ban the in-modes and change the present and the future...

A click sounded.

Max's injured mind established a network connection and joined Earth's cyberspace, moving towards the only remaining target.

A minute passed, then another. Everything swam before his eyes.

She couldn't have changed the implant code... She couldn't have... She had no reason to...

A dull flash, accompanied by debilitating pain. Max saw a corner of a bright and spacious room and overcoming fatigue, established a mental connection with another person's implant.

"Catherine Rimp?" His lips moved and his heated whisper repeated the mental phrase. "Please don't turn off the implant... No, please don't look for me. There's no point. There's no time... Accept this data. I decrypted and processed it... The Alpha Catastrophe is not a tragedy but an opportunity..." His lips were going cold. "An opportunity for everyone... You'll understand..." His voice was fading. "Pain. Too late. My brother and sister..."

The data continued to arrive for another four and a half minutes.

✳ ✳ ✳

Earth
Europe Megacity
Head Office of the Rimp Cybertronics Corporation

"How's the deal coming along?" Catherine Rimp stood by the panoramic window and watched the rivers of lights flowing through the streets of the megacity.

"Kalganov can't understand the reason for our actions and is acting paranoid," replied Mac Taylor.

"Never mind that. Has he agreed to sell the ships?"

"Yes. Nobody needs them anymore, really. The fight against the Martian dust hasn't succeeded."

"Complete the deal as quickly as possible! Don't give him a chance to change his mind! All the documents must be completed by tomorrow."

"Catherine, may I ask why we're buying cargo and passenger transports? The colonization of Mars is now in doubt and such investments..."

Catherine Rimp turned around. She looked tired and thin after the last few days.

"She's barely sleeping," thought Mac Taylor as he met her gaze.

"No. The information is secret," She snapped. "I will tell you everything in time. Did you find Johan Ivanov-Schmidt?"

"Yes, he's at reception."

"Invite him in; no, wait." She sat down at her desk. "How is Bourne?"

"He's in a coma."

"Has he got a chance?"

"Our specialists think that he has. But the situation is critical at the moment."

"Have you found his family?"

"A brother and a sister. They're both at our corporate specialist clinic."

"Keep me updated regarding their condition. And now, please invite our guest to step inside."

"Should I stay for the meeting?"

"No. Send in the android."

Mac Taylor left and a minute later, the office door opened.

"In here, please. Come in and have a seat." It was hard to distinguish the robot accompanying Johan Ivanov-Schmidt from a human. He was a prototype of the new model, Hugo-BD12.

The young astrophysicist looked confused and nervous. No wonder! A personal invitation from Catherine Rimp could mean either a dizzying ascent or a crushing fall. He had no idea what they were going to discuss.

"Johan, you published your hypersphere theory in the Layer several years ago." Catherine Rimp went straight to the heart of the matter. "From what I have been told, you provided a theoretical explanation for the possible existence of an alternative space-time, which possesses physical processes that are impossible in our continuum."

"That's true... but the scientific community laughed at me."

"Nevertheless, you uploaded a conceptual diagram of the hyperdrive to the Net?"

"Yes. In the hope that someone would take an interest. Alas, I have not received a single offer."

"Has the invention been patented?"

Johan nodded, still not sure why he had been invited to the head office of the powerful corporation.

Catherine Rimp frowned. "So, Mr. Kalganov, the law doesn't apply to you?" She thought with a shadow of resentment. "To take openly available information and build an engine without even informing the inventor."

"Before we get down to business," she gave Johan an intense stare, "I would like to make you a proposition. Rimp Cybertronics will buy the patent for the hyperdrive and you will be our leading specialist in the hypersphere."

Johan froze in surprise, the blood draining away from the young astrophysicist's face. He forced himself to nod without even asking about the price.

"Excellent. While we're talking, my lawyers will prepare all the necessary documents. Will one million credits satisfy you?"

"Certainly... Please, I want to know, why the sudden interest? My theory was mocked..."

"It's much more complicated than that, Johan. Your discovery contained a grain of truth. But someone decided to go all in, against everyone. To gain absolute power over the world and the future course of our civilization."

"I don't understand!" Johan half stood up from his chair in agitation.

"You don't need to." Catherine Rimp decided not to elaborate. "This is politics. Your calling is science. Are you ready to start work?"

"Certainly."

"Then let's begin. I have familiarized myself with your theory but I would like to hear a brief summary of it again, in simple language and without all the formulas and equations."

Johan Ivanov-Schmidt gathered his thoughts for several seconds.

"I watched the recordings of Alpha's disappearance thousands of times," he began nervously. "Having analyzed the video, I studied the evolution of the signatures and tried to create a mathematical model of the event. Through a series of complex calculations, I determined that for several nanoseconds, the colonial transport's propulsion system generated extremely powerful energy flows at the time of its overload. The equations confirmed that in that moment, the ship possessed energy characteristics that were impossible for our space. This triggered a rip in its metric and the expulsion of the ship to a higher energy region, which I called the hypersphere."

"So every hypersphere jump is comparable to a catastrophe?" Catherine Rimp inquired with a frown.

"No! Only in Alpha's case!" Johan exclaimed. "I was able to isolate the anomalous structures in the ship's energy matrix. I hypothesized that they were the ones that triggered a tear in the space metric. Further calculations have shown that if the generators that I have developed are positioned correctly, their overlapping signatures will lead to a similar phenomenon. I called it a 'high frequency field'. In my opinion, any material object located within the boundaries of the field will be transported into the hypersphere."

"Can the process be reversed?"

"This has not yet been proven in practice," Johan admitted. "I have designed a second generator contour which creates a field with the opposite characteristics. I have called this part of the hyperdrive the 'low frequency generator'. When it is switched on, it should produce a reverse jump, an expulsion of the object into 3D space, although I must point out that a similar phenomenon may occur when the onboard energy stores are depleted."

"A ship that runs out of energy will be expelled back into our space?"

"That's right. That's what the calculations say."

"What do you think the hypersphere is?"

"I think the hypersphere is a carrier of gravitational interconnections. But without building a prototype of the hyperdrive and undertaking test flights, I can't say anything for certain," Johan gestured helplessly.

"What if I provided you with some documented evidence?"

"From where? How was it obtained?!" The young scientist went pale.

"Lives were lost for it," Catherine Rimp replied without going into the details. "The lives of very good and noble people. Here." She handed Johan a microchip. "Hugo will show you the way out." She signalled to the android. "Please familiarize yourself with the content. Treat the information with all seriousness. I expect preliminary conclusions or at least comments by morning." Her every word, which brooked no arguments, was filled with not only strong business acumen but also a strange intensity that the young scientist didn't understand. "I can assure you that the information is genuine."

A fierce struggle was taking place in Catherine Rimp's heart.

She had lived a difficult life. She had bid farewell to her dream of the stars and resurrected it from the ashes of lost hopes. She had experienced failures and victories. Her will controlled the largest corporation in the Solar System. Perhaps she hadn't changed much on the outside since that memorable conversation in the restaurant, but the daily struggle had gradually hardened her.

Catherine Rimp increasingly preferred the company of humanoid machines to real people. She attended the meetings of the great powers less and less frequently as her dream drifted further out of reach, until three people had burst into her life, reminding her of the goals and values that she had lost and wounding her as deeply as could be possible.

Max, Johnny and Samantha Bourne.

They had become her Rubicon, the waters of a dark river whose opposite shore was shrouded in the mist of an unknown future.

She had seen many things in a different light, through their eyes.

The Layer was slowly but inexorably devouring humankind. Billions of people preserved in the in-modes could no longer tolerate the real world.

What then about space, what about survival on other, hostile worlds?

But if it wasn't space, then who or what had made Max Bourne into a man?

Max had nearly died. Even now, his life was hanging by a thread. He had fallen victim to the unrestrained technology race, but at the last minute had found the strength to carry out the most important act of his life and to consider the billions of other people.

Now his thoughts echoed the worried musings of Catherine Rimp:

"Do I have the right to make a decision on my own? Can I live with the uncertainty, not knowing what befell the people who travelled to other worlds? Will the people follow this new and quite foreign idea?"

There was another option. To leave

everything as it was. To carry out research and tests but once a clear result was obtained, would there be anyone left on Earth who would be able to leave the safety of the in-mode and the decay of the Layer, to lift their heads and look up at the stars?

The fates of the Bourne family screamed 'No!' In another ten to fifteen years, the process of mass degradation would become irreversible. Nowadays, there are still some people who want to leave Earth and who are ready to fight, but who are unable to put their desires into action. Tomorrow they will go into the Layer and gradually lose themselves in their desires, drown and sink to the bottom.

"I have to decide today." Her thoughts were interrupted by a signal.

"Come in!" She turned around.

Johan Ivanov-Schmidt stood in the doorway.

"Come in."

"Ms Rimp, I have analyzed the data."

"Please give me the essence, without emotions and extraneous questions. What did you learn from the recordings?"

"Some of my suppositions were confirmed!" Johan switched on the cyberstack. "Here, take a look!" He pointed to the image of a hemisphere containing a network of thin green strands. "This is one of the devices that I designed together with the hyperdrive!"

"What do these lines mean?"

"The instrument reacts to strong gravitational sources. As per my hypotheses, these power lines correspond to the strongest gravitational interactions between 3D objects in the hypersphere!"

"Meaning that navigation in the hypersphere is possible?" Catherine Rimp reached the immediate and correct conclusion.

"Yes, if the ship follows the mass detector readouts, along the line that shows the current shortest distance between the two star systems.[13]" Johan confirmed.

It was a chance.

The last link that Catherine Rimp was missing in her chain of thoughts.

Johan continued to elaborate on the underpinning theories while she mentally grasped the opportunity itself and went further, assessing the information obtained from Max Bourne.

Following the course lines forming a complex network, the *Vancor* had visited ten star systems (twice in some cases), where it had

---

[13] The hypersphere theory is explained in more detail at the end of the book.

discovered seven planets with an oxygen-containing atmosphere. Without a doubt, the scout ship's journey consisted of a series of 'blind punches'. It was impossible to distinguish one navigational line from another in the hypersphere. There was no reliable way to determine which star system the strand led to.

In this way, there was approximately a 70% chance that a spaceship performing a 'blind punch' would be able to find a planet suitable for human habitation once it returned to 3D space.

Catherine Rimp stood still, deep in thought, not noticing that the android prototype from the Hugo series was following Johan Ivanov-Schmidt's explanations closely, occasionally glancing at the graphs, diagrams and equations that appeared on the holographic monitor.

"People will never agree to interstellar flights with such a percentage," she thought. "They won't follow the corporation or the World Government since they don't trust us."

She saw only one solution, however cruel and cynical it seemed at first. She roused herself and turned resolutely to the astrophysicist. "Johan, how long will it take to manufacture and install one hyperdrive?"

"Six to seven months, I think. Do you have ships? Is there a colonial program already?!" He asked suspiciously. "Are there people crazy enough to risk a 'blind punch' through another space and time?"

"We have ships. Twenty colonial transports, ready for loading." Catherine Rimp did not look away and added firmly. "Leave the rest to my conscience. I know what needs to be done."

Earth. Year 2214
Russia Megacity.

The two cloud levels split the city into three uneven parts.

Down below, within the industrial fog, stretched the endless kingdom of the technosphere, which formed a continuous communications shield.

It was a very different view above the billowing toxic fumes.

The buildings rising higher than the 500 meters above sea level seemed to grow from the yellowish gray haze and climbed towards the low leaden skies in huge steps of the megasuburbs.

Winding interlevel roads circled around the residential complexes, looking like gray fossilized vines that enveloped the buildings in a deadly grasp.

At an altitude of one kilometer, above the

second cloud layer, the upper part of the megacity consisted of huge reinforced concrete platforms containing green parks and the houses of Earth's wealthiest citizens, hidden under transparent domes.

Down below was a hell for billions, while up above stretched an artificially created heaven for the select few.

The three megacity spaces differed in everything, as though the notion of height had become not only a physical measure but also a way to grade society.

In truth, both the rich and the poor, the ambitious and the apathetic were united by the Layer, whose dreams had nothing to do with reality.

Earth was dying slowly and inexorably.

The middle city levels were the only place where real life took place, difficult but at least unrelated to the cyberspace. It was where the active part of the population was concentrated and where it was involved in real sectors of the economy. The life of the inhabitants of the capsule apartments was tough and often monotonous. According to statistics, only a small fraction could ever escape to the castles in the clouds, while millions were constantly under the threat of industrial fog emissions, which rose every year.

Until recently, the Mars Project had been their beacon of hope for a better future but after its collapse, all the megacities on Earth were full of gloomy and explosive sentiments. Many could not cope and gave up, landing in the in-modes and being immediately consumed by the Layer.

However, if one looked closely at the dazzling advertisements that recently begun to light up the dark clouds overhead, one could see that the inhabitants of the middle city levels now had another way to escape their murky and hopeless lives.

Above the average bustling city, home to several billion people, a spectacular laser show painted images of paradisal planets, which according to the advertisers, had been visited by *Vancor*, the first hypersphere scout ship.

More specific information was displayed beside the ghostly images of the distant worlds. Ten 'sending companies' were currently offering their services to anyone who wanted to leave the overpopulated ancestral homeland in search of the promised land.

Ten transport ships, equipped with a hyperdrive and the best colonial equipment, waited for their passengers. Nine of them were in orbit between Earth and the Moon, while the Krivich Colonial Transport was currently docked at the Space Vegas Station and taking on passengers. The next ones on the list were Cassiopeia and Nobel. The names of the other seven ships weren't yet being disclosed — their turn in the spotlight would come only after the abovementioned space leviathans had started their journey, each one capable of carrying up to 300,000 cryogenically frozen colonists to the stars...

...The stars that could not be seen from the surface of Earth, choking in its toxic industrial emissions, the stars that seemed as distant and imaginary as the laser-drawn views of the planets that circled them. The fact that the automated scout ship had managed to perform a series of extradimensional jumps, use its probes to explore some of the advertised worlds and ultimately return to the Solar System, seemed more luck than a planned and completed route, but this was kept quiet, giving billions of people a completely different idea.

Thanks to the hypersphere theory published by the astrophysicist Johan Ivanov-Schmidt, stars had become accessible to anyone who wished to travel to them. This was the main point being emphasized by the advertising companies, who had purchased the massive colonial transports after the collapse of the Mars Project.

Looking up from below, like from the

window of a capsule apartment, for example, the offer to leave Earth didn't seem so crazy or deluded when compared to the deadly gray and urbanized space.

Hope dies last... It was the straw that every person's mind desperately clung to, every person who had ever lifted their gaze to the leaden skies, where glowed the images of other realities, located dozens of light years away from Earth.

Only a narrow circle of people knew that the space anomaly discovered by Johan Ivanov-Schmidt had not been fully explored and contained not only the possibility of crossing the light speed barrier but also numerous unknown dangers.

The laws of hypersphere navigation remained to be discovered, and it would have to be done by the crews of those colonial transports, whose ads appeared on every information channel on the planet.

Every power anomaly line in space leads to a real, star-sized physical object — so proclaimed the hypersphere theory, but was life possible at the other end of the 'blind punch' made through the space-time anomaly?

The advertisements proclaimed that

YES, IT WAS POSSIBLE.

People were charged money and carefully placed into cryogenic capsules. The colonial transports were then towed beyond Pluto's orbit, from where they started their journey. Sometimes it was several ships per month...

Thus began the era of the Great Exodus, sending hundreds of millions of people into the unknown. Not a single ship returned to Earth in over fifty years, and after a half a century, the colonial boom weakened and then eventually died out altogether.

The fate of the ships that never returned remained a mystery, just like who was really behind the actions of the sending companies...

Epilogue

BEYOND Neptune's orbit, a spaceship drifted among the asteroids and dwarf planets of the Kuiper Belt[14].

It looked broken, static and dysfunctional. There was no air on board. The engines didn't work. A name could still be made out on the burnt armor plates: *Normandy*.

A well-trodden path led through its drift zone, used by the colonial transports being towed to the edges of the Solar System.

Each time that a space tug appeared in the effective scanning area, some of the *Normandy*'s subsystems came alive. A mysterious force would

---

[14] **Kuiper Belt** (sometimes called Edgeworth-Kuiper Belt) – a region of the Solar System extending from Neptune's orbit (30 AU from the Sun) to approximately 55 AU from the Sun. Pluto, formerly considered a planet, is now classified as a dwarf planet in the Kuiper Belt.

subtly slip aboard the colonial transport and scan the data stored on the central computer, looking through the lists of colonists.

This continued until the day that the mysterious visitor found what they sought.

The *Normandy*'s signature flared dully. The engines of the ancient cruiser lit up by short bursts and the ship performed a carefully calculated maneuver, following the Fugitive Colonial Transport.

The laser communication system switched on. Following the colonial transport at a respectful distance, the *Normandy* carried out a direct broadcast for 24 hours. The information was received through the technical access port and, bypassing the main information channels, used roundabout ways to get to cargo hold No. 17, where among the various equipment lay containers with the humanoid models Hugo-BD12.

The transmission ended after a day.

The *Normandy* changed its course. A short time later, the ancient cruiser entered a dense cluster of asteroids and disappeared in a silent explosion, while the Fugitive Colonial Transport continued its journey. It had to perform a 'blind punch' through the hypersphere.

What would humanity meet on the other side of the abyss? Would they find a habitable planet?

The first artificial intelligence of planet Earth, which had loaded its consciousness into the android's neural network, didn't have a definite answer but knew that a new era was beginning, and it wanted to share the fate of its creators.

Before entering energy-saving mode, it reviewed the report that it had received from the onboard computer:

Cryogenic capsule 10482. Catherine Rimp.
Cryogenic capsule 10483. Max Bourne.
Cryogenic capsule 10484. Samantha Bourne.
Cryogenic capsule 10485. John Bourne.
All vital indicators in normal range.
Time until the hyperdrive is turned on: 2 hours and 17 minutes.
All class A cybernetic systems must be switched off during the jump to avoid damage.

The android complied with instructions. An 'off' sign appeared on his internal monitor.

It had chosen its path and dreamt of only one thing — to start a new cycle of self-development in a new world, together with the people that it trusted.

Final edition of June 2017
Russia, Krasnodar Krai.

Author's website: https://livadny.ru

P. S.

During the Great Exodus, 7,023 colonial transports left the Solar System. As of Inhabited Galaxy Year 3800, the fate of 49 of these ships is known:

1. Alpha — after a 'blind punch' through the hypersphere, in 2207 it landed on the second planet of a gas giant in a star system in the Orion Nebula. The planet is referred to as the Temple.

2. Krivich — successfully landed on planet Elio in 2216. During exploration of the nearest star systems, the crew of the scout ship crashed on and colonized the planet Eres.

3. Fugitive — emergency landing on the planet Dabog in 2218.

4. Nobel — emergency landing on the planet Rogue in 2224. During the First Galactic War, the colonial transport became a sanctuary for AIs, which later occupied the planet.

5. Zeiss — successfully landed on planet Grjunverk in 2227. Employees of the Genesis Corporation left Earth on board this colonial transport. Later, the

inhabitants of Grjunverk colonized a planet called Zoroaster, where for centuries flourished genetic engineering, forbidden in the Inhabited Galaxy.

6. Cassiopeia — successfully landed on planet Cassia in 2230.

7. Pursuer — successfully landed on planet Kjuig in 2231.

8. Worm — emergency landing on planet Kjuig in 2231.

9. Rizenberg — successfully landed on planet Kjuig in 2260.

10. Hope — emergency landing on planet Rock in 2247.

11. Orion — was dragged into the vertical hypersphere. The fate of the colonial transport remains unknown.

12. Danais — date of landing on planet Dansia has not been established.

13. Wargaze — successfully landed on planet Wargaze in 2234. The population of the colony was destroyed by the Haramminams.

14. Bristol — successfully landed on planet Demetra in 2242. The planet had already been colonized by families of Insects, who had fled Dyson's Sphere after it was destroyed by the Harbingers.

15. Project Elcom — in 2247,

eleven colonial transports (serial numbers were used instead of numbers) performed a reverse jump within a gas and dust nebula. The colonists found refuge on the asteroids in the young star system.

16. Miriam — successfully landed on planet Ganio in 2280.

17. Erigon — successfully landed on planet Erigon in 2231.

18. Yuna — emergency landing on planet Yunona in 2219. The planet later joined the Earth Alliance and during the First Galactic War was one of the strongholds in Hammer's Line, a chain of worlds that protected the Solar System from attacks by the Free Colonies' fleet.

19. Terra — successfully landed on planet New Earth in 2216. The planet was part of the Earth Alliance at the beginning of the First Galactic War.

20. Shiran — successfully landed on planet Shiran in 2271. Part of the Shiran Cluster.

21. Saud — successfully landed on planet Saud in 2274. Part of the Shiran Cluster.

22. Mertab — successfully landed on planet Mertab in 2275. Part of the Shiran Cluster.

23. Zymani — successfully landed on planet Zyman in 2277. Part of the Shiran Cluster.

24. Aravia — successfully landed on planet Aravi in 2279. Part of the Shiran Cluster.

25. Algiers — successfully landed on planet Algiers in 2280. Part of the Shiran Cluster.

26. Sax — emergency landing on planet Athena in 2240.

27. Sargon — successfully landed on planet Sargon in 2232.

28. Erlizaph — successfully landed on planet Erliza in 2235.

29. Arax — emergency landing on planet Arax in 2253. The colonial transport performed a 'blind punch' through the vertical hypersphere.

30. Cassandra — crashed on one of the planets in the Necklace after being dragged into the vertical hypersphere.

31. Ark — landed on planet Ancor in 2249. The colonists were deported from the planet by the Earth Alliance forces during the First Galactic War.

32. Valerian — successfully landed on planet Varl in 2231.

33. Hope-2 — successfully landed

on planet Y-406 (O'Hara star cluster) according to the united star catalog in 2227. The colony's population was captured by the Insects and partly killed and partly deported to another star system.

34. Freese — landed on planet Freeside in 2025. The colonists were deported by the Earth Alliance forces during the First Galactic War.

35. Alexandria — the date of landing on planet Alexia (in the O'Hara cluster) was not established.

36. Octavia — launched in 2231. Fell into the vertical hypersphere and was found on one the planets in the Necklace system.

37. Atlas — made an emergency landing on planet Aqua (a former colony of the Delphon race) in 2257.

38. Rusich — successfully landed on a planet located in the modern Corporate Periphery. The history of the colony is unknown. Its civilization is developing in isolation with no contact with the rest of humanity.

39. Eden — landed on an Earth-type planet in 2240 in an area of low star density in the O'Hara cluster.

40. Phobos — emergency landing on planet Phobos in 2253.

An article on the hypersphere theory is available on my website, https://livadny.ru/?p=534.

End of Book One

Want to be the first to know about our latest LitRPG, sci fi and fantasy titles from your favorite authors?

Subscribe to our NEW RELEASES newsletter:
http://eepurl.com/b7niIL

Thank you for reading *Blind Punch!*
If you like what you've read, check out other LitRPG
novels published by Magic Dome Books:

Dark Paladin LitRPG series by Vasily Mahanenko:
The Beginning
The Quest

**The Dark Herbalist LitRPG series
by Michael Atamanov:**
Video Game Plotline Tester
Stay on the Wing

The Neuro LitRPG series by Andrei Livadny:
The Crystal Sphere
The Curse of Rion Castle
The Reapers

**The Way of the Shaman LitRPG series
by Vasily Mahanenko:**
Survival Quest
The Kartoss Gambit
The Secret of the Dark Forest
The Phantom Castle
The Karmadont Chess Set
Phaman's Revenge
The Hour of Pain (a bonus short story)

Galactogon LitRPG series by Vasily Mahanenko:
Start the Game!

Phantom Server LitRPG series by Andrei Livadny:
Edge of Reality
The Outlaw
Black Sun

**The Game Master series
by A. Bobl and A. Levitsky:**

The Lag

You're in Game!
(LitRPG Stories from Bestselling Authors)

The Naked Demon (a paranormal romance)
by Sherrie L.

More books and series are coming out soon!

In order to have new books of the series translated faster, we need your help and support! Please consider leaving a review or spread the word by recommending *Blind Punch* to your friends and posting the link on social media. The more people buy the book, the sooner we'll be able to make new translations available.

Thank you!

Till next time!

www.ingramcontent.com/pod-product-compliance
Lightning Source LLC
Chambersburg PA
CBHW071637260626
47170CB00001B/138